MY
CHILD IS
MISSING

BOOKS BY LISA REGAN

MY CHILD IS MISSING

LISA REGAN

bookouture

Published by Bookouture in 2023

An imprint of Storyfire Ltd.
Carmelite House
50 Victoria Embankment
London EC4Y 0DZ

www.bookouture.com

ISBN: 978-1-83790-575-1
eBook ISBN: 978-1-83790-573-7

For Sean House. You've always been the best one.

ONE

It starts as a whisper, a story that children tell each other on the playground and at slumber parties to scare one another. There's a creature in the forest. Or maybe it's a man, seven feet tall, and as big as a tree. He lurks and watches, always there, just out of sight, but ready to pounce. If this mythical thing captures you, you disappear. Or you die. No one knows for sure. The story changes over time as the lore grows and spreads, as more whispers join the chorus, until it is more than a story. It's a legend.

The legend of the Woodsman.

I hear people talking about it in stores, restaurants, the city park. Parents tell their children the Woodsman isn't real. There's nothing to worry about, they say in soothing tones. I can see in their faces that they're fed up with this nonsense, with their children having nightmares over a stupid story. I can tell that they believe what they say. The Woodsman is not real.

They're wrong.

I know this because I am the Woodsman, and I am coming for their children.

TWO

Josie was jolted awake by screams. Her body sprang to a standing position. It was part instinct, but she was also vaguely aware of being propelled to her feet by some unseen force. Her eyes snapped open to blinding daylight and she realized she had been jostled out of her seat by a crowd of people cheering. Blinking, she tried to get her bearings. Spread out before her was a baseball field filled with seven- and eight-year-olds in uniforms and helmets that looked too large for their heads. She was in the stands sandwiched between her friend, Misty DeRossi, and her former mother-in-law, Cindy Quinn. All the parents were hollering and pumping their fists in the air. One of the boys sprinted around the bases. Josie blinked again, trying to see if it was Harris, Misty's son.

Beside her, Misty screamed, "Go, go, go, go!"

On the other side of her, his grandmother, Cindy, yelled, "Run! Run!"

The boy slid into home base. His helmet tumbled off, taking his hat with it, revealing blond hair with a whorl at the back of his scalp identical to that of Josie's late ex-husband, Ray Quinn.

Misty let out a resounding whoop and then threw her arms

around Josie's neck, squeezing hard. At home plate, Harris jumped to his feet and began high-fiving nearby teammates and one of the coaches. Then he ran off the field and directly into the arms of Josie's husband, Noah Fraley. As the crowd quieted, Josie heard Harris's voice. "Did you see, Uncle Noah? Did you see?"

Noah's reply was swallowed up by one of the coaches hollering for the next player to come to bat. He spun Harris around and set him back onto the ground, waving him toward the bench where his teammates waited with high fives. The smile on Noah's face made Josie's heart thump.

Harris wasn't related to either of them, not by blood or marriage, and yet they both loved him fiercely. After Josie had separated from her first husband, Ray, he had started dating Misty. He died and later, Misty gave birth to Harris. Back then, Josie was grappling with a lot of complex emotions over the dissolution of their marriage and later, Ray's death. She was ashamed to say now that she had taken them out on Misty. Until Harris was born. Josie hadn't expected to love him so much but the instant she held him, she knew she would do anything to protect him. Over time, she and Misty grew closer. When Josie and Noah became a couple, Noah easily became part of the found family dynamic among Josie, Misty, and Harris. Now, Josie couldn't imagine their lives without Misty and Harris. The ease with which Noah had come to love and dote on Harris had only made Josie love him more.

As Misty and Cindy sat back down, so did Josie.

"That was so exciting!" Cindy said.

Gleefully, Misty clapped her hands together. "It really was!"

When Josie didn't add anything, Misty turned to her. "You okay?"

She managed a smile. "Sure, yeah."

"You fell asleep, didn't you?"

Josie felt a flush creep up her neck to her scalp.

Misty laughed. "How could you fall asleep here?" She looked around them. Parents and other family members were crowded into the bleachers, shoulder to shoulder. "There aren't even backs to these seats!"

Josie opened her mouth to give some kind of answer, but more shouting erupted below near home plate. The father of one of Harris's teammates screamed at the umpire. "Let him swing! You didn't give him enough swings!"

The crowd bristled. Someone below them told him to shut up and sit down. Another man stood up, cupped his hands around his mouth, and yelled, "He's out! He got six pitches! All the kids get six pitches!"

The father who'd started the dust-up turned toward the stands, searching for the man who'd called out and finding him instantly. They began shouting at one another.

"Not again," Cindy muttered.

Noah and several of the coaches from each team intervened, trying to defuse the situation before any more parents got involved. Before Harris started playing organized sports, Josie had had no idea just how heated things could get among the parents or how quickly a confrontation could spiral out of control.

"This is ridiculous," Misty sighed.

The knot of men that had gathered behind home plate quieted enough so that Josie could no longer hear what was being said, but the argument continued. The crowd grew restless as they waited for it to be resolved. Several people took out their phones to check messages and social media. By this time, Josie had formulated a response to Misty's question. It was a tried-and-true excuse for her exhaustion: she was tired because of work. Both she and Noah were investigators for the Denton City Police Department. Denton was a small city tucked away in the mountains of central Pennsylvania. The center of it lay along the banks of a branch of the Susquehanna River but the city limits sprawled out from there, encompassing a lot of rural area. The city's population had been growing steadily for the last ten years. Josie, Noah, and their colleagues often worked long and unpredictable hours. The last three months had been even more grueling than normal.

Before she could say anything, Cindy's elbow bumped gently against her side. "Still having trouble sleeping?"

"A little," Josie admitted. "Work, you know."

Pointedly, Misty said, "Have you been seeing Dr. Rosetti?"

Josie's muscles stiffened. "I, uh, really don't want to talk about this right now."

Cindy said, "If you're not, you should talk to her."

Her face felt hot. Sun-poisoning hot. Stiffly, she said, "I am seeing her. I never stopped seeing her."

Josie had started seeing Dr. Rosetti for therapy after the death of her grandmother. She didn't like it. She had never liked it, but she went because she knew she had a lot of childhood— and now adult—trauma that needed to be addressed. Drinking hadn't worked. Alienating everyone in her life hadn't worked. Operating solely on sex and rage hadn't helped either. She'd finally come to the conclusion that the people she loved deserved more from her, and that she should make some effort to learn to cope in a healthy way. Plus, while solving a case connected to her grandmother's death, she'd met a courageous little girl who had taught her about tolerating her discomfort. Josie had made that girl a promise that she'd go to therapy.

Slowly, Misty said, "Have you talked to her? About your insomnia?"

Through gritted teeth now, Josie said, "You can talk about him, you know. You can say his name. I'm thinking about him twenty-four hours a day as it is—there is no moment in which I am not thinking about him—so bringing it up isn't going to upset me. Just say it."

Cindy patted Josie's knee. "I'm sorry, hon. We're just worried about you."

Misty said, "Are you not sleeping because you're having nightmares about when Mettner died?"

Josie felt an instant wave of relief wash over her at the sound of his name. It had been three months since her friend and colleague Detective Finn Mettner died in the line of duty, while holding Josie's hand, and everyone around her acted like he'd never existed. Even at work, where his desk remained untouched since the last time he'd been there, no one said his name. No one talked about him. He was the elephant in every room. It was as if people were afraid to talk about him because it might set off some explosion of grief even though Josie was not the type to explode. Not from grief, anyway. She was a champion at bottling things up. Still, the more people walked on eggshells around her, avoiding the topic of Mettner's death, the worse she felt. A couple of times she'd tried to bring him up at work, to Noah, Detective Gretchen Palmer, and their Chief, but then their press liaison, Amber Watts—who had been Mett's girlfriend—walked in and everyone shushed her. Evidently, they were treating Amber the same way they treated Josie, which was to say they never spoke of Mettner.

But he was real, she kept saying to herself. *He was real. He was my friend. I loved him. I watched him die.*

Not saying his name, not acknowledging his absence, made it feel like he had never existed.

Of all the horrible things she'd felt in the wake of his murder, that was worst of all.

"Not nightmares," Josie said. "Not like I had when my grandmother died. It's just... I'm there with him again." She pressed her palms together. "I can feel his hand. I see his eyes—"

She broke off, not willing to get into the rest of it here in such a public space. She didn't want strangers to hear about how she had watched his face change from shock to realization and then to resignation before the life drained from his eyes completely, even though that was what kept her up at night.

Misty slid a hand across her shoulders and pulled her in for a side hug. "I just want you to know I'm here for you. You can talk to me about Mettner."

Josie felt the sting of tears behind her eyes and mumbled a thanks. Much to her relief, the crowd of adults had dispersed on the field below, and play was resuming. Everyone's attention returned to the game. Josie's eyes tracked Noah's progress from home plate to behind the dugout of Harris's team. She watched as he fished his cell phone from the back pocket of his jeans and looked at it. Frowning, he looked up from its screen and searched the crowd for her. Josie stood up. They locked eyes. She knew from his expression that they wouldn't be here for the remainder of the game, nor would they be joining Harris, Misty, and Cindy for a post-game dinner.

Misty said, "What's going on?"

"I don't know," said Josie.

As she made her way to the bottom of the bleachers, her own phone buzzed in her pocket. She took it out and saw a text from the Chief of Denton's police department, Bob Chitwood.

Need you both ASAP.

She found Noah at the side of the bleachers. "I just talked with Gretchen," he said. "Two kids have been reported missing."

THREE

The address Gretchen had given Noah was to a house in a rural area of Denton. It was several miles from the center of town along a little-traveled two-lane road that wound its way deep into the mountains. While Noah drove, Josie checked her phone. It was nearing three in the afternoon, which meant they had over five hours of daylight left. That counted in their favor when it came to searching the forest. Gretchen had texted the names and ages of the missing children first: Kayleigh Patchett, sixteen and Savannah Patchett, eight. Sisters. Next, a photo of the two girls flashed across Josie's phone screen. They stood side by side in front of a bright red door, each wearing a sports uniform of some type. Even though Josie and Noah tried to go to as many of Harris's sporting events as possible, Josie's knowledge of kids' sports was dismal. Kayleigh looked like she was in a softball uniform. She had straight, shoulder-length dark hair, almost black like Josie's, and a round face with a smattering of freckles across her nose and cheeks. In the photo, she gave a stiff smile that didn't reach her brown eyes. Savannah, on the other hand, had a grin that went on for days. Her uniform looked more like what kids wore to soccer, if Josie had to guess. Unlike her sister, her hair was curly. Even her loose ponytail couldn't contain her curls.

Josie said, "What did Gretchen tell you?"

"The kids went for a walk in the woods this morning while the parents were out grocery shopping. Never came back. Parents searched for them but found nothing. After a few hours, they called 911." There was a pause. Josie looked away from the photo of the Patchett sisters long enough to see a muscle ticking in Noah's jaw.

"What is it?"

"We had a new report yesterday from the state police. Last fall, in Lenore County, two teenagers went into the woods. Only one came out. The other died. The kid who survived said someone attacked them but couldn't give a description. They went out in the dark, apparently. No leads. I talked to Heather."

"Heather Loughlin?" Josie asked. "From their criminal investigative division?"

"Yeah. She said initially they thought that the kid who survived made it all up but then two other kids went into the woods about three weeks ago up in Montour County."

Josie felt the first stirrings of nausea deep in her stomach. "Let me guess. Only one came out."

"Yeah. Same thing. They went for a walk in the woods in the dark. One of them got attacked and died. The survivor didn't see anything that could help Heather or her team. Again, no leads."

"What was the cause of death?" asked Josie. "Was it the same in both cases?"

"Blunt force trauma to the head. I don't know much more than that. Didn't seem important until now."

"I don't remember seeing either of these cases in the press," Josie said.

"They weren't. You know how it is—not every death gets

picked up by the press, especially with local news outlets having to cover such a large area of Central Pennsylvania."

Lenore County was about a half hour south of Denton. Montour County was about two hours north of Denton. The cases were nowhere near each other and certainly nowhere near Josie and Noah's jurisdiction.

So why did Josie's gut feel like someone had filled it with concrete?

She took one last look at the faces of Kayleigh and Savannah Patchett before switching from her text app to Google Maps. Frowning, she said, "How many is this, Noah? For us? Here in Denton."

He didn't need an explanation. He knew exactly what she was talking about. "In the last three months? We've had three kids get lost walking in the woods on their own and a few weeks ago, a pair. All located thanks to Luke and Blue."

Josie punched the address of the Patchett home into Google Maps. She was already familiar with the area, but the satellite view confirmed her suspicions: behind the Patchett home was an area of forest that stretched for miles.

Josie said, "Gretchen called Luke already?"

"He's meeting us there."

For the first time, the prospect of running into Luke Creighton didn't make Josie the least bit uncomfortable. Luke and his bloodhound, Blue, had started working with the Denton PD as their K-9 liaison months earlier. Their department had not been able to afford its own K-9 unit, and City Council had turned down the Chief's most recent request for one. Chief Chitwood had found an alternative, partnering with a nonprofit organization that supplied search-and-rescue dogs at nominal fees to police departments that could not afford their own. It just so happened that the handler he'd chosen was Josie's ex-fiancé. Seven years earlier, their relationship had ended in an ugly and public way. Josie and the team hadn't taken well to his return to Denton at first, but after he and Blue saved Josie's life, the tide started to turn. So far, Luke and Blue had found all of the kids who had recently wandered off and gotten lost in the woods around Denton.

"We need radios," Josie said.

"Back seat."

She took off her seatbelt and turned, leaning into the back and rooting around for their radios. She found them under a plastic bag from a local pharmacy. She plucked that up with the radios. Once she was seated again, she opened it and peeked inside. Heat crept into her cheeks as she saw the three new pregnancy tests inside.

Noah glanced over at her. "Those are for you."

She couldn't tear her eyes from them. Her heart sped up a little. "Thanks," she said. "But I—" She broke off. She felt his eyes on her as she tied the bag closed and returned it to the back seat.

"You already got your period," he said. It wasn't a question. There was no recrimination in his voice. Not even a note of disappointment. There was nothing at all in his voice to make her feel badly but she still did.

"Right before the game started," she mumbled.

They'd only begun talking about having kids three months ago after Mettner died. At first, Josie had told him she just wanted to think about it, to make the choice of whether or not to have children without letting fear cloud her judgment. When Josie was three months old, she was abducted by a woman so evil, she made Satan look mild in comparison. That same woman, Lila, had burned down Josie's family home to cover up the crime. Josie's twin sister, Trinity, survived but the authorities had told Josie's parents that tiny Josie perished in the fire. No one had even known that Lila was there that day. Lila had brought Josie to Denton. She was hell-bent on getting her ex-boyfriend, Eli Matson, back. She used Josie, telling him

that she was his baby. Back then, there weren't mail-in pater-
nity tests or anything that the average person could avail themselves of in order to prove parentage. Eli had fallen instantly
in love with Josie and raised her as his own. But his love had
cost him his life, leaving Josie in Lila's care until finally, when
Josie was fourteen, Eli's mother, Lisette Matson—the only
grandmother Josie had ever known—had gotten custody.
Lisette had given her a good life after that but the damage that
Lila had done in those intervening years was permanent, and
for as long as Josie could remember, the lasting effects of the
trauma that Lila inflicted on her was the filter through which
Josie made all decisions—including whether or not to have
children.

Josie had been convinced that she would be a horrible
mother to any child she bore since Lila was the example she had
grown up with. Only after Mettner's death had she come to see
how ridiculous this logic sounded. After Mettner's funeral, Josie
had told Noah she wanted to think about having children but
then, less than a week later, she worried that waiting to decide
was just her subconscious way of continuing to put off having
children because she was still secretly afraid. They hadn't
exactly decided to go for it. They were taking a "let's try and see
what happens" kind of approach. So far, nothing had happened.

Noah's palm was warm on Josie's knee. "Hey," he said,
drawing her out of her thoughts. "It's only been a few months.
Don't worry. We'll keep trying. Those pregnancy tests will
keep."

She gave him a wavering smile.

He squeezed her knee. His eyes stayed on the road. "Josie,
I'm sure this isn't something that happens immediately for most
people. Let's give it some time."

"What if it—what if it doesn't happen?" she said. "Ever?"

He gave her a quick glance. "You already know the answer
to that. I never wanted anything more than you. If we have a

baby, I will love that baby like no one has ever loved their kid before, but I don't need kids to be happy. Just you."

She swallowed over the lump in her throat, feeling embarrassed for needing his reassurance, again.

He flashed a grin. "To be honest, I'm kind of having fun trying, aren't you?"

It was true. They'd never been so physically connected, so on fire, as they had been since they started trying to get pregnant. Her thoughts briefly turned to that morning, a different kind of blush staining her cheeks as she remembered the feel of him against her, inside her. First, in bed. Later, in the laundry room.

"I can't argue with that," Josie answered.

"Hey," Noah said, turning onto the Patchetts' road. "Ask Gretchen if they checked the house yet."

She returned her attention to her phone, typing the question out to Gretchen. Her answer came back in seconds. Josie read it off to him. "Yes, first thing. House was clear."

Whenever they got a call for a missing child, procedure dictated that they search the child's home even if that wasn't the last place the child was seen. It was the unfortunate consequence of missing child reports turning out to be cases in which the children weren't missing at all. Sometimes, they were hiding. Other times, they'd been harmed or killed by their parents and then hidden inside the home. Searching the house first eliminated these two possibilities. It also gave investigators a chance to observe the parents' behavior. If their child was truly missing, they wouldn't have an issue with the police searching their house. If something more nefarious was happening, they might object to the search or otherwise show signs of stress that could indicate they were involved in the disappearance.

The road narrowed, trees rising up on both sides like sentries. There were several residences along the way, but they were spread far apart, each one set on four or more acres with long driveways that snaked through pine trees. Most of the homes weren't visible from the road, their presence marked only by mailboxes.

"This is it," Noah said as they crested a hill and saw a Denton PD cruiser parked near a driveway. The uniformed officer stood outside his vehicle near a white mailbox. He waved to them as Noah turned their SUV into the driveway. A ribbon of asphalt cut through a large grove of eastern hemlock trees, curving to the left ahead. Noah followed slowly, around the bend and up an incline.

"I cannot even imagine how they deal with this driveway when it snows," Josie muttered.

Noah banked to the right as another curve in the driveway appeared. "Someone has to plow them out."

Finally, a house came into view. A two-story rancher with tan siding and a two-car garage. Josie recognized the red front door from the photo of the Patchett sisters. It overlooked a small front stoop bracketed on either side by flowerbeds freshly mulched and dotted with pink peonies and purple geraniums. A stone walkway veered from the stoop in the direction of the garage. A fastidiously cut front lawn lay between the house and more trees, mostly hemlocks and various species of pine. Beside the garage, on a concrete slab, sat an old pickup truck with a plow on the front.

"Must do the snow removal themselves," Josie said.

She turned her attention to the other vehicles gathered at the front of the garage. Two police cruisers, Gretchen's unmarked car, and a minivan. Nearby, a group of people stood in a loose circle. Josie recognized Gretchen's short, spiky brown and gray hair immediately. While a few of the uniformed officers milled around, Gretchen spoke with a civilian couple. Josie knew they were a couple by the way they held onto one another. The man was tall and round. A baseball cap covered his head. A blue T-shirt that read "Soccer Dad" hung down over his wrinkled khaki cargo shorts. On his feet were a worn pair of slides. He looked like he'd been in the middle of changing when the police showed up. Or maybe that was how he always dressed. Josie recognized Kayleigh Patchett's round cheeks, soft chin, and wide mouth in his face. On Kayleigh, they were far more pleasing. The woman clinging to his body was smaller and more smartly dressed in a floral-print silk blouse, black slacks, and a pair of tan ballet flats. Her curly brown hair was pulled back into a loose ponytail but a halo of frizz had escaped. Savannah Patchett was the spitting image of her mother.

Noah parked the SUV behind one of the cruisers and they hopped out, jogging over to the group. They produced their police credentials, offering them to the parents. They barely glanced at them. The woman looked back and forth between Josie and Noah, her eyes wide and hopeful. The man batted their IDs away. His voice boomed across the space between the house and the trees. "I don't care who you are! Find my damn kids!"

FOUR

"Dave!" the woman admonished. Two circles of pink appeared on her cheeks. She tried to pull away from his embrace, but he held her tightly against his side, one meaty hand clamped on her shoulder.

"Shut up, Shel! I'm sick of all this talk. Talk, talk, talk. Where are our damn girls?"

Gretchen ignored his outburst altogether. She held her notepad in one hand and pen in the other. She used the pen to indicate the couple. "Quinn, Fraley. This is Shelly Patchett and her husband, David. As you know, their two daughters are missing. Kayleigh is sixteen, and Savannah is eight."

"Both went missing at the same time?" asked Josie.

David Patchett rolled his eyes. "More damn talk!" he said under his breath.

"Yes," Shelly said, her voice high and nervous. She looked toward Gretchen.

Giving a reassuring smile, Gretchen said, "While we're waiting for the K-9 unit, why don't you tell Detective Quinn and Lieutenant Fraley what you've told me."

Shelly wiped a tear from her cheek. "This morning Dave and I got up late."

"What time was that?" asked Noah.

"Around eight," said Shelly. "We try to sleep in on weekends if we can. It's usually impossible with games and practices. We had a rare morning off today. Dave and I went grocery shopping around nine. We came home around ten, maybe ten fifteen? The kids weren't answering us."

"Which is not unusual," Dave said, calmer now. "They scatter when it comes to helping us unload groceries."

Shelly shot him a disapproving look, extricating herself from his arms. This time, he let her go. "Savannah loves to help but Kayleigh will usually hide. Anyway, we got everything put away and they still weren't coming when we called them. We found a note in the living room from Savannah."

"Can we see the note?" asked Noah.

Gretchen produced it from the pages of her notebook. On a plain piece of copy paper, eight-year-old Savannah Patchett had written:

We went for a walk in the woods. Savannah.

Two hearts had been drawn under her name. As Josie expected, the letters were large and awkward, spread apart in some places and crowded together in others. It reminded her of the cards that Harris made for her and Noah.

Noah said, "Do they do this on a regular basis? Walk in the woods?"

Dave motioned to the trees all around them. "Well, yeah. That's all there is to do out here. We put up a playset for Savannah but she's kind of outgrown it. The girls practice as much as possible in the yard—soccer for Savannah and softball for Kayleigh—but they get bored and sometimes wander into the woods."

"That's not entirely true," Shelly said, "Savannah's been afraid of the woods the last several months so I'm kind of surprised that she went."

"Why is she afraid?" asked Josie. "Did something happen?"

Both parents shook their heads. Dave said, "Some stupid story going around school. Something about a bogeyman."

"The Woodsman," Shelly offered. "All the kids started talking about him one day. He takes kids and never brings them back to their moms."

Dave rolled his eyes. "Yeah, yeah, and he's ten feet tall and eats fully grown deer for breakfast and leaves his mark in the woods to warn people to stay away."

Although she'd never heard those particular details, Josie was well aware of the lore of the Woodsman that had been making its way through the schools of Denton. It had been months since Harris had sat in her lap and confessed to having nightmares about a man the kids at school called "The Woodsman." It had been a rumor going around the elementary school. A shadowy man lurking in the woods who stole children and never brought them home to their moms. Josie had instantly deemed it a silly child's story, like the kind kids made up on playgrounds and at slumber parties. When Josie was a little girl, her classmates used to claim that if you said a particular phrase three times while looking into a mirror, a woman would appear behind you and "get you." Naturally, they all tried it. None of them were ever "gotten." In fact, nothing ever happened.

Harris had gone through a phase where he had nightmares about the Woodsman. Misty, Josie, and Noah had finally gotten him to stop believing in the Woodsman three months ago. Or at least, he'd stopped having night terrors.

"What school does Savannah go to?" asked Josie.

"Wolfson Elementary. She's in second grade," Shelly said.

"My…" She hesitated, never sure how to refer to Harris when speaking with other people. She settled on, "Nephew goes there as well. Same grade. We heard all about the Woodsman from him."

Dave mumbled, "It's so damn stupid."

Shelly shot him another look, this one a mixture of irritation and incredulity. Redirecting her attention to Josie, she said, "Kayleigh kept telling Savannah they would take a walk together so she could show her that there's no reason to be afraid, but Savannah was always too petrified. Until today, I guess."

Noah said, "Kayleigh is sixteen. I assume she has a phone? Have you tried contacting her?"

Shelly looked down at her feet. "She doesn't have it with her."

Dave added, "We're very strict about the phone. You see how kids are with them these days. How much trouble they get into with these phones."

The three of them nodded. They knew better than anyone what types of terrible things happened as a result of teenagers having unlimited and constant access to cell phones. In Josie's experience, most problems that arose had to do with bullying. Then there were situations in which pedophiles and sex traffickers posed as young people and used social media to groom teenagers, eventually convincing them to meet. It never ended well. No matter how much outreach the Denton PD did to educate students and parents at local schools about these issues, bad things continued to happen.

Gretchen cleared her throat.

Dave glanced at her and then said, "Kayleigh was being punished. No phone for a week. So no, we didn't contact her because we couldn't."

"But we looked for them," Shelly said, voice getting higher. "For hours."

Josie asked, "You said you got home from the grocery store around ten. At what point did you begin searching for them?"

"We waited until eleven thirty. We had no idea what time they'd left so we figured we'd give them a little bit of time in case they were on their way back. I thought they must be getting hungry for lunch by then because it didn't look like they'd eaten anything but cereal while we were gone."

Dave said, "Kayleigh never does her dishes no matter how many times we remind her."

Another look of frustration from Shelly went unnoticed by her husband.

"It's not like them to not come home," Dave added. "When we couldn't find them after a few hours, we panicked and called you guys."

"You did the right thing," said Josie.

Noah asked, "There's a pretty big forested area behind your house—and every other house on this road. How big was your search area?"

Shelly and Dave looked at one another. Shelly opened her mouth as if to speak but closed it again. Dave scratched his temple. "Uh, I'm not sure because Shel got lost for a bit."

Sheepishly, she said, "I ended up down that way." She pointed in the direction of Central Denton. "Behind one of our neighbors' houses."

Dave said, "I was headed directly away from the house for a while, but then she texted me and said she didn't know where she was, so I turned back."

"We have Androids so we don't have the Find My Phone app," Shelly explained. "And Google Maps doesn't exactly work in the middle of the forest. Spotty service. I was trying to tell him where I was but in terms of landmarks, there's not much besides trees."

Dave said, "I stayed on the phone with Shel but then I got a little confused out there, too. Eventually, I found the house again. She got into a neighbor's yard."

"That's when we realized we needed help," Shelly said.

Behind them, tires crunched over gravel. They all turned to see Luke's old, dirt-covered pickup truck pulling in behind Noah's SUV. He hopped out, leaving his door open long enough for a large bloodhound to jump out of the truck. As Luke approached them, Blue dutifully loped along at his side. While Blue was sweet and adorable, Luke was an imposing figure, six feet, lean and muscular. Now that he was a civilian and no longer a state trooper, he wore his brown hair to his shoulders. Stubble darkened his cheeks. When they were together, Josie had liked his close-cropped hair and clean-shaven face but now she thought this more informal, relaxed look suited him more. He lifted a hand to wave at the Patchetts, and Josie noticed Shelly visibly recoil at the sight of Luke's hands.

Josie and her team were so used to the sight of them, they barely registered just how unsightly and damaged they appeared. During the case that had ended his career as a state trooper and his relationship with Josie, as well as sent him to prison for a stint, he had been tortured. Both his hands had been smashed to bits. Silvered scars ran like thick, ropy veins across both his hands from the multiple surgeries he'd undergone. The doctors had done their best to piece his fingers back together but still, the index and middle fingers of his right hand were flattened, and the top knuckle of his left pinky stuck outward at an unnatural angle.

With Luke still out of earshot, Dave Patchett whispered, "What happened to him?"

With a stiff smile, Gretchen said, "An accident. I assure you that his injuries do not impact his work at all."

"Yeah," Noah said, a note of defensiveness in his voice. "He's the best. So is Blue."

Josie looked at her husband, stifling a smile. Months earlier, when Luke had joined their team, the tension between him and Luke had been palpable. Josie was glad it was behind them now.

Whatever their history, Luke and Blue were an invaluable and much-needed addition to Denton PD.

Chastened, Dave looked down as Luke and Blue joined them. If Luke had seen their looks of horror, he didn't show it. Blue nudged one of Josie's hands with his head, and she rewarded him with a scratch behind both floppy ears. Once introductions were made, Luke said, "Blue will need an item of clothing from one of your girls."

Shelly disappeared into the house to find something. Luke addressed Dave. "Do either of your daughters have any medical conditions I should know about before we get started?"

Josie saw a flicker of hesitation cross Dave's face. Then he said, "No. Nothing. They're both very healthy."

"Do you know what they were wearing when they went into the woods?"

"Uh, no. They had already gone out for a walk when we went out."

Shelly came running from the front door, a small soccer jersey in her arms. "This is Savannah's," she said as she reached them. The front of it was covered in dirt. The number 12 had been stitched onto the back. "Will this work?"

Luke smiled. From his belt, he unhooked a harness and lead. Blue sat obediently, tail wagging. Kneeling, Luke slid the harness on and clipped the lead to it. He murmured a few words into one of Blue's ears. Then he took the jersey from Shelly Patchett and let Blue sniff it, giving the dog some last instructions. Within seconds, Blue was tugging at the lead, pulling Luke around to the back of the house.

"He's got it," Luke said, jogging after the dog.

Josie watched his form recede. "I'm going to go with them," she said.

FIVE

Blue moved swiftly, head swinging back and forth, nose twitching. Gone was the playful, lumbering sweetheart Josie knew. In his place was a dog driven with purpose, singularly focused on Savannah Patchett's scent. At the back of the Patchetts' home was the playset that Dave had told them about. It was a huge wooden structure shaped like a pirate ship. Beside it, discarded sports equipment trailed to the edge of the yard where the grass ended and the forest began. No fence separated the two. Josie scanned the perimeter to see if there was some well-worn path that the kids used to go into the woods, but there was nothing.

Blue found a small area where the overgrown weeds had been tamped down slightly and surged over it into the woods. Luke followed, laser-focused on the task at hand. Josie trailed behind them, giving them enough space so that she was not a hindrance to their search. In a soft voice, Luke offered Blue occasional praise and encouragement. The ground beneath them began to incline. Fallen branches, gnarled tree roots, brambles, knee-high brush, and large stones littered the way but none of it impeded Blue. Josie had been on searches with him and Luke a handful of times now and she was always surprised by how quickly and nimbly Blue navigated even the trickiest terrain. The late-afternoon sunlight filtering through the trees dappled every surface. Under the thick foliage, the air was cooler but at the pace they were moving, Josie started to sweat within minutes. Ahead of her, she saw perspiration on Luke's shirt forming a V in the center of his back. He stopped near a group of boulders to give Blue some water, pulling a bottle and collapsible bowl from the backpack he carried.

He offered her a bottle but she refused. "Save it for Blue."

Luke smiled. "He's been heading pretty much in the same direction, west."

Josie said, "According to the parents, they were looking in the opposite direction when they searched earlier."

"You have any idea how far this patch of woods goes?"

Josie thought about the Google map she'd studied on the way to the Patchetts' house. "About three miles to the west, give or take. It comes out on Kelleher Road. Gretchen already sent patrols out there to search from that direction as well as the north and south sides."

"Any structures?" he asked as Blue resumed his search.

"Not along that road. Not for another five or six miles, at least. It's pretty remote the further you move away from the city."

Luke made a noise of acknowledgment and continued on. Blue zigzagged between trees and hopped over rocks. A few times Josie was startled by the movement of other animals nearby—squirrels, rabbits, and even a small group of does which Blue scared, causing them to scatter. Blue barely gave them a glance, too focused on following Savannah Patchett's scent. Josie sidestepped multiple piles of animal excrement, each time relieved to see that the droppings were from neither coyote nor bear. They came to a ravine, and Blue sniffed along its edge but continued onward. Josie leaned over the precipice to make sure no one was lying below, but there was nothing but more brush and rocks. Luke and Blue had just taken a left behind a large oak tree when she finally heard Blue bark. Then came Luke's voice. "Josie!"

After that, a bloodcurdling scream.

Josie broke into a sprint, feet flying over a large rock. Blue sat to attention next to a dead tree trunk that had fallen across a shallow ravine. His worried eyes followed Luke as he knelt beside the tree, peering into the small opening between the trunk and the earth. Another high-pitched scream of terror sounded, sending Luke back to his feet. Face pale, he met Josie's eyes.

"It's her," he said. "The younger one."

Josie nodded. She handed him her radio. "Call it in."

While he took a few steps away and spoke into her radio, Josie got down on her hands and knees and stared at the face of Savannah Patchett. Her curls frizzed wildly around her face. A smudge of dirt streaked one of her tear-stained cheeks. Eyes wide with terror, she shrank from Josie, curling more tightly into the tiny ball she'd made herself into. Behind her was only a wall of dirt. She didn't scream again though, which Josie counted as progress.

"Savannah," Josie said. "My name is Detective Josie Quinn. I'm with the Denton Police Department. I'm here with my friend, Luke and his dog, Blue. We came to take you back to your parents."

Savannah stared at Josie, unblinking.

Josie repeated her words and then extended a hand to the girl. "Can you come out here with me?"

Savannah didn't move.

Josie said, "You're safe, Savannah. We won't hurt you. If you'd like, I can get your parents on my radio, and you can talk to them before we do anything else. Would you like that?"

No response. No movement. The girl's eyes stayed locked on Josie's face, suspicious, terrified.

Luke walked back to Josie but stayed out of Savannah's sight. Josie motioned for him to hand back her radio. After a couple of minutes, Shelly Patchett's voice filled the air. It sounded as though she was crying. "Savannah? Savannah? Are you there? Baby, please talk to me."

Josie got onto her chest and shimmied along the ground, getting as close to Savannah as she dared. She held out the radio, pointing at the various controls. "Press here when you want to talk."

Savannah looked at the radio but didn't take it. Shelly continued to speak, begging her daughter to respond. Josie wriggled closer to the girl, arm aching as she held out the radio. "I'll press the button," she said. "You talk."

She depressed the button and held the radio close to Savannah's face. The girl licked her dry lips and said, "Mom?"

Shelly's voice came back, several octaves higher than before. "Oh baby! Thank God. Thank God you're okay. You go with the police officers, okay? They'll bring you back to us."

Josie held the button down once more and Savannah squeaked out an "okay."

Extricating herself from beneath the tree, Josie sat back on her heels and pocketed her radio. She held out a hand to the girl. "Are you ready?"

Several seconds ticked by before Savannah slowly crept out. She wore blue cotton shorts, the back of which was covered in dirt. One of her elbows was bloodied. She looked all around, taking in Josie, Blue, and Luke, then studying the rest of the area before trying to stand up. Both her knees bore fresh, bloody abrasions. Her white T-shirt featured the logo of her school's soccer team as well as a large tear in the side. Her legs trembled and collapsed under her. Josie caught her before she fell, holding her upright. She was about the same size as Harris.

Blue whined. Josie said, "Are you hurt, or are your legs stiff from being in that little space for so long?"

Savannah shook one leg and then the other, studying the matching cuts on her knees. Slowly, she inched away from Josie's touch. "I fell and got cuts," she mumbled. "But I also feel stiff."

"Do you think you can walk?" Josie asked her.

"I can give you a piggyback ride if you want," Luke offered.

Savannah stared at him wordlessly. A small kernel of trepidation burrowed into the pit of Josie's stomach. She had rescued her fair share of kids after they'd been lost in the woods. Usually, they were freezing or wet from rain or they'd injured themselves too badly to walk, but their spirits, particularly after being found, were high. Even the quieter ones perked up when told they'd be reunited with their families within an hour.

Savannah seemed stunned.

"Did you hit your head, Savannah?" Josie asked her.

She slowly felt the back of her skull. "I don't think so. I fell on my hands and knees." She held up her hands so Josie could see the scrapes striping the meaty parts of her palms.

"Do you think you can walk?" Josie asked again.

When she didn't answer, Josie wondered if she was going into shock. A glance at Luke's worried face told her that he was concerned about the same thing. Turning to Savannah, she added, "Or I can give you a piggyback ride. It might be faster. We want to get you back to your parents as soon as possible. We'll also need to get you checked out by the paramedics to make sure you're okay."

Blue whined again, longer this time. He stood up and walked over to Savannah, whimpering as he paced back and forth in front of her. She watched him, her face still guarded.

Josie said, "What's he doing?"

Luke knelt and held out a hand to Blue. "Come here, boy."

But the dog didn't obey. He simply stood in front of Savannah and whined again.

Luke met Josie's eyes. "He, uh, knows when something is wrong."

The dog was worried about Savannah. It only confirmed Josie's uneasy suspicion that something was not right. Josie said, "Savannah, what happened out here today?"

Josie, Luke, and Blue all watched as tears silently streamed down the girl's cheeks. Positioning herself directly in front of Savannah, Josie squatted so they were eye to eye. "Savannah?"

No answer, only more tears and a slight quiver of her lower lip.

Josie softened her tone and tried a different question. "Savannah, where's your sister? Where is Kayleigh?"

Her words were a sudden screech, pushed out on the edge of a sob. "He took her!" she cried. "He took her away!"

SIX

Josie's entire body stiffened. The dam of her emotions broken, Savannah fell forward and threw her arms around Josie's neck. Her small body shook in Josie's embrace. Tears soaked through the shoulder of Josie's T-shirt. Stroking Savannah's hair, Josie whispered soothing words into her ear. "Okay, Savannah. I'm glad you told me that. I'm here to help. I'm going to try to find Kayleigh, okay? I'll do everything I can to try to find her. So will my team."

Another sob, followed by another shriek. "You can't!" Savannah wailed. "You can't find her. She's gone. Once the Woodsman takes you, he never brings you back!"

Luke said, "What did she say?"

Josie wasn't sure she had heard correctly. "Savannah, I need you to calm down. We need to talk about this. What did you just say?"

Savannah pulled back, looking into Josie's eyes. Her nose was bright red, eyes glassy. Gulping a breath, she said, "The Woodsman. He took Kayleigh and once he takes you, he never brings you back."

Luke said, "Who is the Woodsman?"

"It's not important," Josie mumbled. She was less concerned with the lore of the Woodsman than she was with the fact that Kayleigh Patchett had been abducted.

"It is important!" Savannah insisted. "He took her!"

"Josie?" said Luke quietly. "Who is the Woodsman?"

Josie shook her head. "It's nothing. Just a story going around school."

Beneath Josie's hands, Savannah's thin shoulders trembled. "It's not just a story! It's not! He took my sister."

Josie looked at her earnest face. She tried to quell her own panic. If what Savannah said was correct, and the sisters had encountered a man who kidnapped Kayleigh, the police had already lost precious hours trying to locate her. Taking a deep breath, Josie said, "Savannah, I believe you that something happened to Kayleigh. My team is back at your house. Not far from here. If you tell me what happened, I can radio to them and have them start looking for Kayleigh right away."

Again, Savannah looked all around them, as if she expected someone—the Woodsman?—to jump out from behind a tree at any moment. Blue whimpered again. One of Josie's hands let go of Savannah's shoulder and patted the gun at her waist, reassured that it was still there.

Josie added, "I promise you are safe with me, Luke, and his dog, Blue. We won't let anything happen to you."

Savannah gripped one of Josie's wrists with both hands. They were cold and clammy, in spite of the warm May evening. "The Woodsman took my sister."

"A man took your sister?"

Savannah nodded.

"What did he look like?"

"I don't know."

Josie said, "Did you see him?"

Savannah shook her head slowly. "Not his face or anything.

I just saw... like, something move. He was wearing yellow, like a yellow shirt or jacket or something."

Josie released Savannah's other shoulder, attempting to give the girl some space, but Savannah kept her hands clamped over Josie's wrist. "Savannah, can you tell us what happened?"

Standing several feet away from them, Luke shifted from foot to foot. "Josie," he said. "It will be dark before we know it. We should get going."

She silenced him with a raised palm, keeping her eyes on Savannah. Though the sun was fading, they still had a couple of hours before it turned completely dark.

"We were walking," said the girl. "I was scared of the Woodsman. I get nightmares a lot. I usually go into Kayleigh's room at night, and she hugs me in bed until I fall back to sleep. She always said he wasn't real, but I didn't believe her. Last night I had another bad dream and so I went into her room again. In the morning, Mom and Dad were out. Kayleigh said she would prove to me that the Woodsman wasn't real. We could go for a walk in the woods together and she could show me there was no one out here. We walked and walked and walked. I stopped to pick a flower and when I turned around, she was gone. I yelled her name and then I heard all this noise."

"What kind of noise?" asked Josie.

"Like trees breaking or something," Savannah replied. "And Kayleigh screamed."

"Could you see her?"

She shook her head. "I couldn't tell where she was. I looked around and around, but I didn't see her. But then, between these two trees, I saw this huge guy run across. He had on a yellow shirt or something. Maybe a jacket—oh! And blue jeans! I saw his blue jeans!"

"That's good," Josie said. "What else can you tell me?"

"I heard Kayleigh again. She said, 'He's got me! He's got me!' and then she screamed for me to run so I did. I just ran and ran and ran until I couldn't hear her anymore. I fell. Three times. I got scared. I didn't know which way was the right way or the way back to the house and I was afraid if I kept going, he would get me, too, so I hid under that tree."

Under his breath, Luke muttered, "Good lord."

Josie patted Savannah's hands. "I'm glad you told me. You did a good job. I just have a few more questions."

"Josie," Luke protested.

Blue grunted.

"Quick ones," Josie said as Savannah's grip tightened on her wrist. "Do you know how long ago this happened?"

Savannah stared at her, uncomprehending. Josie remembered how bad Harris was at estimating time at this age and rephrased. "You said you walked and walked and walked before this happened. Had you stopped at all before that? To rest or anything?"

Savannah shook her head.

"So you didn't need a rest before that?"

Another headshake.

"Good," said Josie. "Do you have any idea what part of the woods this happened in?"

"I don't know the parts of the woods," Savannah said, her voice almost a whisper.

Josie smiled. "Your parents said you and Kayleigh walk out here sometimes. Are there any markers—certain trees or rocks—that you recognize or use to tell how far from home you are or where in the forest you are?"

"I don't know. Kayleigh usually knows where we are. Well, sometimes we get lost, but she always finds the way back to the house."

"Okay," Josie said. "You're doing great, Savannah. One more question. What was Kayleigh wearing today when you two left the house?"

"Um, shorts. Black ones, and her blue hoodie."

"Under her hoodie?" asked Josie.

Savannah's lower lip trembled. "I don't remember."

"That's okay, that's all right," Josie said quickly. "How about her shoes?"

"Sneakers."

"Great. What color?"

"White."

It was enough to start with, enough for an Amber Alert. Josie smiled. "You did an awesome job, Savannah. Let's start walking back. I'm just going to need you to let go of my hand for a few minutes while we walk, so I can call my team on the radio and let them know that they need to start searching for Kayleigh immediately."

Reluctantly, Savannah peeled her hands from Josie's arm. Luke approached, holding out Blue's leash. "I have to keep my dog on his lead, but if you want, you can hold onto the middle part of it, and we can let him lead us both back. I'll hold it here, and you can hold it there. This way you're always between me and Blue and you can't get lost again."

She stared up at him, eyes moving from his face to his hands. Unlike her mother, she didn't recoil. Only curiosity flared in her eyes. She said, "Are your hands okay to hold onto the leash?"

Luke smiled. He lifted one of his hands and flexed it. "Oh yeah. I've had lots of practice. They look bad but they don't hurt."

Savannah glanced back at Josie, as if for reassurance. Josie nodded and Savannah walked over and grabbed Blue's leash. Josie stood up and the three of them began walking. Josie hung back until she was out of earshot of Savannah. She got Noah on the radio and began briefing him as quickly as possible.

"Get an Amber Alert out as soon as possible," she concluded.

"Roger," came Noah's response.

As the last squawk of the radio sounded, she thought she heard the snap of a twig somewhere behind her. She froze, scanning the forest all around, but saw nothing. Her eyes strained against the dimness of evening encroaching. There was nothing. No movement. No sound either, beyond the ambient noise of birds, insects, and a few toads. After a few moments, she turned away and ran to catch up with Luke, Blue, and Savannah.

SEVEN

Savannah clung to her mother like a barnacle, her long legs wrapped around Shelly's waist. Dave gathered them in his arms, holding them close. Tears poured down both parents' faces. While Luke took Blue over to their vehicle for some food, water, and rest, Josie gathered in a tight little knot with Noah and Gretchen.

"Did you tell them?" asked Josie.

Gretchen sighed. "They haven't stopped crying since."

Noah said, "Dad got us one of Kayleigh's pillows for Blue to scent, but Josie, it's going to be dark within the hour."

She glanced over at Luke, who sat on the tailgate of his truck with Blue beside him. He stroked the dog's back. "They can work in the dark. I talked to Luke on the way back. He's ready to go. So is Blue. We just need lights. Did you call the state police? Can we get a helicopter out here? They've got infrared. Besides Blue, that's probably our best bet to find her."

"I called the Chief," said Gretchen, opening her notebook and paging through it. "He's trying to get it. Can't make any promises."

"Josie," said Noah, hesitating. He looked over at the Patchetts.

She sighed. "I know, but we have to try everything."

What none of them needed to say out loud was that if a man had taken Kayleigh Patchett, there was a very high chance that she was dead already, in which case the infrared sensors would not pick up her body heat. With each step that Josie took back toward the Patchett home, the dread in her stomach had grown heavier.

Gretchen tapped her pen against a half-filled page in her notebook. "What are we looking at here? A random guy skulking around in the woods? Sees Kayleigh and on impulse, decides to attack her?"

"There's no way to know for sure," Josie said. "But on the way over here, Noah mentioned a couple of cases from Lenore and Montour Counties that sound similar. Two kids go into the woods and get attacked."

Gretchen used her pen to scratch her temple. "Yeah. I heard about those, too. I think it's too soon to say this is related to that, though."

Noah said, "We have to consider that maybe someone was out there stalking these girls and as soon as they got separated, he went after Kayleigh."

Josie said, "If we don't find her tonight, we have to entertain both possibilities: either it was a random guy out in the woods who saw Kayleigh and took his opportunity, or it was someone stalking her. First thing in the morning, we do a line search."

A line search was a way to look for evidence, usually outdoors, by having several people line up side by side and walk slowly across a designated area together, scanning the ground in front of them for anything that was significant to the case.

Noah looked behind Josie where the forest was shrouded in darkness. "A line search? That's a lot of ground to cover."

Josie nodded. "Especially since we don't really know where

Kayleigh was last seen by Savannah. Blue should help us with that, though. The Amber Alert should be going out any minute. Everyone will know we're looking for this girl. We can get the press involved. Call on the community. People will show up to help with a line search. They've done it before here in Denton."

"Sadly," Gretchen sighed. She scribbled something on her notepad.

Josie continued, "If we don't locate her, then we should check her phone, laptop, any electronic devices she uses. Talk with her friends and classmates. Take another look at her room. Have a much longer conversation with her parents. We also need to take a closer look at the map of this area. Did you hear anything from the patrols you sent out to cover Kelleher Road, since that's where this patch of forest ends?"

Gretchen nodded. "They didn't see anything. I stationed units on all three sides of the area though."

"Great," said Josie.

Noah added, "As soon as you radioed in, I sent units to canvass all the residences on this road. If the Patchetts are walking out in these woods regularly, it stands to reason other residents are as well. Could have been a neighbor."

"We also checked for registered sex offenders within a five-mile radius," Gretchen said. "There are a few. We've got a unit checking in with them."

"I think we should be looking at property records in a five-mile radius, at least, tonight. We should call Mett. He can—"

She broke off. Horror stabbed at her diaphragm, freezing the oxygen in her lungs. The air around them went still. It was as though the entire world had stopped spinning, although Josie was vaguely aware of muffled conversations coming from where the Patchetts stood and where the uniformed officers milled around. Both Gretchen and Noah stared at her, wide-eyed and stunned. Every breath she took felt like fire in her chest. She started to count the seconds off in her mind, gauging how long the awkwardness lasted. When she got to ten, she tried to speak again, but all that came out was a choking sound.

Gretchen looked down at her notebook and tapped her pen against it. "Boss," she said, voice cracking.

Now the words came, fast but still scratchy. "Please don't call me that," said Josie. "Please."

Gretchen met her eyes and Josie saw the question in them.

Before their current Chief of Police, Bob Chitwood, arrived in Denton, Josie had been the interim Chief. In fact, she was the one who had hired Gretchen as a detective. Everyone on the force had gotten into the habit of calling her "boss" during that short tenure, and no matter how many times she'd corrected her colleagues afterward, it stuck.

Josie swallowed. She could barely push the words out. With them, the memory of Mettner's last moments came racing back. "Mett said that. Right before he died."

"I'm sorry," Gretchen said. "I didn't know."

Noah inched closer to her and rested a hand on her shoulder. "It's okay, Josie. Do you have any idea how many times I've almost called him or texted him? I've actually typed the words into my phone, nearly hit send, and then remembered he was gone."

"You don't think it's something you would forget," Gretchen said. "But when someone is that much a part of your life, turning to them becomes so automatic that you can't help it."

Josie's throat felt thick with words she could not get out. Gretchen was right. It had been the same way for months after her grandmother's death. Josie had picked up the phone to call her or automatically turned up the road to her assisted living facility to pop in before remembering that she was gone. The Denton PD hadn't had such a large, high-stakes investigation since Mettner's death. At times like these, they had relied on him. The Chief had authorized overtime so they were getting additional uniformed officers to come in and assist, but it wasn't lost on any of them that the person they could have used most was Mettner. His absence wouldn't impact the physical search, but it would certainly slow down other aspects of their investigation.

"Josie," Noah prodded.

She shook her head, like a dog shaking off water, trying to focus on the task at hand. She pushed all the emotions associated with Mettner deep down inside a secret compartment in her mind and shut the lid. A girl's life was at stake. Josie could not afford to let her personal emotions slow the search. She had a job to do.

"I'm okay," she said. Then she turned and called out to Luke, "You guys ready?"

"Whenever you are," he replied.

Noah squeezed Josie's shoulder. "I'll get some flashlights."

EIGHT

No one sees me. I have learned how to traverse the woods as quietly as possible, taking careful steps, avoiding animals and other natural dangers. I have learned how to be patient and watch, sometimes for hours. No one ever expects me, even when they've come looking for me. I lay my traps and wait. When they come, it's always in twos, because that is part of the legend, which is ever-evolving. I hear it talked about when I walk among them in my regular life. They have no idea that they are talking about me right in my presence.

They come in twos but I only want to snare one.

That is part of the fun. Keep them or kill them?

Sometimes things happen too fast for me to make the decision. Their heads crack and the thrill of the night is over. But my legend lives on because I let the other one escape.

Someone has to keep telling my tale.

NINE

The frantic race to keep up with Blue was much harder beneath a rapidly darkening sky. Although Blue was surefooted—as was Luke with his headlamp leading the way—the rest of them were not. Josie and Noah had gone along for the search while Gretchen stayed back at the house to coordinate the various facets of the investigation. The air had cooled considerably but as they made their way through the forest, sweat began to bead along Josie's hairline and pool at the base of her spine. A few times, small animals darted across their paths, startling all of them except Blue, who was so focused that nothing got through to him except Luke's commands.

Josie's calves were burning by the time Luke and Blue stopped. She and Noah had fallen pretty far behind. Noah said, "Did Blue alert? I didn't hear him bark."

Fear tickled the back of Josie's neck. She knew that Blue had both an active alert, which involved barking, and a passive alert, which involved simply stopping and laying down next to his find. She was pretty sure Luke used the passive alert for cadavers. But as their flashlights crisscrossed over Luke's back,

Josie saw that Blue was standing beside him, drinking from the collapsible water bowl.

"You guys okay?" Luke asked as they drew up beside him.

"Yeah," Josie said. "How's Blue?"

Luke knelt and took up the bowl, tucking it back inside his backpack. "He's fine. We're good to go."

Noah pointed his flashlight ahead of them. "Look."

From between two birch trees, Josie saw the light pass over a slash of yellow. "Is that the road?"

"Looks that way," said Luke.

"That's got to be Kelleher Road," said Noah. "I'll call it in."

He got on the radio as Luke murmured instructions to Blue, who took off at an easy jog once more, after Kayleigh Patchett's scent. In seconds they were in the middle of Kelleher Road. Looking to her right, toward the stretch of road that led back into town, Josie saw headlights in the distance as well as the red and blue flash of a Denton PD cruiser's emergency lights. The headlights blinked twice.

Noah said, "They see us. They'll hold position there."

Josie expected Blue to stop along the road. Surely he would lose Kayleigh's scent here. Her abductor could have been parked along this deserted stretch of road, brought her back to his vehicle, stuffed her inside and taken off. Instead, Blue kept going, plunging into the trees on the other side of the road.

She and Noah had no time to talk or even think as they followed Luke and Blue through what was now full darkness. Soon, the *thwap-thwap* of helicopter rotors filled the night air, faint at first, then louder.

"Looks like the state police sent their helicopter," said Noah.

Josie nodded, saving her breath. They were both soaked through with sweat and out of breath by the time Luke paused the search again to give Blue some rest and more water. The helicopter was nearby, circling their position. The glow of its spotlight gave the area around them a dull glow.

Noah had to raise his voice to be heard over the rotors. "How many miles do you think we've gone?"

Luke shrugged. "Hard to say."

"The distance between the Patchetts' house and Kelleher Road was three miles, so we've gone at least that far," Josie said.

"How far can Blue reasonably go, Luke?" asked Noah.

From under his headlamp, he smiled. "Oh, a good, long way provided we stop for rest and water." He bent and scratched behind Blue's ears. "I'll let you know when he's ready to quit if we haven't found Kayleigh Patchett by then."

They were off again, this time climbing. It was getting harder for Josie to catch her breath. Her jeans, soaked with perspiration, chafed against her thighs. Blisters had started forming on her toes. Her lower back and feet ached. There was something else, too. Something she couldn't quite identify. A feeling of unease that had nothing to do with the case. But there wasn't time for her brain to examine it.

Until Luke and Blue stopped abruptly. Pushing his body in front of Blue, Luke waited until Josie and Noah had drawn close enough for them to hear him hiss over his shoulder. "There's a man up ahead!"

Heart pounding, Josie unsnapped her holster and pulled out her gun, positioning the flashlight under the barrel. Noah did the same. She pushed past Luke and Blue. "Get behind a tree," she told Luke.

She wondered if this was the abductor or if it was some random person just wandering around in the woods. Surely, whoever it was, he'd heard them. They hadn't made any effort to conceal their approach. Between their flashlights and the nearby helicopter, they weren't exactly quiet. She and Noah fell instantly into formation, him panning the left side of the forest ahead while Josie took the right.

"Denton Police," Josie called out, trying to yell loud enough to be heard over the helicopter. "Please come out where we can see you."

No movement or sound came from ahead of them.

"There!" Noah said, stopping. "Right there."

His flashlight beam froze on the shape of a man leaning his back against a rock face. His chin dipped downward. One of his feet was tucked up behind him, the sole against the wall.

Josie's heart gave a little stutter and then kicked into overdrive, a racehorse galloping in her chest. She lowered her weapon. "Noah," she croaked. "That's the Standing Man."

She couldn't see his face clearly, but she heard the confusion in his voice. "What?"

"It's not a real man. It's a rock formation. If you approach from this direction, it looks like a man leaning against the wall."

Noah took tentative steps forward until he had a clearer view of it. He, too, lowered his pistol. Turning to her, even in the low light, she could see that his face had paled. "This is the place, isn't it?"

The helicopter noise subsided a bit as it circled wide, away from their current position.

Now Josie knew the source of the unease that had plagued her as they'd continued to forge through the woods. "Yes," she said, the word nearly getting strangled in her throat.

From behind them, Luke's voice sounded. "Everything okay?"

"Yes," Josie called. "You two can come out."

As Luke and Blue approached, Josie shone her light onto the Standing Man. "Rock formation," she said.

Luke studied it for a long moment. Then his face went ashen, too. "Oh Josie. It was here, wasn't it?"

She couldn't talk so she simply nodded. Eight years earlier, she had solved the most famous case in Denton. That, too, had started out with a missing teenage girl, but it had ended in the discovery of one of the most prolific serial killer teams in history. The entire city had been shattered. Solving the case had come at great personal cost to Josie and many other people, including Luke, who had almost died and lost his spleen. She hadn't been back to the mountain since the conclusion of the case. It had been too painful.

Luke said, "But I thought the city bulldozed this entire..." He broke off, not finding the right word.

In her mind, Josie filled it in: *mass grave.*

Noah said, "The city bought up all the property the remains were found on and tore down all the structures. They took everything, even some of the trees. Planted a field of flowers. That's what we'll find ahead. If Blue keeps heading in that direction."

Josie could feel Luke's eyes on her. "You gonna be okay?"

She thrust her chin forward. Inside, she gathered the old traumatic memories and pushed them deep into the mental box where her trauma from Mettner's death lived. Nothing was going to get in her way of helping to find Kayleigh Patchett.

"I'm fine," she said, surprised at how strong her voice sounded. "Let's keep moving."

Luke gave Blue a command and the dog resumed his long search. As Josie watched them go, she felt Noah's hand on her shoulder. His touch sent an instant wave of comfort through her body. Some of the tension knotting her shoulder blades released. He pointed his flashlight ahead. "Let's go."

TEN

Moments later, they reached the field. The silver light of the moon illuminated rows of tulips, peonies, irises, geraniums, and wildflowers across the top of the mountain, dropping off where the land dipped back downward. Blue tromped right through them, undeterred by their heady scents. Soon the helicopter swept across, its spotlight bringing the colors of the flowers briefly into relief. Air pressed down on them, bending the stalks of the flowers. Then the helicopter circled away again. Josie had to admit, the field must be beautiful in the daytime. In a sense, they were on hallowed ground. So many young girls had rested here, lost and forgotten until the day Josie arrived. It was here that she had committed the final act of violence on this mountain.

She hoped.

As if reading her mind, across from her, Noah said, "Why here?"

She knew he didn't expect an answer. She was glad when they crossed back into the tree line and began their descent.

"You think he walked her all this way?" Noah said. "We're miles away from the Patchetts' home."

"Or she got away," Josie said hopefully. "And she's been running since."

"She would have been found by now," Noah said.

Luke and Blue had gained so much ground that Josie could barely make out the white of Luke's shirt. "Come on," she said. "Let's catch up."

She and Noah broke into a run. Josie kept the square of Luke's back in view as they slid down an embankment. The rear of a small structure came into view. A log cabin. New. Josie quickly counted the windows at its rear, all small and above eye level. Luke and Blue jogged around to the front of it. Noah stopped, taking up position at the back, and waved Josie onward. Along the side of the cabin was a large blue tarp, covering some sort of object or objects. Josie got on the radio and alerted them to it, advising that she was going to look beneath it. She held her breath, wondering if she'd find Kayleigh's body underneath. In one swift motion, she tore the tarp away. Her flashlight beam illuminated what looked like several car jacks, jack lifts, and some pieces of plywood. No body.

Breathing a sigh of relief, she radioed her findings and continued to the front of the cabin. It was well-lit by exterior spotlights. At the bottom of the steps leading to the front door, Blue sat patiently, looking back and forth from the door to Luke.

"He pulled toward the door," said Luke.

The helicopter drew closer.

Josie spoke more loudly. "Did he alert?"

"He followed her scent toward the door but no, he didn't alert."

Josie looked around, noting a broad gravel driveway that snaked up from between more trees and then sprawled into a flat area almost double the size of the cabin. An old Toyota Highlander sat on one side and a pale El Camino on the other. Now the helicopter was overhead, hovering, its spotlight on the cabin's front door. Its rotor wash kicked up leaves, dirt, and gravel all around them. Before Josie could say or do anything else, the front door opened, and a man stepped out. He was bare-chested, save for several tattoos that Josie couldn't discern from where she stood. Sweatpants hung low on his hips. He looked up at the helicopter, one arm shielding his eyes from the spotlight.

Luke pulled a reluctant Blue to the side as Josie approached the steps, shouting to be heard over the 'copter. She wasn't sure if he heard her words but as soon as he took in her clothing and the gun she held, he threw his hands up. Leaving his front door ajar, he moved slowly down the steps to where Josie stood, keeping both palms aloft.

"What's going on?" he shouted.

Up close she could see that at least some of the tattoos on his chest and arms were crudely drawn and in black ink. Prison tattoos, most likely. His torso was sculpted and lean. Beneath piercing blue eyes, his jaw was strong and square. Josie estimated him to be in his late thirties, early forties.

"Are you the only person here?" Josie asked.

He nodded.

"There's no one in the house? No one else?"

"No one. Just me." He looked over at Blue, who stared up at the open doorway as if there was a treat on the other side of the threshold, if only he could cross it. Josie's radio squawked. Gretchen was sending the marked units positioned closest to their location. Their ETA was five minutes.

"Detective Josie Quinn, Denton PD. We're searching for a missing girl. Our K-9 unit followed her scent here."

The man raised a brow. "Here? You think there's a girl in my house?"

"What's your name?" Josie asked, still speaking loudly to be heard over the helicopter.

"Henry Thomas," he said.

"This is your place?"

He nodded. "Can I lower my hands?"

"Keep them where I can see them," said Josie.

He lowered them to his sides and looked around, from the helicopter to Luke and Blue.

"Do you live here alone?" Josie asked.

"Yes."

She gestured behind them, at the Toyota and El Camino. "Who do those belong to?"

He gave a little smile. "Me."

"Both of them?"

"You can check the registrations, but yes. The El Camino doesn't drive. Hasn't moved from that spot in months. I'm restoring it." He pointed to the Toyota. "That is my everyday vehicle."

"Any pets inside?" asked Josie.

"Not unless you count the fieldmice I can't seem to get rid of."

Blue and red emergency beacons strobed through the trees from the direction of the road. The end of the driveway wasn't visible from where they stood but within seconds, two marked units pulled in, one behind the Toyota and one behind the El Camino.

Henry said, "You want to have a look inside?"

"We need your permission to search the premises," Josie said.

He nodded. "You have it."

She pointed to one of the marked units where the officers were spilling out. "I'm going to have to ask you to wait over there with one of my colleagues."

He nodded and walked toward the officers. Josie signaled for one of them to stay with him. Luke moved closer, Blue at his side, eyes fixed on the door to the cabin. "Can we go in?" he asked.

Josie was relieved when the helicopter lifted and began

circling again. It was still loud but not deafening. "Not yet," she said. "I'd like to clear the house."

He nodded. She motioned for two of the uniformed officers to follow her into the cabin. Once at the front door, they dropped into tactical formation with Josie at the lead. Inside, the cabin was small but new. Had City Council begun selling off portions of the land? Who would buy property or build out here where so many murders had occurred?

Shaking off the questions, she focused on clearing the cabin. The living room bled directly into the kitchen. The furniture was old and mismatched, as if each piece had been bought on a different occasion from a thrift store. There was no television, only a beat-up laptop sitting on one of the couch cushions, open. Its screen glowed with the Netflix menu. A frozen pizza slow-cooked in a toaster oven on the kitchen counter. At the back of the cabin was a small bathroom, with only a standing shower, and two bedrooms. One was clearly Henry Thomas's sleeping quarters with its full-size bed and rumpled blankets. Josie noted there was only one pillow. A phone, watch, and lamp sat on the bedside table. Along one wall was a dresser, made in a different style and from a different wood than the nightstand. On top was a neatly folded pair of jeans and a tan shirt. The closet was filled with more clothes as well as shoes. In the other bedroom were about a half-dozen cardboard boxes marked "Dad's stuff." One of them sat open. A glance inside revealed a pile of foothold traps used for trapping small game. They looked old, the metal rusted. Josie and the other officers found no doors to a cellar or entrances to an attic. Based on the structure of the cabin, there didn't appear to be an attic, but Josie was certain the place had a crawlspace beneath it.

However, inside the cabin, there was no sign of Kayleigh Patchett.

Josie and the patrol officers exited the cabin. She radioed Noah to come around the front. Seconds later, he was beside her. He looked over at where Henry Thomas stood beside a uniformed officer, watching them with his penetrating gaze.

"The house is clear," Josie said. "I'm going to follow Blue and Luke inside, for what it's worth. We need to find the access point to the crawlspace under the cabin."

"It's in the back," Noah said. "I saw it while I was covering the rear of the building."

Josie swallowed, wondering if that was where they would find Kayleigh and if she would still be alive. She suppressed a shudder thinking of the dark, dank conditions that surely existed beneath the cabin. Josie had never done well with dark, enclosed spaces, not since her childhood.

Noah said, "I'll handle the crawlspace while you go with Luke and Blue."

"Thank you," she said.

His hand brushed hers as they parted, the movement small and quick so that no one else could see. He knew how much anxiety it caused her to be up on this mountain looking for another teenage girl and discussing spaces that made her claustrophobic just thinking about them.

Josie signaled to Luke, who gave a command to Blue. The dog surged up the steps and into the cabin. Josie followed the two of them, watching while Blue explored every inch of the living room and kitchen, then each bedroom, and the bathroom before turning around and heading back outside. Ignoring the other officers and Henry Thomas, Blue sniffed around each one of Thomas's vehicles before finally coming to rest between them and giving a short bark.

Luke praised Blue, rewarding him with a large rope toy before turning to face Josie.

She said, "What does this mean?"

Wordlessly, Luke dropped to his hands and knees and looked under each car. Josie followed suit, adding her flashlight to his headlamp. Their lights shone on nothing but gravel and some weeds poking up from it. As they stood back up, Luke said, "Check the cars."

Josie walked toward the patrol cars. A uniformed officer stood next to Thomas, who leaned casually against the side of the police cruiser, arms crossed over his bare chest, as if he hadn't a care in the world. He gave her a small smile that seemed almost smug. Was he gloating because he'd gotten away with something, or was it because he knew they'd find nothing?

"We'd like to search your vehicles," Josie said.

He waved a hand with a flourish. "Be my guest. They're both unlocked."

With a nod, Josie walked back to the cars. She searched the El Camino while one of the uniformed officers searched the Toyota. Kayleigh was not in either one of them.

Luke and Blue waited near the front steps to the cabin. When Josie shook her head to indicate that nothing had been found, Luke's face fell. As Josie strode toward him, Noah's voice came over the radio, sounding slightly out of breath. "Crawl-space is clear. No sign of Kayleigh. No freshly overturned earth or anything."

"Roger," Josie said into her radio. "The house and vehicles are clear as well."

"She's not here," said Luke.

Josie knelt and scratched behind Blue's ears. Tail thumping, he dropped his rope toy and licked her cheek. "I've never known you to be wrong, boy."

Luke said, "Blue is damn near perfect, but he's given false alerts before. Kayleigh was here. That he lost her scent in the driveway tells me that she left here in a vehicle."

"That's what I'm thinking." Josie stood up and looked around at the scene. The helicopter had gone, thankfully, searching the rest of the area. From across the driveway, Henry Thomas stared at her, expression placid. His eyes never left her, even when Noah appeared beside her once more, covered in dirt and cobwebs.

Noah pushed a hand through his thick brown hair, dislodging some sort of dust. "Let's call in the ERT," he said. "Have them process the house and impound the cars."

Josie nodded. "I'll ask Gretchen to go back to the station and get the warrants started. Luke, you and Blue should go home and get some much-deserved rest. One of the marked units can take you back to the Patchetts' home."

"You guys were amazing, as always," Noah added, reaching out to shake Luke's hand.

Josie watched them go. "How do you want to do this?" she asked Noah.

"I'll stay here until the ERT arrives with the warrants. Make sure the scene is secure."

"Good," said Josie, her gaze finding Henry's once more. "I'd like to take Mr. Thomas to the station and ask him some questions."

ELEVEN

Henry Thomas was too relaxed. He sat at the cigarette-scarred table in one of their interview rooms, shoulders leaned back as far as the chair would allow, legs splayed out, chin dipped to his chest. Josie watched him on the CCTV from the viewing room adjacent. She adjusted the sound on the computer to confirm that he was snoring. In her experience, the only people who snored in interview rooms were guilty people. Innocent people were usually so freaked out by being in one of them that they paced or tapped their feet or drummed their fingers on the table. Frequently, they shouted for someone to please hurry and come talk with them.

Henry Thomas had done none of those things. He was the most cooperative person of interest that Josie had ever seen. When she had asked him at the scene to come with her, he'd agreed without question. She had walked him into the cabin and watched him put on a shirt and shoes and grab his wallet. He had handed over his phone for them to peruse, along with his passcode. He hadn't protested at all when she put him in the back of a cruiser and sent him to police headquarters ahead of her with instructions for him to be shown into an interview room to wait for her.

Now, he was snoring.

A knock sounded at the door and then their desk sergeant, Dan Lamay, poked his head inside. "Boss," he said.

Josie winced but Lamay didn't seem to notice. "Just Josie, please, Dan."

If he registered her words, he didn't show it. Instead, he opened the door wider to reveal a box of pizza in one hand. "I got it plain, like you asked. Had to go to that all-night place by the college. I didn't think they'd be open around now but they were."

Josie managed a smile. "Thanks, Dan."

She took the pizza from him and went into the interview room. Henry startled when she entered, legs kicking out. He blinked and sat up straight, running a hand through his thick hair. Josie put the pizza on the table and slid it toward him. "Thought you might be hungry," she said.

Slowly, he leaned in and opened the box, peering inside. "You guys didn't happen to turn off my toaster oven, did you? I'd hate for my place to burn down."

"My colleague did, yes," Josie answered. She took the chair closest to him, angled to face him. As he wolfed down a slice of pizza, she read off his Miranda rights which he acknowledged before grabbing another slice.

She waited for him to ask for a lawyer, but he didn't.

"Mr. Thomas," she said. "Do you know why you're here?"

Around a mouthful of pizza, he said, "You think I did something to some girl?"

Josie took out her phone and pulled up the photo of Kayleigh Patchett, turning the screen so he could see it. "Kayleigh Patchett. Sixteen years old. She was abducted in the woods a few miles from your home earlier today. Our K-9 unit followed her scent to your home."

He grunted.

"Do you know her?"

"Nope."

"Have you ever seen her before?"

"Nope."

"The cabin? That yours?" She already knew the answer, of course. She had looked him up in every database she could access as soon as she got back to the station. Property records showed that he'd purchased it a year earlier in cash. It hadn't cost much, probably due to its location. Josie didn't know many people who would want to live on land where over a hundred dead girls had been unearthed.

"Yeah," said Henry. "It's mine. Bought it outright with money my dad left me. He died about two years ago."

"The traps in your spare bedroom," said Josie. "Were those his?"

"His name's on the boxes, isn't it?"

"You don't trap?"

"Don't have a license. Besides, there's a lot of rules you have to follow. I don't have the patience."

"Did you ever trap with him?" Josie asked.

He shrugged. "Sure, when I was a kid."

Changing tack, Josie said, "Tell me about your movements today. Starting with when you woke up until we came to your door."

With a sigh, he closed the pizza box and pushed it away. "I woke up around seven. It's my day off. Showered, shit, shaved. Put my clothes on. Drove to town. Had breakfast at the Denton Diner. Came home. Worked on the El Camino. Watched Netflix."

"You have a receipt from your meal at the diner?"

"Do you get receipts when you go to a diner?" he asked.

"You paid cash." She'd be able to verify his trip to the diner.

The Denton Diner kept extensive surveillance inside and outside of their building.

Changing the subject, Josie asked, "Where do you work?"

He smiled. "Are you really going to act like you didn't look me up? Come on, you know all about me, don't you? Including what I got sent up for."

One of the other things her extensive searches had turned up was that the crime for which he'd been in prison had been committed in Denton. Detective Finn Mettner had handled the case. She had known, of course, that there would be times on the job that they'd have to look back on cases that Mett had handled or that they'd handled with him but still, seeing his name was like a spear to her heart. She'd only been able to read the bare essentials of the file before her eyes blurred with tears. She had no time for tears. Not tonight.

"I know what the police databases say, but a few things entered into a computer don't always tell the full story, wouldn't you agree?"

He sat back in his chair again, legs spread wide. This time, he crossed his arms over his chest and regarded her with a look of interest. "Are you still talking about my job?"

"What do you think?" Josie asked. She waited a few beats, keeping her eyes locked on his, and then added, "You know how this works, Henry. I ask the questions. You answer them. Where do you work?"

He looked away. "I work for the park commission. City park. Sanitation. I clean up after the good citizens of Denton."

"Henry, I'm not interested in wasting your time—or mine—so let's get right to Kayleigh Patchett."

"The girl you're looking for."

"Our K-9 unit alerted on your property." Josie didn't mention that Luke thought it was a false alert. Thomas didn't need to know that. She went on, "She was in your cabin. This will all go a lot faster and a lot smoother if you just tell me what happened."

"What happened is I came inside from working on the car, put in a toaster pizza, turned on Netflix, and the next thing I know a damn helicopter is hovering over my cabin. I look outside and you're there. That's what happened."

"How do you know Kayleigh?" Josie pressed.

He leaned forward, putting his elbows on his knees and clasping his hands loosely together. "I don't know anyone named Kayleigh."

Josie tapped against her phone and brought Kayleigh's photo back up. "How about this girl? How do you know her?"

"I don't. I've never seen her before."

Now it was Josie's turn to sigh. "Henry, she was inside your house."

There was a beat of silence. He stared at Kayleigh's smiling face. Then he turned his gaze back to Josie. "I don't lock my doors, Officer."

"Detective," Josie said.

"I don't lock my doors, Detective. Maybe she did come to my house. Maybe she went inside. Didn't find what she was looking for and left."

"You said you were out front working on your car most of the day," Josie pointed out.

"If she really was in my cabin like you say, she came and went before I got home from the diner."

Josie tapped the phone screen again before it went black. "Kayleigh Patchett was abducted."

"If you're looking for a kidnapper," Henry said, "it's not me."

"You sure about that?" asked Josie. "Your conviction for unlawful restraint suggests otherwise."

He laughed, the sound low and quiet. "You cops love to

twist things. Do they teach you that at the police academy, or what?"

"The nineteen-year-old woman you forced into a basement at gunpoint seven years ago—do you think she would agree with you? Would she say that I was twisting things?"

"You have no idea what you're talking about," Henry said, showing the first signs of strain. A light sheen of sweat broke out across his forehead.

"Like I said, some facts entered into a computer don't always tell the full story," Josie said. "What am I missing, Henry? Because the way I see it, you spent five years in prison for unlawful restraint of a young woman. Today, a girl not much younger than her was abducted. We know she was at your home because our dog followed her scent there."

His voice rose an octave. "I didn't kidnap anyone. That nineteen-year-old? She was my buddy's girlfriend. He owed me money. I went to his house to get it. She was there. I made her go into the basement to keep her out of my way. I didn't hurt her. The DA couldn't get me on the robbery charge so he used the unlawful restraint charge and that little bi—" He stopped himself, taking a deep breath. "That woman threw me under the bus out of loyalty to her boyfriend. It was a personal problem with a friend of mine. That's all."

Josie nodded along as he spoke. "Fair enough."

Henry shifted in the chair as if he was trying to find a more comfortable position, folding and unfolding his arms and drawing his feet in, knees pressed together.

Josie added, "But still, it's not a stretch to think that you are capable of abducting a teenage girl. You're out of prison less than two years. Alone on the top of that mountain. A guy like you? I'm sure you've got needs. It must be hard to meet women with that conviction in your past. Maybe you got frustrated, thought it might be easier to take what you wanted. Saw an opportunity, went for it. It's been known to happen."

"Are you crazy?" he said. "Trying some cop mind-fuck on me? I don't need to 'take' anything from anyone and I'm not touching jailbait. You think I want to go back inside?"

"I think there's something you're not telling me."

"We can sit here all night and all day tomorrow and I'm still going to tell you the same thing. The truth. I do not know that girl. I've never seen her before. I didn't do anything to her," he shot back.

Josie waited a couple of seconds, staring directly into his eyes. Then she leaned forward, entering his personal space. "My team is processing your home as we speak. They've impounded your vehicles." At this, his skin went pale. Josie continued, "They're combing over every inch of your property and your cars. What are they going to find, Henry?"

He swallowed, Adam's apple bobbing up and down. "No-nothing," he stammered, his facade of cool disinterest fully gone now.

Josie reshaped her features into a semblance of concern. "You must know how this works already, Henry. Don't make it worse for yourself. Tell me what they're going to find. If you say they'll find nothing and later I find out that there was something, you'll be in even bigger trouble."

He pulled his feet in and pressed his knees together. His face hardened. "I want to leave now."

She couldn't hold him, not any longer than it would take for her team to execute the warrant and that would only be a few hours. "I can have a patrol officer take you home. You won't be able to enter until my team is finished. I just want to give you one more chance to get things out in the open, Henry, to get ahead of this. Where is Kayleigh Patchett?"

He crossed his arms tightly over his chest again. "I already told you. I don't know."

TWELVE

Killing takes practice. Once I've done it a couple of times, I realize that it's not the killing that brings me joy. What satisfies me is the swell of fear that keeps driving kids into the woods to find me. It's the kind of fear you get in a haunted house or on a roller coaster. You know that once it's over you'll be safe. They come into my domain with a false sense of security, a sort of thrill in their pursuit of me, someone that they've deemed fictional. If they knew the truth, they'd never go into the woods again.

Some of them I've watched and let go. The watching was enough. Knowing how much power I had over them was enough to sate me.

But a legend doesn't remain a legend by letting their prey escape, unscathed.

THIRTEEN

Josie's eyes burned. Her legs ached. The rank scent of stale sweat reached her nostrils every time she lifted her arms. The café down the street where they usually got their coffee wasn't open yet, so she'd brewed coffee in the first-floor breakroom and carried it up to her desk in the second-floor great room. She sipped it as she settled into her chair. The bitterness made her eyes water. It was just about four a.m. Sunday morning by the time Noah, Gretchen, Chief Chitwood, and their press liaison, Amber Watts, tromped through the door. Silently they filed in, Noah, Gretchen, and Amber taking their places at their desks. The Chief stood in the middle of the room, arms folded over his thin chest, watching them. As haggard as Josie felt, the rest of them looked much worse. Even Amber, who'd been asked by the Chief to come in the night before when the Amber Alert went out. Then again, she'd looked perpetually exhausted since Mettner died. Josie suspected she wasn't sleeping much anymore either.

Josie looked at Noah and Gretchen, eyes carefully avoiding Mettner's desk. It was just as it had been when he'd died. None of them had had the heart to touch a thing on it—except for the reports and official documents they needed. The Chief had told Amber that she could take his personal effects from it when she was ready, but she hadn't touched the desk either. None of them talked about Mettner's desk. Most of the time, they all avoided even looking at it. Except that when Josie was the only one there, she did, remembering the way he used to sit, the way he'd swipe and scroll on his phone, sending everything he'd recorded on his notes app in the field to his work email so that he could then transfer it to his reports. The way he used to tidy up his desk at the end of every shift, putting his pens back into their holder, and making sure the edges of all his stacked files lined up just so. He'd throw out any paper coffee cups or takeout containers and then he'd pull his small wastebasket from under his desk and set it in plain view so that the cleaning staff didn't have to go searching for it. Then, after he started seeing Amber, he'd walk over to her desk—if she wasn't there—and scribble a note on the top sheet of her Post-it pad. Josie had never read the notes, but she'd always noticed the way Amber smiled when she came in the next day and read them.

A burning flared in Josie's stomach. Shutting down thoughts of Mett, she turned her focus back to her colleagues. "Where are we?"

Gretchen sighed. "Let's start with the standard stuff. Canvass of the Patchetts' neighbors turned up nothing. The nearby sex offenders our patrol units checked in with didn't raise any red flags. There were only three and they all had alibis for the day. A property record search didn't turn up anyone in the area that we didn't already talk with—including Henry Thomas. He's the only one up on that mountain."

Josie said, "Tell me you found something in Thomas's cabin."

Noah brushed some dirt from his polo shirt. "The ERT took a number of DNA samples from what Hummel thinks were sweat and saliva but those things take a long time to process. It doesn't help us right now."

"What about hair?" Josie said.

"Hummel found several long, dark hairs. Some in the living room, some in the bathroom. They could belong to Kayleigh but of course we've got to have them analyzed at the lab," said Noah.

Before Josie could speak, Gretchen said, "I already took a sample of Kayleigh's hair from her hairbrush and buccal swabs from both parents so we can get a familial DNA match if the hairs in Thomas's cabin belong to Kayleigh. Noah called me as soon as Hummel found the first hair."

"Did any of the hairs in the cabin have roots?" asked Josie. Without the root, the lab would not be able to get sufficient DNA from a strand of hair in order to test it. In 2019, a scientist in California had made huge advances in extracting DNA from rootless hair, but the technique wasn't widely used enough in law enforcement to be of any help to Denton PD in this case.

"We got one root," Noah said.

"I'll ask that DNA testing be expedited," The Chief said.

Josie said a silent thank you to the heavens. If they could match Kayleigh's hair to the hair found inside Thomas's cabin, it would be definitive proof that she had been inside his home. It might be enough for an arrest warrant. "What else?" she asked.

"Hummel found a few different sets of prints that didn't match anything in AFIS," Noah said. "But we don't have prints on file for Kayleigh so we can't confirm whether any of them match hers."

"What about the vehicles?" asked the Chief.

"Officer Chan worked on those back at the impound lot while the rest of the ERT handled the cabin," Gretchen replied. "She found a few sets of unknown prints on the inside and outside of both but again, we can't match them to Kayleigh without a set of her prints. No blood evidence. She found several short brown hairs in both vehicles but given their length and the fact that they're significantly darker than Kayleigh Patchett's hair, they probably belong to Thomas. Chan also found traces of DNA in the Toyota—what looks like sweat—on the driver's headrest but it is most likely that of Henry Thomas. She found a lot of different DNA in the El Camino but that thing is from 1970 and from what we've been able to gather, it had multiple owners before Thomas bought it so I'm not sure how useful that will be. It's going to take forever for them to test all the samples. Anyway, the ERT sent everything to the state police lab. They're still working on getting the GPS reports from the Toyota."

"But we don't have enough to arrest or charge him," said Noah.

"Yet," muttered Josie.

Gretchen said, "I assume you got nothing from the interview."

Josie recapped the interview for them. "He's definitely lying about something. I couldn't get anything out of him. If I had more to work with, something to rattle him, I could bring him back in and try again. It would be even better if we could get a DNA match and just arrest him."

Noah said, "We could use that as leverage to try to get him to tell us what he did with Kayleigh."

"With her body," said Gretchen. "If Thomas is behind this, she's already dead. He would have had enough time to kill her and dispose of her body before you guys arrived at his cabin."

A solemn moment of silence filled the room. Then Josie said, "That doesn't change anything about how we do our jobs. We find Kayleigh Patchett. Period."

"If he killed her and dumped or even buried her body some-where nearby," Noah said. "Couldn't we have Blue do a cadaver search? He's certified for it."

Josie took another sip of her coffee, trying not to wince at the acidity. "There were so many remains in that area, and as much as we tried to recover them all after the missing girls' case, the FBI told me there were likely still fragments all over that mountain. It's possible Blue would alert to a number of places and then we'd spend all our time digging."

Gretchen said, "It would probably make more sense to just look for any area that appears to be newly turned-over dirt."

The Chief said, "Amber, where are we with the line search? Do we have enough volunteers to start at dawn?"

Amber looked at her tablet. "I've been coordinating with Sergeant Lamay since last night. We're ready."

"I want one line search starting in the Patchetts' backyard and another starting at Henry Thomas's cabin, but let's keep a lid on Thomas as a suspect for now."

Amber nodded. "You got it."

Gretchen said, "How sure are we that Thomas is involved in this? I know that Blue followed Kayleigh's scent to his cabin—"

"Into his cabin," Josie said. "Someone took her. If it wasn't Thomas then why would the abductor walk her all the way to his cabin?"

"That was a hike," said Noah. "Over the mountain. Miles from where she was taken. Why would anyone else but Thomas go to all that trouble?"

"Because their vehicle was there?" Gretchen said. "Blue lost her scent there. She had to have been put in a vehicle and taken elsewhere."

The Chief pointed to a nearby wall. "I want a map of the area up here by this afternoon and I want it marked. The Patchett house. Where Savannah was found. The approximate path that Blue took to locate Kayleigh. Thomas's cabin."

Josie said, "If Thomas was all the way down near the Patchetts' place on foot, he was very far from home."

Gretchen said, "Why would he be that far down the other side of the mountain?"

"Maybe he was hunting," Noah said. "Not for animals but for people. There wouldn't be many of them up near him but where Kayleigh was taken is relatively close to that long residential stretch. There's a lot more chances he'd run into someone in that section of the woods."

"You think this could be connected to the cases that the state police are looking at?" Gretchen said.

"What cases?" said the Chief.

Noah told him what little information he'd shared with Josie earlier.

"One of you can look into those," the Chief said. "But for now let's focus on Thomas since Blue followed Kayleigh's scent to his cabin."

Josie thought about the old traps she had seen in Thomas's spare bedroom. "Did you find any furs in his cabin?"

Everyone stared at her. "What?" said the Chief.

She looked at Noah. "There were traps in his residence. The kind trappers hunting for furbearers use. He said that they belonged to his father, but he also admitted that he knew how to trap. He could be doing it illegally. Maybe he set traps near where the Patchett girls were walking. He might have been out checking them and seen Kayleigh."

Noah said, "You think that he took her because he didn't want to get in trouble for trapping without a license?"

"I doubt that's why he took her," Josie said. "He was in prison for five years for forcing a nineteen-year-old girl into a basement at gunpoint and holding her there. We know he is capable of something like this—abducting Kayleigh Patchett. I'm just saying maybe their paths crossed by accident because he is trapping illegally. Did you find any furs on his property?"

"A few," Noah said. "But they were in boxes marked 'Dad's

stuff' just like the traps. It was hard to tell how old they are. They could have been his dad's."

The Chief said, "We can swap theories about how this went down, but that doesn't tell us where to find this girl. It's most likely that he killed her and dumped her body somewhere, but that's not the only possibility. This guy's got an interest in teenage girls. A criminal history. We know she was at his place but we can't find her and the dog lost the scent, indicating that she was taken by vehicle from Thomas's cabin, so we need to consider that she might have been trafficked. You get into this guy's phone?"

Noah sighed. "It was clean. Phone calls and texts to buddies of his, mostly about meeting up at a bar now and then. Phone calls and texts to his boss. He's got a sister who lives in Oklahoma. He calls her once a month. Food places, doctors' offices. Nothing that raises any red flags."

Josie said, "We need to look into his buddies, though. What about his laptop?"

"The ERT is still working on that," said Noah.

Gretchen reached into her jacket pocket and pulled out a cell phone with a sparkly purple cover. "For the sake of due diligence, we also need to look closely at Kayleigh Patchett. Since we don't have any trained experts in-house who could do a forensic download, I've already prepared a warrant for her phone records in case there are things she's deleted from the actual phone that would still show up in records. We need to make sure that no one was threatening or stalking her and that she hadn't come into contact with anyone who might have wished her harm. Anyone grooming her over the internet who might have gotten the bright idea to spy on her in the woods and take her."

"Yes," Josie said. "Also, it seems unlikely, but we should see if there is any connection between her and Henry Thomas."

"Good point," said Noah. "Maybe this wasn't random at all.

Maybe Thomas was so far from home because he was specifically going to find Kayleigh Patchett."

"We have to entertain every possibility," Josie replied.

"The bos—Josie's right," said Gretchen. "If Mett were here —" She broke off. The silent seconds that ticked by were like bombs going off. Everyone's heads swiveled toward Amber.

Without looking up from her tablet, Amber said, "If Finn were here right now, he would be challenging every single one of your assumptions and telling you that even though this guy— Henry Thomas—looks good for this abduction, you don't have enough evidence to prove it. So you better make sure you turn over every rock and eliminate every other possibility before you throw all your resources behind the case against Thomas."

Josie felt a warmth spread through her center. Her admiration for what Mett had always brought to the team was tempered by a strange sort of longing for her felled colleague and the way he had always challenged her at every turn. Mett had made her a better investigator, she realized, and she missed that. It was one of the many things she missed about him.

"That's true," said Josie.

More silence. When it stretched into awkwardness, Amber glanced up from her tablet, staring at them. "Better get to work then."

FOURTEEN

The Chief sent Gretchen home for a few hours of sleep. Noah worked on tracking down the names of Henry Thomas's associates and doing background checks on them while Josie went through Kayleigh Patchett's phone and laptop, which her parents had given them permission to do. They'd even given the Denton PD Kayleigh's passwords, which was concerning to Josie. The fact that they had such control and supervision over their daughter's electronics told Josie that she was unlikely to find anything of use on either one of them. If there was any activity that Kayleigh wished to hide, she likely would not conduct it on a device to which her parents had unfettered access.

The first thing she noticed was that there were no social media apps on the phone, which was odd since they usually came pre-installed. Were the Patchett parents really that strict? Josie made a mental note to ask them when she saw them next. There were frightfully few contacts, but Josie made note of their names. Most of the non-family names were followed by some description like Felicia (from English class); Braelyn (from softball); Hector (from work). Had Kayleigh done that herself or did her parents insist on it? Braelyn from softball had texted Kayleigh telling her she should quit the team if she wasn't going to play like she wanted to win. Kayleigh had responded by saying her parents wouldn't let her. Since her parents had full access to her phone, this seemed like an intentional barb.

The only contact whose name did not have a qualifier was Olivia. Moving to the text messages, Josie found that the majority of texts were between Kayleigh and Olivia. Based on the messages, it appeared that Kayleigh went to school with and worked with Olivia. There were multiple texts coordinating rides to and from work together. Josie made another mental note to find out where Kayleigh worked. There were also texts scheduling sleepovers, shopping trips, nights out to the movies.

Days before Kayleigh's abduction, there were two exchanges about changing shifts at work. Nothing gossipy. Nothing that Josie typically saw on teenagers' phones in her line of work, although most of the time, the personal and often incriminating stuff was in their social media accounts. Josie found it hard to believe that Kayleigh had no accounts. Usually kids whose parents restricted them from having social media had secret accounts, and simply used friends' phones to log in. Josie would have to ask Olivia about this.

Next, she checked the photos. There were fewer than Josie expected to see on the phone of a teenager. She scrolled through dozens of selfies occasionally punctuated by photos of Kayleigh side by side with another teenage girl. Olivia, perhaps? The girl was taller and more striking than Kayleigh with bright blue eyes, red hair, and a smattering of freckles across her nose. Josie briefly studied the background of each photo. One looked as though it was a school; another a restaurant; several looked to be outside. Scrolling through the rest of the photos, Josie found that the only other person who appeared in them was Kayleigh's younger sister, Savannah. Kayleigh photographed her doing just about everything: practicing soccer in their backyard, napping on the couch, eating a red popsicle that stained her lips, trying on makeup, playing board games, dancing. There were dozens of selfies of the two sisters, cheek to cheek, making funny faces or laughing. There were also selfies of the two side by side in a bed with Savannah sound asleep, her head on Kayleigh's shoulder, while Kayleigh held her phone up above them, smiling contentedly.

Finding nothing of interest in the photo gallery, Josie searched the rest of the phone, making a list of the apps that were installed on it. There was no tracking app installed, like Life360 which would tell them where Kayleigh's phone was at any given time. Nor were there the more exhaustive apps like Bark or FamiSafe which would monitor her activities on the phone as well as location. Josie's eyelids were drooping, her pen faltering when she came across a second calculator app.

"Gotcha," she muttered.

Noah looked up from his computer screen. "What was that?"

"Kayleigh Patchett has a calculator vault app. You know, the ones that look like a calculator but actually hide photos?"

"Yeah. See them all the time. You need a password to get into it. I doubt her parents know it," Noah said.

Josie opened the app, which looked and operated just like a calculator. She knew it was a vault app because she'd seen it on the phones of people they had arrested or investigated before. There were a number of them out there. She knew that this one in particular usually had a four-digit password and that you had to press the percentage sign and then the equal sign in order for the app to register that you were signing in to your hidden vault of photos. "Her best friend might know the password," said Josie. "If we can get her to tell us. I'm just going to try the old standbys."

She started punching numbers into the app, followed by the percentage and equal signs.

Noah laughed. "You mean the ones teenagers use thinking they're so clever that no one would ever figure it out? Like four zeroes?"

"That didn't work," Josie said. "But yeah."

Teenagers were sneaky and they often thought that they knew more than everyone else, but most of the time, they just weren't very savvy—or they thought that adults made things so complicated that they would never try the simplest solution. It was like using the word "password" for your password. Josie looked up from the phone screen, studying Noah briefly. She tried to imagine them in fourteen or fifteen years with a teenager of their own. Before her brain could invent all the possibilities that went along with that thought, she returned her focus to Kayleigh's calculator app. Next she tapped in the numbers one, two, three, four, followed by the percentage and equal signs. There was a brief flicker and then a folder opened with several photos in it.

"Got it!" Josie exclaimed.

"It was one, two, three, four, wasn't it?" said Noah.

"Of course it was."

There were only about a half-dozen photos in the vault, but they were all of Kayleigh and a boy. As Josie swiped through them, she realized that none of the photos showed his entire face clearly straight-on. Three showed him in profile. One showed him from the back, walking down a Denton city street in jeans and a hoodie pulled up over his head. One showed him driving a car, only trees out his window, his face turned away so that only his ear and the back of his head were visible. One photo showed a pair of hands clasped together, fingers intertwined. The angle was strange. Swiping through them once more, Josie wondered if he had even known that Kayleigh was taking the photos. They had an almost covert quality about them, as though he had been unaware they were being taken. Josie tried to zero in on any identifying features like a tattoo or a scar. Anything she could use to identify him in person, but there was nothing. All she could tell was that he was thin with shaggy brown hair; he was old enough to drive a car; and he liked hoodies.

"What's in the vault?" asked Noah.

"A secret boyfriend, by the looks of it. How far did you get with Henry Thomas's associates?"

He leaned back in his chair and stretched his hands over his head. "I have a solid list here. I just have to go rattle their cages."

Josie checked the clock. "It's almost dawn. Why don't you get something to eat and then start running them down? I want to talk to the Patchetts before the line search begins."

FIFTEEN

The road to the Patchett home was lined with cars for miles. Two vans from the local news station, WYEP, sat at the mouth of the driveway. A young reporter was giving a live update as Josie pulled in. Halfway to the house, she was stopped by a uniformed officer who was tasked with taking the name and checking the ID of every person who came onto the property. The line search would begin in the Patchetts' yard where Savannah and Kayleigh had entered the woods. Denton PD would keep a list of the volunteers from the community. It wasn't unheard of for a child abductor or a killer to return to the scene and blend in with the crowd of onlookers, watching police work, or for them to offer help.

Josie drove up to the house and found a parking spot behind a group of vehicles. The sky had grown lighter, the horizon a flaming orange with pink undertones. People milled around everywhere, waiting for the line search to begin. Amber and the Chief stood near the side of the house, directing people into the backyard. Josie waved an acknowledgment and made her way inside the house.

The living room was spacious and decorated in white and

blue. A white sectional took up most of the room. On one corner of it, Dave Patchett slept on his back, head turned to the side. His mouth was open, a line of drool hanging from the corner of his lips. Savannah lay alongside him, her head resting on his chest. Sweaty strands of hair were plastered to her flushed cheek. Josie felt a wave of relief seeing Savannah safe and secure in her father's arms, followed by the prickle of worry that her sister might not make it home. The thought that Kayleigh might already be dead kept floating to the surface of her mind, unwanted, taunting her.

Shelly waved Josie over to the unoccupied section of the sofa, motioning for her to sit. Josie remained standing and watched as Shelly gently nudged Dave awake. When he saw Josie, he extricated himself from Savannah. She didn't stir, not even when he tucked a blanket around her. Swiping a hand down his face, he lumbered to the other side of the sectional and settled in beside Shelly. They clutched at one another and looked up at Josie with trepidation on their faces. It broke Josie's heart.

"Do you have news?" Dave asked, blinking.

"I'm afraid not," said Josie. "We have not located Kayleigh yet."

"Your friend," Dave said. "The other lady—"

"Detective Palmer," Josie said.

"Right," said Dave. "She told us about the dog. That guy in the cabin. You didn't find anything?"

"She showed us his photo," said Shelly. "We've never seen him before."

"I'm aware," said Josie. "We're still looking into him."

Dave said, "You think this guy is the Woodsman?"

Suppressing a sigh, Josie said, "Mr. Patchett, the Woodsman is not a factor in our investigation."

"But the kids won't stop talking about him," said Shelly.

"Savannah's been having nightmares. Obviously, we thought it was just a story. Until yesterday."

"It *is* just a story," Josie assured them. "The person who took Kayleigh is a human being, not a mythical figure. We're looking for a man, not a character from children's folklore."

"Don't you think you should be taking this more seriously?" said Dave. He pointed to Savannah. "My daughter woke up screaming last night because the Woodsman took her sister."

"Again," Josie said, trying not to let her impatience show, "the Woodsman is not real. What we are taking seriously is evidence, which is why we're about to conduct line searches outside. We'll be looking for anything that might lead us to Kayleigh. In the meantime, I need to ask you some questions about your daughter."

Shelly looked over at Savannah, who slept on, snoring slightly.

"Your daughter, Kayleigh," Josie clarified.

"Right," said Shelly.

"Like what?" Dave asked.

Josie decided to start with the easy stuff. "Where does Kayleigh work?"

Shelly said, "The Timber Creek restaurant."

Dave said, "Why do you need to know that?"

Shelly squeezed his arm. "Honey, please."

Glancing at her, he said, "No. Why are you turning this onto Kayleigh? She was kidnapped. You should be looking for her kidnapper."

"We are looking for her abductor," Josie assured him, keeping her tone calm and even. "I'm sure you can understand that in a case like this, we have to consider every possibility, no matter how remote it may seem. Although it doesn't appear that Kayleigh was targeted, we must consider the possibility that her abduction was not random."

"What are you saying?" said Dave.

Shelly sighed and pushed him away from her. "She means that someone might have been stalking Kayleigh. Followed her into the woods and taken her. Right?"

"More or less," Josie said. "While some of our questions may seem intrusive, it's crucial that we don't miss anything. The faster we get answers to our questions, the faster we can move the investigation along."

Dave still seemed reluctant, but Shelly nodded eagerly. "What else do you need to know?"

"Who is Kayleigh's best friend?"

"Olivia," answered Shelly. "Olivia Wilcox. They go to the same school—Denton East High—and they both work at Timber Creek as hostesses. Kayleigh sleeps over at Olivia's a lot. They go to the movies together, shopping, that sort of thing."

Josie took out her phone and pulled up one of the photos of Kayleigh with the redhead. She had transferred the photos she needed to show the Patchetts from Kayleigh's phone to her own. "Is this Olivia?"

"Yes," said Shelly.

"I noticed that there are no social media apps on Kayleigh's phone," said Josie.

Dave said, "We don't allow her to have social media."

Josie said, "You've never allowed her to have social media, or she had accounts and no longer uses them?"

"Never," said Shelly. "It's a distraction. We wanted her to focus on softball."

Josie thought of the nasty text exchange between Kayleigh and Braelyn from softball. *My parents won't let me quit.* "Does Kayleigh enjoy softball?"

"She doesn't understand the benefits," Shelly said. "It keeps her healthy, in shape. Teaches her teamwork. Keeps her out of trouble."

Josie thought about the fact that Kayleigh hadn't had her

phone when she was abducted. "What caused you to take Kayleigh's phone from her yesterday?"

The parents looked at one another, some silent communication passing between them. Dave gave a small nod and then Shelly turned back to Josie. "She was reading smut on this app she has on her phone. It's called StoryJot. People upload their own stories. We let her download it because she wanted to read fan fiction about characters from one of her favorite video games. It was all pretty innocent at first. It kept her occupied."

"Then we came to find out that the stuff she was reading on there was basically porn," Dave said. "She left her phone out with some story on the screen at the kitchen table and Shelly saw it."

"Then I looked at her reading history," said Shelly. "It was story after story of sex stuff."

Dave added, "We told her once that it wasn't appropriate, but then she kept reading it so we told her we were taking her phone for a week."

Josie could remember every girl in her high school reading Anne Rice's Sleeping Beauty series precisely because it was scandalous and racy. It had been released before Josie was born but had seen a resurgence when she reached high school. She and most of her classmates devoured anything that adults deemed too mature for them. The more inappropriate, the better. Even kids who didn't like to read were glued to those types of books. In Josie's experience, the fastest and most sure-fire way to get a teenager to read something was to tell them they couldn't.

Shelly wrung her hands together. "I know what you're thinking. She's sixteen, she's not a baby. I've had the sex talk with her. She's not completely sheltered. It's just that this stuff she was reading was really over the top. It was... disturbing. Not something a young woman should read. Maybe not even something any woman should read."

Changing the subject, Josie asked, "Is Kayleigh dating anyone?"

"No," Dave answered immediately.

Shelly said, "She doesn't have time. Not with school and work and softball."

Josie felt a small prick of guilt for what she was about to do but it could not be avoided. She punched the passcode into her phone again and swiped until she found the clearest profile photo of the boy that Kayleigh had had in her vault. "Do you know who this is?"

Both parents leaned in to study it. "No," said Dave.

"Should we?" asked Shelly.

"You can't see his face," said Dave. "How could we even tell?"

"Who is he?" Shelly said.

Josie explained where she had found the photos concluding with, "From these pictures, it appears that Kayleigh may be dating this person."

Dave shot up out of his seat. "Son of a bitch."

Shelly looked over at Savannah, her forehead creasing. "Dave!" she hissed.

He paced back and forth in front of his wife. "She lied to us. Again." He stopped moving and looked at Josie. "How long has this been going on?"

"I was hoping you could tell me," Josie said. "From what I was able to tell from the details attached to those photos, they were taken at various times in the last year."

"Oh God," Shelly said.

"You didn't know?" Dave asked, whirling on his wife.

She pressed a hand to her chest. "No, I didn't know. How would I know?"

Josie said, "Mr. Patchett, you said she lied again. What else had she lied about?"

He glared at Shelly.

She sighed and looked away.

Dave answered, "She lied about a school assignment. Something she had written for her English class. We thought that was bad, but it was certainly nothing on this grand a scale... a secret boyfriend. How do we find out who he is? Do you think he's the one who took her?"

"I'll start by asking her friends if any of them knows who he is, maybe speak with the principal and see if he's a student at her school. If we can't figure out his identity from there, then we go to her workplace and see if anyone there recognizes him. There aren't a lot of contacts in Kayleigh's phone and not many text exchanges other than with Olivia. Do you know the names of any other kids she hangs out with regularly?"

A look passed between Shelly and Dave. He said, "She doesn't talk much with anyone on the softball team anymore, not outside of practice."

Shelly looked at her feet. "Kayleigh always had trouble making friends. All she ever wants to do is sit in her room and read. That's why we signed her up for softball. She tried soccer and volleyball, but she wasn't very good. She did a bit better at softball. For a while she seemed to get along well with all the girls but in the last year, she stopped hanging out with them. Or anyone, really, even from school. Except Olivia."

Josie rattled off some of the names she had seen in Kayleigh's contacts, concluding with Felicia (from English class). "Do you know any of those kids?"

Dave said, "Just Felicia, but they're not friends."

Shelly said, "Just classmates."

Dave said, "You found those photos on her phone. What about her laptop? Was there anything on there that we should know about?"

"No," said Josie. "It appears she uses it for schoolwork and to play some online games."

Josie's cell phone chirped. She looked at the screen. Dave

and Shelly Patchett stared at her with heartbreaking hopeful-
ness. "The line search is starting soon," she said. "Before I go, I
was wondering if I could have a look inside Kayleigh's bedroom.
I know my colleague took a look yesterday, but I'd like to see it
for myself."

Dave said, "You're looking for stuff like those photos, aren't
you?"

"I'm looking for anything that might help us find Kayleigh
or direct us to someone who can help us find her."

Shelly stood up. "Come on. I'll show you."

SIXTEEN

Josie followed Shelly out of the living room and up a set of stairs to a long hall. The walls were dotted with framed photos. One or two were of the entire family—at Disney World and at a beach—with Kayleigh unsmiling in each one. The rest of the photos were of Savannah. Candid shots of her dressed up for Halloween, eating an ice cream cone, in a Christmas play at school, holding up a lost tooth, and playing soccer. Toward the end of the hall, there was a single framed school photo of Kayleigh. Again, she was unsmiling. They passed three closed doors before arriving at the end of the hall. There was a doorway but no door. Shelly motioned to the room beyond. Josie stepped inside and looked back toward the hallway to confirm that what she was seeing was correct.

"No door?" she said.

Shelly's face flushed. "We took it off. Only temporarily. Kayleigh snuck out a few times at night. We caught her coming back in. We gave her a couple of warnings but that didn't work. Dave got mad and just... took the door. He says he'll put it back up when he can trust her again. I thought she was going to see Olivia, but now I wonder. Maybe she was out with that boy."

"Does Olivia live near here?" asked Josie.

"No, but Olivia has her own car."

"Does Kayleigh drive?"

"No. Not yet. She wants to get her license, but we've had so much trouble with her lately—academically, on the softball team, reading stuff she's not supposed to read, sneaking out—Dave didn't want to reward her by letting her get her license, he said."

"What about you?" Josie asked pointedly.

Shelly smiled tightly. "Do you have children, Detective?"

"No," said Josie, silently adding, *not yet.*

"It's a lot more challenging than you think," Shelly said. "You think you've got everything under control and then you realize they're sneaking out of the house in the middle of the night!"

Josie thought about the texts between Kayleigh and Olivia. It was possible that Kayleigh had used her phone to have Olivia —or the mystery boyfriend—meet her at the bottom of the driveway and then deleted the evidence from the phone. Gretchen had already forwarded the warrant for her phone records to her carrier. They just had to wait for them. Maybe they could get them expedited, seeing as Kayleigh was missing.

"Do you mind if I look in drawers and under the bed and such?" asked Josie.

Shelly leaned against the doorframe, hugging herself. "Of course. Whatever you need to do."

A full-sized bed took up most of the room. A purple comforter was rumpled at its foot. Beside it was a small wooden nightstand with two drawers. It looked like it had been spray-painted, also purple. Josie snapped on a pair of gloves and began looking through the drawers. It was mostly makeup, chargers, pens, hair accessories, and books. She counted a half-dozen paperbacks, half horror and half romance. Based on the nearly naked men stretched across their covers, Josie wasn't sure her parents knew she had them. Josie took each one and fanned its pages, looking for anything that might be lodged inside. There was nothing.

Spotting the covers of the romance novels, Shelly's face flushed. "Oh my God!" she said, striding across the room to get a closer look. "Where did she get these?"

Josie ignored her question and kept searching. She took each drawer from its seat and looked inside the shell of the nightstand. After that, she checked under the mattress, the bed, in and around the small desk in the corner of the room and even among the heap of softball equipment tossed on the floor. In the closet were more books stacked along the floor. More romance and horror as well as mysteries and thrillers this time. Shelly looked on with dismay as Josie checked each one, finding nothing of note. Josie riffled through the clothes hanging up and upended each shoe she found. On the shelf above the clothes was an old blanket, a bin full of nail polish, and a stuffed elephant that looked as though it had seen better days.

"That's Ellie," said Shelly as Josie lifted it from the shelf.

"Ellie the Elephant?"

Shelly gave a weak chuckle. "Yeah, it was her favorite stuffed animal when she was younger. She had lots. She gave them all to Savannah except this one. Naturally, Savannah wanted this one the most. We tried to convince Kayleigh to let her have it, but she just couldn't be nice and do it."

Josie didn't think it was too much to ask for Kayleigh to be able to hold onto at least one piece of her childhood rather than give her little sister everything, but she kept silent. She gave Ellie's body a gentle squeeze, feeling nothing but stuffing. Ellie's trunk was a different story. Beneath her fingers, Josie felt several small objects. She checked the seam of the trunk until she found the slit. Moving over to the bed, she carefully removed the items from Ellie's trunk. There were rolling papers, Dutch

Master cigars, a lighter, and a baggie, its corner knotted, with what appeared to be marijuana inside it.

"What is that?" Shelly asked, voice going up an octave.

"It's marijuana," Josie said.

She put her hands over her face. "God. I don't believe this. I do not believe this! Where would she get this?"

Josie didn't tell her that marijuana use among teenagers in Denton was rampant. She would have been more surprised if she hadn't found it in Kayleigh's room. Josie texted Hummel and asked him to come inside to collect it. "I'll have to take this into evidence," she said. "My colleague will be in to do that."

As she snapped off her gloves, her phone chirped again. The line search was starting.

SEVENTEEN

Behind the Patchett home there were easily thirty people lined up side by side, several feet apart from one another. The Chief was gone, off to supervise the line search at Henry Thomas's cabin, but one of their uniformed officers, Brennan, had taken over to coordinate the search. Josie took her place in line. While she waited, she checked her phone to see if there were any updates from Noah. As she pulled up the messaging app, the screen blurred. She blinked, feeling the grit of exhaustion in her eyes. She'd been awake for nearly twenty-four hours, and she still had several hours to go before she could go home and rest— not that she'd been sleeping much lately anyway. These were the hours in which Mettner's absence was most noticeable. No one wanted to replace him, but the truth was, they needed a fourth investigator. Josie had seen a stack of résumés on the Chief's desk but there had been no discussion of hiring anyone new.

Amber nudged her way into line beside Josie. Somewhere down the line, Brennan began to shout instructions. "Stay in line. It's very important that you stay lined up and move together with no one getting ahead or falling behind. You can stay a few feet apart from each other but stay side by side."

Ahead of them, atop the tree line, the sky was a periwinkle blue. Behind them, it was a fiery orange-red as the sun began its ascent into the sky. Josie looked over at Amber but she was staring into the woods, pulling the lapels of her jacket more tightly around her. Josie was so tired, she hadn't even noticed the chill in the air. It would burn off as soon as the sun was overhead.

"We will move slowly, in a line, all together at the same pace," Brennan went on. "As you walk, you'll want to look at the ground directly ahead of you and then left and right so that the entire area between you and your fellow searchers has been checked."

Someone along the line called out, "What if there's a tree right in front of us?"

"Search the ground beneath it and then carefully and slowly, while keeping pace with the line, go around it as best you can," Brennan answered. "Then immediately resume your place in line. The same goes for any other obstacles."

Josie studied the patch of forest directly ahead of her. Other than some thick brush, it would be several feet before she was forced to go around a tree. She couldn't say the same for everyone else. There were some dense parts of the woods they were about to search. It was going to be a long morning.

Brennan paced back and forth in front of the line, one of his arms held high over his head. "Remember, Kayleigh was last seen wearing a blue sweatshirt and a pair of black shorts, as well as white sneakers, according to her younger sister. If you find something, whether it is clothing or anything else you think is important, call out. Loudly and firmly. Raise your hand and keep it up so we know which one of you hollered. Do not touch anything. Simply alert us that you've found something and raise your hand. The rest of you should stop as soon as you hear this alert. We've got three officers following behind the line. One of them will come over to you so you can show them what you've found. We will determine whether or not it should be marked as evidence. If we mark it, and you're close to it, simply go around it when the line begins moving again. Do not move unless the line is moving. Does everyone understand?"

There were mumbles of agreement up and down the line.

Brennan took a long stick from one of the uniformed officers and held it up. "We've got a pile of sticks in case you want to use them to move aside any brush or undergrowth as we search."

A few people stepped out of line and walked over to Brennan to take sticks. Amber followed and returned seconds later with two sticks. She handed one to Josie, who mumbled a thanks. Josie waited for her to take her place in line a few feet away, but she was close enough for Josie to feel her breath against the side of her neck. "Do you have your gun?" she whispered.

"What?" Josie said, lowering her voice to match Amber's. "Please tell me you're not worried about the Woodsman."

Amber laughed softly. "No. I'm worried about bears."

It was a legitimate concern although Josie's Glock wasn't going to stop a bear. However, she didn't tell Amber that. "Yeah," she said. "I've got it. The other officers are armed, too."

"I know," said Amber. "But I'm not walking beside any of them."

"Well, then," Josie said. "Consider me on bear duty."

Brennan instructed them to begin, and the line began moving as one, each person focused on their lane, eyes fixed on the ground. The progress was slow. As they got deeper into the woods, the terrain was more difficult. Some searchers had to skirt ravines, detour around boulders, and climb over downed trees. The sun climbed higher in the sky, heating the air around them. No one spoke. There were no calls or shouts about findings. A sheen of perspiration covered Josie's face. She estimated that they'd traveled almost three miles when Amber put her hand in the air and called out, "I think I found something."

The line stopped moving. Josie looked from her lane over into Amber's while Officer Chan jogged up from behind them. "What do you have?" she asked.

Amber pointed to a large, flat rock at the base of a birch tree. Josie saw several round droplets, the color of rust. "It looks like blood."

Wordlessly, Chan moved in to mark it. Once she gave the signal, Brennan instructed the line to move on. Amber edged her way around the birch tree so as not to disturb the blood evidence. Seconds later, Josie heard her ask, "Do you think that was her blood?"

"We won't know until the ERT tests it. It may not even be human," Josie said automatically.

"Does that mean yes?" Amber whispered.

Josie kept her eyes straight ahead. She didn't answer. The line hadn't moved more than five or six feet when a heap of leaves and twigs appeared at Josie's feet. There was something about the pile that didn't seem natural. Josie raised her arm and called, "Found something."

The line stopped. She felt all eyes on her. Chan made her way over and looked at the mess. "This?" she asked.

"Yes."

Amber said, "It's just some downed branches."

"No," said Josie. "Look closer. There." Careful not to disturb anything, she knelt and used her stick to point to two branches, no thicker than a baseball bat, that had been bound together with a vine. They formed an L shape. At the other end of one of them was more vine, loose and uncoiled where it had likely been tied to another branch.

"Someone made this," said Chan. She threw down an evidence marker, pulled a camera from the bag at her waist, and started snapping photos.

"Kayleigh's not—she's not under there, is she?" Amber whispered.

Chan stopped taking pictures. She and Josie exchanged a glance. "I think Blue would have found her last night," said Josie. She didn't remember seeing this heap, but it was possible that they'd passed it and Josie simply hadn't noticed it. Blue had been moving so fast, it had been getting darker, and without a careful, close look, it would have appeared to be a pile of leaves, just like Amber had said.

Chan said, "I'll check just in case."

She produced a pair of gloves and pulled them on before kneeling and carefully removing leaves, sticks, and loose vines from the center of the pile. Josie took a deep breath, relieved that the scent of decomposition wasn't in the air, although a body probably would not last several hours this deep in the woods without scavenging animals having a go at it, even if it was hidden beneath leaves and sticks.

Murmurs went up and down the line of searchers as Chan worked. Clearing some of the leaves, she picked up another branch, this one clearly sharpened by human hands. A small piece of blue fabric hung from its point. She studied it momentarily and set it aside. Josie leaned in as she reached the forest floor beneath the debris. There were some droplets of blood and a cluster of purple wildflowers that had been crushed into the mud, but no Kayleigh.

Chan stood up. "I'm going to get one of the other ERT guys out here right away, but we have to keep on with the search. We've got a lot of ground to cover."

Josie looked up and down the line, noting the wide eyes and ashen faces of the other searchers. "Not her," she called to them.

As the message spread through the line, Josie could practically feel the relief like waves lapping at her sides.

"What is this?" Amber asked.

"Whatever it is," Chan replied, "it's destroyed now. I'll know more when my team sorts it out."

Josie took another look at it. Spear. Cloth. Branches tied with vines. Leaves—for cover, most likely. Glancing upward at the trees next to the pile, she saw more vines hanging. They'd been tied to a much thicker tree branch overhead. Now their remnants dangled, swaying in the light breeze.

"It's a trap," Josie said.

"What?" said Chan.

Josie pointed to the hanging vines. "I'm not sure how it was shaped or the kind of trap it was, but it looks like a trap. It was hanging from up there. But look, those vines were snapped so either it broke, or someone tried to tear it down."

"Or it was tripped and broke," Chan said. "It's made of hardly anything. No paracord. No metal. No heavy rocks. Nothing that would hold up to an animal."

"But it was enough to hurt someone," Amber said, keeping her voice low. "There's blood."

Had Kayleigh somehow tripped the trap and gotten stuck in it? Injured? Was that the noise that Savannah had heard? Had the person who built it been nearby, waiting? But there had been blood behind them, going toward the Patchett house. Had she been injured and then attempted to run home before the abductor caught up with her?

"We can talk about this later," Chan said firmly. "Let's keep going."

EIGHTEEN

Josie dozed in the passenger seat of Gretchen's car. It was warm, even for May, and the line search had left her sweaty and disheveled. While Gretchen went into Komorrah's Koffee, Josie turned the air conditioning on full blast, hoping to dry the perspiration that had formed in every crease of her body. The cold air felt incredible and within moments, her eyes were drooping. When Gretchen opened the driver's side door, Josie jumped. Her knees banged into the dashboard. If she noticed, Gretchen didn't mention it, instead climbing inside and handing Josie a large flat white latte—her newest obsession. The heat of the cup stung her palms, but the smell of espresso and cream made her mouth water. Or maybe it was the anticipation of the infusion of caffeine about to hit her body.

From the other side of the car came the crinkle of a paper bag. "I got you two cheese Danishes," said Gretchen. "'Cause I know you haven't eaten in hours."

"I think you're my soul mate," Josie said, taking the bag and hungrily devouring one of the cheese Danishes in two bites.

Gretchen laughed, setting her own drink in the center console. Another Komorrah's bag appeared in her hands. From

it, she produced a pecan croissant which she ate far more deli-
cately than Josie had hers. "I think your husband would have
something to say about that. Speaking of which, he briefed me
on his progress before he left."

"He must not have turned up much among Henry
Thomas's associates if he didn't call or text me himself," said
Josie.

"No, he didn't," Gretchen said. "What about you?"

Josie had met up with Gretchen after the line searches. The
Chief hadn't found anything on his side, which had started at
the Thomas cabin and proceeded halfway toward the Patchett
home. The two lines had met in the middle. The only findings
were the drops of blood and the bizarre trap that Amber and
Josie had found. She described it to Gretchen. "Chan said
they'll type the blood to see if it matches Kayleigh's blood type
and she'll try to reconstruct the trap—or whatever the hell that
thing was—oh, and I talked with the Patchetts. They had no
idea about the secret boyfriend."

"So his identity remains a mystery," Gretchen said.

"Looks that way." Josie told her about the conversation she'd
had with Kayleigh Patchett's parents as well as the fact that
she'd found marijuana hidden in Kayleigh Patchett's room.

"Typical teenage stuff," said Gretchen.

"Yes," Josie agreed. She thought of the array of family
photos in the upstairs hall and how ninety percent of them were
of Kayleigh's younger sister. There were eight years between
them. Surely, the Patchetts had taken photos of Kayleigh before
Savannah arrived. Why weren't any of those framed and
displayed? "But do her parents come down so hard on her
because she breaks their rules, or does she break their rules
because she is trying to get their attention?"

"Could be a bit of both. Neither of us is in a position to
theorize."

Although Gretchen had twins that she was in touch with—

her daughter, Paula, lived with her—they were now in their twenties, and both had been adopted as infants and raised by other families. Josie hadn't even entertained the notion of having her own children until recently. Both their own mothers had been brides of Satan—hardly examples of good parenting.

"That's true," said Josie.

"You think we need to look more closely at the parents?"

"I'm not sure. I just wonder if in any of Kayleigh's adventures, she met someone who might have wanted to do her harm."

"We'll need to talk to someone besides her parents," Gretchen said. "Friends, coworkers, classmates."

"Yeah, I'd like to start with her friend Olivia, but let's keep the focus on Henry Thomas for now since Blue led us to him. What did Noah tell you about Thomas's associates?"

Gretchen put on her reading glasses and took out her notepad, flipping until she found the page with the notes she'd taken while speaking with Noah. "He talked with five different guys—contacts from Henry Thomas's phone. One of them was a counselor who helps convicts transition back into society. He was the one who helped Thomas get the job at the city park. He said Henry was never particularly remorseful about what he did but he was very intent on staying out of trouble from here on out."

"Isn't that what anyone would say to a guy who was helping them get a job?" Josie asked.

"That's what I think, but based on Thomas's cabin, which is clean as a whistle, and the fact that he was so cooperative, there is likely something to what the counselor said."

Josie gulped down some more of her latte and fished the second Danish out of the bag. "He's clean and cooperative not because he intends to do no wrong this time around but because he intends not to get caught. There's a difference. I'm telling you, he was too smug. He's hiding something and he's hiding it really damn well."

"Agree," said Gretchen. She flipped another page. "Two of the guys Noah talked with are in a pool league with Thomas. Wednesdays at Brews and Cues. They said Thomas started coming in there regularly about a year and a half ago. They got friendly with him. He's good at pool, evidently. They claim they don't see him outside of pool league. Neither of them has a criminal record. They've both got alibis for yesterday."

"The other two guys?"

"One Thomas met in prison. That guy has an alibi. He was in a holding cell in Bellewood sleeping off a drunk and disorderly all day. The other guy is a coworker. They sometimes go to the strip club together."

"Nice to know Foxy Tails is still in business," Josie said with a sigh. She'd had occasion to visit the club many times as a police officer. None had been pleasant. "Does the strip club coworker have an alibi?"

Gretchen turned another page. "He worked seven to three yesterday, so he's got one for most of the day. Another park employee was with him the entire day except for lunch, which was a half hour."

"We can pretty much rule him out then," said Josie. "Criminal record?"

"No. Also, Noah spoke with Henry Thomas's boss who had nothing to say about him except that he is reliable and stays out of trouble."

"Is there anyone left?" asked Josie. "Anyone Noah didn't talk with?"

"One guy," said Gretchen. "Morris Lauber, sixty-two. Lives in an apartment in Southwest Denton."

NINETEEN

I went unnoticed by the police for so long. I was as careful as I could be but I never expected to remain unseen forever. Now I watch as the first flurry of news reports come in. Not about me. Not yet. Only about what I've done. This is my first time seeing my work on television. A new thrill. I like this taste of fame, even if it doesn't have my name on it yet. I am nothing if not patient, and if they do not begin to give me proper credit, I'll just have to raise the stakes. Even with so much scrutiny, I know where to find fresh victims.

TWENTY

Josie's calves burned as she followed Gretchen up the eighth flight of steps in Morris Lauber's apartment building. Although most of West Denton was upper middle class with almost no crime at all, and South Denton was more of a business district than a residential area, also with little crime, Southwest Denton had distinguished itself as one of the seediest and most run-down areas of the city. One main thoroughfare in particular was made up mostly of old apartment buildings over laundromats, takeout food places, and pawn shops. Almost all of them were six stories or more. Morris Lauber's building was ten and he lived on the tenth floor. They'd tried the elevator but after waiting for fifteen minutes in a hot, windowless lobby that smelled like piss and hot wings, they decided to take the stairs.

"Have you been jogging?" asked Josie as they reached the ninth floor. "You're not even huffing."

Gretchen glanced back at her. Josie could see that her face was bright red and covered in sweat. "Paula's got me out running almost every morning. Trying to get me on this health kick." She squeezed a roll of skin beneath her Denton PD polo shirt. "Wants me to lose some of this because I'm prediabetic."

"That's great," Josie said.

"No, it's not," Gretchen replied, trudging up the last flight of stairs. "It's terrible and I hate every second of it. By the way, if you could not mention that pecan croissant the next time you see her..."

"What pecan croissant?" Josie said.

Gretchen reached the door and twisted the knob, pulling it open. "Maybe we are soul mates, after all. You should let Noah down easy though. I like that guy."

Josie laughed softly as they passed through the doorway. She was relieved to feel cooler air once they were out of the stairwell. Lauber's apartment was in the middle of the hallway. The interior of the building was in much better shape than the exterior and the lobby. Fresh white paint coated the walls of the hallway. Polished hardwood floors gleamed. Wall sconces hung between apartment doors. The faint smell of bacon mixed with something more florid. Perfume, maybe.

"This place isn't so bad," Gretchen muttered. "Maybe they'll fix the elevators next."

She knocked on Morris Lauber's door. Beyond it, they heard footsteps. Then a beat of silence. Something passed over the peephole. Next came a muttered, "Shit." The door opened slowly, just a sliver, and half of a grizzled face with brown eyes peeked out.

"If you're looking for the guy with the feral peacock, he's in 23."

Gretchen held up her credentials. "We're looking for Morris Lauber, but let's unpack that later."

"Shit," he said again.

"Are you Morris Lauber?" asked Josie, also presenting her credentials.

"Yeah, that's me."

"Can we come in?" asked Gretchen.

"I'd really prefer it if you didn't. See, my girlfriend will be home soon, and she won't be happy to see me talking to the cops."

"Why?" asked Josie. "Have you done something wrong?"

"No, no. I wouldn't break the law. You can look me up. I don't have a record. A few speeding tickets but that's it."

Gretchen looked at her watch. "What time does your girlfriend get home?"

He told her.

"That's in twenty minutes. We'll be gone in fifteen," she promised him. "If we see her, we'll tell her we're looking for the guy in 23."

This seemed to mollify him. Slowly, he opened the door. Inside was a living room that bled right into a kitchen just big enough to accommodate a table and chairs for two. The place was clean and neatly kept. The furniture was dark, dated, and scuffed in places but Josie could see the touch of Lauber's girlfriend in the fresh flowers sitting in a glass vase on the pitted coffee table and the stack of romance novels on one of the end tables. Morris muted the television and sat down on his couch. Kayleigh Patchett's face flashed across the screen, but Morris didn't react, instead reaching for a half-full bottle of beer on the table. He put it to his lips and hesitated. "I guess I shouldn't drink this with the police here."

Josie said, "Mr. Lauber, you're in your own home. We've interrupted your afternoon. Do as you like."

This garnered a big smile. Gretchen looked at her watch again. "We're here about Henry Thomas."

Slowly, he put the beer down. Then he ran a hand down his stubbled face. "Oh no. Henry get himself into some trouble again?"

"We were hoping you could tell us," said Josie. "We found your phone number in his phone. Looks like the two of you talk pretty regularly."

"We do. I knew his dad. He and I used to trap together. I

was always around, watched Henry grow up, practically. Then he got in trouble on account of that girl, and he went to prison. Broke his dad's heart. Right before Henry got out, his dad passed. I helped him with the estate and everything. Finding a lawyer, going through his dad's things, selling the house, helping him buy the cabin. I ain't no dad, but I try to be there for him."

"I'm sure his dad would appreciate all you've done for him," said Josie. "How often do you see Henry?"

"We usually get together once a month. He comes here or I go to his place. Sometimes we hit the bar. Depends. Just shoot the shit. I complain about Darcy—that's my girlfriend—and he complains about work."

"Henry isn't dating anyone?" asked Gretchen.

"Says he doesn't have time for it." Morris laughed. "But that boy doesn't do nothing but go to work and watch Netflix, so I don't know what he's talking about. I think he just doesn't want the frustration of having to answer to another person."

"When was the last time you saw him?" asked Josie.

"Oh, about a week ago. Say, is Henry okay?"

"He's fine," said Josie.

Gretchen said, "Mr. Lauber, what kind of trouble do you think Henry got into that might bring us here?"

He shrugged. "Hell if I know. Bar fight, maybe? He's got a temper on him, that's for sure."

Josie said, "You said you trapped with Henry's father. Did Henry trap as well?"

"Sure, when he was younger. He was good at it but never took a liking to it. Got bored with it real fast. Never did get his license. Is that why you're here? Was he trapping illegally?" His brow furrowed. "That's really something for the game commission, not regular police."

"That's not why we're here," said Gretchen. She pointed to the television which now showed aerial views of the line searches that had been conducted earlier that morning. The chyron on the bottom of the screen read: *Searches Underway for Abducted Denton Teen.* The camera cut back to the anchor at the news station. Kayleigh's school picture appeared over her shoulder. "That's why we're here."

For a moment, Morris looked stunned. His whole face went slack as he stared at the screen. "Wait," he said. "You think that Henry had something to do with that missing girl?"

"Do *you* think he had something to do with her?" asked Josie.

He shook his head, eyes still locked on Kayleigh's face. "No. No. Not Henry."

"He held a nineteen-year-old girl against her will at gunpoint," Josie pointed out. "This girl, Kayleigh Patchett? She was in the woods, only a few miles from Henry's cabin when she was taken."

"That don't mean nothing. Henry wouldn't hurt a young girl. He wouldn't do that."

Gretchen said, "Mr. Lauber, our K-9 unit tracked Kayleigh Patchett's scent to his cabin. Inside his cabin."

"No."

"Yes," Josie said. "Tell us again the last time you saw Henry."

He tore his gaze from the television to look up at them. "I told you, a week ago. Why are you asking me this?"

"Where were you yesterday?" asked Josie.

"What?"

"Where were you yesterday?" she repeated.

He looked everywhere but at them, as if seeking help that was not coming. "I was here. I was right here. I mean, most of the day. I went—I went—Oh shit..."

Josie perched herself on the edge of the coffee table, her knees touching his. "Where were you when you weren't here?"

He slumped. "Checking on my traps."

Josie said, "There's not much the game commission allows you to trap this time of year. What were you after?"

He looked down at his hands, fiddling with the label on the beer bottle. "Coyote is legal all year round."

Gretchen said, "Mr. Lauber, how many motor vehicles do you own?"

He seemed confused by the abrupt change in subject but answered anyway. "Just one. A Ford F-150. It's out back."

Josie knew that Gretchen had already looked this up before they arrived. He was being truthful.

"This is your residence," Gretchen continued. "Do you own any other property anywhere? A cabin, maybe? Is there anywhere else you spend your time?"

"No, no. I'm here all the time. My girlfriend lives here with me. Don't own no other places."

"Great," said Gretchen. "Do you mind if I take a quick look around your apartment?"

"Sure, I guess."

Gretchen disappeared down the short hall while Josie continued the questions. "Where do you keep your trapping equipment?"

"In my truck mostly. I scaled down the last few years. Don't got much left. Just a couple of traps. The other stuff I keep in my storage unit in the basement here till I need it. My girlfriend don't like me trapping. Says it's 'inhumane.'"

"You've got some traps out now. How many?"

"Only two."

"Where are they?"

He scratched his head. "They're over by—wait—I saw the news. That girl went missing near that bad place. The one where all those girls died."

"By Henry's place," Josie said.

He shook his head vehemently. "None of my traps are there. None."

"Mr. Lauber," said Josie. "I need you to be honest with me right now."

"I am being honest with you!"

Josie made a slow scan of the room. "Really? Because I have never met a trapper who could carry out their business in a tenth-floor apartment with—" She leaned to the side and looked down the hall. "Looks like one bedroom. Doesn't give you a lot of room to work. Where would you hang your skinning gambrel or mount your fleshing beam?"

He sighed and hung his head. "Okay, okay. Truth is, Henry lets me use his property. When I catch something, which isn't often. And I got my license. I'm legal. Everything is above board."

"Okay," said Josie. "What about Henry? To your knowledge, does he trap illegally?"

"No. I don't think so. I never saw anything that would make me think that. He never said. I've never seen anything up at his place, and I would have said something if he was doing it without a license or out of season. I'm telling you, he wasn't interested when he was a kid and he's not now."

"You must go to his place a lot," said Josie. "Have you ever seen anyone else there?"

He started shaking his head but then stopped. "Kids."

Josie felt her heartbeat stutter but kept her voice calm. "What do you mean, kids?"

He waved a hand in the air. "Teenagers. They come up that way a lot. In groups, or boys trying to scare their girlfriends—or maybe impress 'em, who knows? You know what happened up there on that mountain, right? The killers? All those girls?"

"Yes," Josie said, the word like a piece of gravel in her throat.

"They come up and want to look around. It's like they think the place is haunted. How else do you think Henry got that place so cheap? No one wants to go up there, much less live up there. I know the city cleared it and planted all those flowers but it's creepy. I don't mind visiting Henry there, but I couldn't live there."

"The kids, Mr. Lauber," said Josie. Gretchen reappeared in the living room. She gave a slight shake of her head. She hadn't found anything.

"Right," he said. "Kids come up there. I've seen them. Henry's is the only driveway up there. I mean, there were a couple of other driveways leading to where the old properties was on the other side of the flower fields, but they're overgrown now and one of 'em's chained so people use his road. They pull right into his place. I guess thinking that no one lives there."

"You've seen them?" asked Josie.

"Sure. Couple of times. Henry goes out and tells them to get lost."

"Did you ever see Kayleigh Patchett?"

"I couldn't tell you. I never got a good look at any of them. Just saw they was teenagers."

Gretchen walked over. "But you could see well enough to know if it was a teenage boy driving or if he had a girlfriend in the passenger's seat."

"I guess, but I wasn't studying them or nothing."

Josie took out the photo of the mystery boy they'd found on Kayleigh's phone and showed Lauber. "You ever see this kid out there?"

He hesitated but Josie wasn't sure if it was because he recognized the kid or because he was nervous about somehow getting the answer wrong. Finally, he said, "I don't know. I really don't know. How am I supposed to tell from the side of his face?"

Pocketing her phone, Josie said, "Were you at Henry's at all yesterday?"

"No."

Gretchen said, "Mind if we have a look at your vehicle?"

He looked at the clock on the cable box. "You serious? My girlfriend will be here any minute. You promised me—"

Josie stood up. "We did, but you've been so helpful that we're going to need a little more from you. A look at your storage unit in the basement, your vehicle, and also, we're going to need you to show us where your traps are located."

He put his head in his hands. "Shit."

TWENTY-ONE

Morris Lauber was considerably more freaked out by the police inquiries than Henry Thomas had been, but he was equally as cooperative. He showed them his storage unit in the basement of the apartment building, pacing nervously outside it while Josie and Gretchen went through its contents. It was neatly kept, almost like a workshop. For a lifelong trapper, he certainly didn't have many traps left, just as he'd said, although he did have all the equipment needed to skin, tan, and cure pelts. Next, he led them to his truck. After taking an initial look in the cab and bed, Gretchen called Hummel and asked that the ERT come out and process it for any evidence of Kayleigh Patchett. Finally, Lauber led them to his traps, which, as promised, were nowhere near Henry Thomas's cabin. Hummel and his team were finished by the time they returned him to his home. When Josie and Gretchen broke it to him that they would need to speak with his girlfriend after all, he showed the most distress he'd exhibited all day.

By that time, Noah had arrived at the stationhouse. Gretchen sent Josie home to sleep while she interviewed Morris Lauber's girlfriend. Everything in Josie wanted to object, to stay for that one last interview, but she knew that there was never just one last interview. Not in big cases like this. She had now been awake for over thirty-six hours and knew that the best thing she could do for Kayleigh Patchett was to go home and get some sleep so that she would be alert and clear-headed when she came back to work on Monday morning. Noah picked her up at Lauber's apartment and dropped her back at her car.

Fifteen minutes later, she was kneeling on her foyer floor, petting their Boston terrier, Trout, while he wiggled his butt uncontrollably and licked her face. Luckily for her, Noah had walked and fed him before he reported for work. Trout waited dutifully on the bathroom floor while Josie took one of the longest, hottest showers of her life. Tonight she felt exhausted enough that she might actually get rest. She was just getting under the covers when the doorbell rang. In the second it took for her to consider not answering it, Trout began barking. As he ran from the bedroom and tore down the steps, Josie dragged her heavy limbs from the bed and followed.

Misty, Harris, and their little chiweiner dog, Pepper, stood on her front stoop. Trout moved past Josie to greet Pepper. The two were old friends. Harris clutched his mother's hand. There were two bags hanging from her other hand along with Pepper's leash. Wisps of hair escaped the loose ponytail she'd tied her blonde hair into, blowing against her cheeks in the light May breeze. "I'm sorry," she said. "I know you've had the worst day." She looked down at Josie's sweatpants and the oversized T-shirt —one of Noah's—that she usually wore to bed. "You've been up since the last time we saw each other, haven't you?"

Josie waved them inside the foyer. Harris dropped to the floor and started scratching behind Trout's ears. Misty stared down at him, brow creased. Josie's mind was slowed from fatigue. It took a moment for her to realize that he hadn't greeted her with his usual enthusiasm, jumping into her arms and yelling out, "Aunt JoJo!"

"What's going on?" she asked Misty quietly.

Dropping her bags at her feet, and letting Pepper off her leash, Misty said, "He wanted us to sleep here tonight. I'm sorry. I hoped you—or Noah—wouldn't mind. I know I should have called but I was afraid..."

Josie smiled. "Have we ever said no to you guys?"

Misty shook her head.

"You have a key," Josie reminded her.

"I know, but I don't like to use it unless you know I'm coming over or we've talked about it."

"Misty, you and Harris—and even Pepper—are family. You know that. What's going on?"

Misty reached down and tousled Harris's blond locks. He kept his attention on Trout, who was now on his back, legs spread wide as he accepted gratuitous belly rubs. Pepper's tail wagged as she observed the activity. Misty lowered her voice to a whisper. "He's terrified, Josie, and I don't know what to tell him. You know he's been having nightmares over this stupid Woodsman thing for months. He was doing better after you and Noah talked with him and told him the Woodsman wasn't real, but now with that girl missing... He was hysterical earlier. I've never seen him so scared."

Josie pulled Misty to her and hugged her tightly. "You guys did the right thing coming here. Stay tonight. Tomorrow. As long as you want."

Misty squeezed back. "Will you talk to him?"

"Of course."

"I'll take this stuff to the spare bedroom," Misty said, picking up the bags.

Josie waited until she was upstairs before getting down on her knees and trying to get Harris to meet her eyes. "Hey, why don't you tell me what's bothering you? Your mom said you were pretty upset earlier."

"You lied to me," he mumbled.

Josie felt the words like a spike in her heart. "What?"

"You lied to me. You said the Woodsman wasn't real, but he is real and he took a girl yesterday and now she's gone and she'll never go back to her mom."

Josie took a deep breath, trying to focus her muddled mind. "Harris, I didn't lie to you. The Woodsman is not real."

Finally, he looked at her, his blue eyes so much like her late first husband, Ray's, that her breath caught in her throat. "He is, too! He took someone! I went to Liam's birthday party today and he told me. I didn't believe him because you and Uncle Noah said the Woodsman wasn't real, but he showed me on the news!"

"Harris," Josie said evenly. "A teenage girl was taken by a bad man yesterday. That is true. She was taking a walk in the woods at the time. That is also true. But the Woodsman did not take her. The Woodsman is not real."

His lower lip quivered. "How do you know?"

Trout squirmed and turned back onto his stomach, ears pointed now as he looked back and forth between them, his soulful brown eyes filled with concern. Bored with them, Pepper wandered off in search of Misty.

"Because the Woodsman is something kids made up, like a ghost story."

"But you said a man took a girl! How do you know it wasn't the Woodsman? The Woodsman is a man! How do you know it wasn't him?"

"Because I—" Josie stopped.

How could she explain to a seven-year-old that he shouldn't be afraid of the Woodsman when a man had, in fact, kidnapped a girl in the woods? It didn't matter that the Woodsman wasn't real. It was a meaningless distinction. The reality was that a man had abducted a girl from the woods. Even if Josie convinced Harris that the Woodsman hadn't done it, what was the alternative? Another bad man had kidnapped her. That wouldn't make him feel any safer. Even though the Woodsman wasn't real, monsters were. The kinds of monsters who hurt children. Josie had dedicated her life to putting those kinds of people in prison. But she couldn't stop them. No one could. She couldn't even tell Harris that Kayleigh Patchett would be found safe and returned to her parents because she didn't know that, and these cases didn't usually turn out that way.

No wonder Misty hadn't known what to say.

How did you reassure a child that the world was safe when it wasn't? How did you convince them that you could control things about the world when you couldn't? She was supposed to be the adult. She was supposed to have all the answers.

She didn't.

Was this what it would be like to be a parent?

"Harris," Josie tried again. "I know that you're scared. It's very scary when bad things happen. A bad person took that girl, and me and your Uncle Noah, and Gretchen, and the Chief and everyone we work with—including Luke and his dog, Blue—we're all doing everything we can to find her as soon as possible."

His voice was small. "What if you can't?"

Now it felt as though some vital piece of her heart had been torn to pieces. She tried not to let her body slump under the weight of the feeling. Trout whined and jumped to lick her face. "It's okay, boy," she murmured, petting his head. She stood up and extended her hand to Harris. His palm was cold and clammy in hers as she led him to the living room couch. She sat and pulled him close to her, one arm wrapped around him. Kissing the top of his head, she said the only thing she could think of: "We keep trying. We just keep trying."

He slid an arm across her middle and rested his head on her chest. She stroked his hair, inhaling his scent. It took her back to when he was just an infant. Back then, his entire body had fit on her chest. As one of his primary babysitters, she'd spent hours rocking him to sleep in the glider chair at Misty's house.

"I'm afraid that the Woodsman will get me, and I'll never see my mom again," Harris whispered.

Josie felt the breath leave her body. Holding him more tightly, she said, "Your mom is one of the smartest people I know, Harris. Everything she does is to protect you and keep you safe. She also has me and Uncle Noah to help her. If we all stick together, we have a very good chance of staying safe."

It didn't seem like enough.

"What if someone took me?"

This was an easy one, which made Josie wonder what that said about her—and the world. She thought about what Noah had said to her months ago during a case involving a married couple. The wife had been murdered and the husband, while upset, wasn't particularly focused on finding the killer. Noah had made it clear that if he were in that situation, he'd respond very differently. *If anything ever happened to you, I'd burn this entire city down finding the person who hurt you.*

If anything ever happened to Harris, if anyone ever took him from them, Josie would burn the entire world to the ground to find him—and punish the person who hurt him. But she couldn't say that. Not to a seven-year-old.

She kissed his head. "Then we would do everything that we could to find you. Absolutely everything, and we would never stop looking. Not ever. No matter what. Not for a million years."

"You can't live for a million years," he said, and she heard the sleep in his voice.

"For you, I would try."

A few more seconds ticked by. Trout jumped up on the couch and snuggled up to Josie's other side. Drowsiness began to overtake her. When she heard Harris's snores, she let herself fall deep into the darkness.

TWENTY-TWO

Josie slept for several hours before memories of Mettner's death replayed in her dreams, the echo of the gunshots that took him startling her awake. She was in her bed with Trout pressed against her. Outside her windows, dawn was just a blue and purple whisper. As the last vestiges of the dream-memory left her, she felt the phantom sensation of Mettner's hand sandwiched between her own. Sitting up, she stared at her palms. How was it that all these months later, she still felt his hand squeezed between hers? She stood abruptly and wiped her hands on her sweatpants. Still under the covers, Trout sighed and shifted. Before the flood of images from the night Mett died inundated her, Josie cast about for one of the breathing exercises her therapist had insisted she try. The only one that worked— sometimes—was the four-seven-eight breathing exercise. She inhaled, counting to four, held her breath for a count of seven, and then exhaled while counting to eight. After several of these, her mind settled, thoughts turning from Mettner to Kayleigh Patchett.

She checked her phone but there were no updates. She turned on the television. The local news was just coming on, its top story Kayleigh's abduction. Josie went to her dresser and began pulling out clean clothes as the anchor recapped the weekend's developments before sending the broadcast over to a reporter in the field. "WYEP's own Dallas Jones is at police headquarters with the latest developments in this case. Dallas, what are you learning at this hour about the investigation?"

Josie stopped on her way into the bathroom and looked back at the television. Dallas Jones was young, only a few years out of college. He was stocky and wore his dark hair slicked back from his face and lacquered into what she was sure was a hard shell. Like most young reporters, he was hungry to make a name for himself, which meant he liked to dig way beneath the surface of every story, even if there was nothing to find. Standing in the municipal lot a few feet from the entrance, he spoke into his microphone. "So far, the police are being very tight-lipped about the results of their investigation, giving only scant details about Kayleigh Patchett's abduction. What we do know is that it happened in the woods behind her house. Police have not given a description or any details at all about the man they think is behind this. However, after speaking with many local parents and students who attend Denton East High School with Kayleigh, it seems there is a fear that this might be the work of someone called the Woodsman."

"Son of a bitch."

Trout's head popped up beneath the blanket. He stood and scrambled to find the edge so that he could get out from under it. Josie walked over and uncovered him. Scratching his head, she murmured, "It's okay, boy. Just me talking to the TV."

She sat and watched as Dallas went on. "Rumors have spread like wildfire in the community of Denton as far back as Thanksgiving that a man called 'the Woodsman' has been stalking children in the forests around the city. So far we have not been able to confirm this with the Denton Police Depart-ment. Whether or not there was any substance to the rumors before, there is certainly a lot of fear now that Kayleigh Patchett's abduction is the work of the Woodsman."

The screen split into two boxes, one showing Dallas Jones and the other showing the anchor back at the studio. Under the two of them the chyron read: *Local Teen Feared Abducted by Man Calling Himself "The Woodsman."*

"This is not good," Josie groaned.

The anchor said, "Dallas, this sounds a lot like a disturbing fairy tale come to life. Have the police indicated whether or not this Woodsman has been active anywhere else in the state?"

Dallas shook his head. "Not at this point. As I said, the police have not given us many details. Right now, they say, their priority is finding Kayleigh Patchett."

Josie turned the TV off and gave Trout a squeeze before snatching her phone from the nightstand. She didn't bother checking the time as she found the name in her contacts. Heather Loughlin slept about as much as Josie did. She picked up after two rings and agreed to meet with Josie at a truck stop along Route 80 in one hour.

With plenty of time before she had to report to work, Josie fed Trout, took him for a walk, and left Misty and Harris a note before driving forty minutes to the truck stop that Heather had specified. The massive parking lot was half filled with eighteen-wheelers. Josie circled the sprawling mini market in the center of the lot, watching as truckers went in and out of its four different entrances. Neon signs promised everything from cigarettes to hot showers. Inside smelled like scalded coffee and bacon. Televisions hung in every corner of the shop, each one tuned to a repeat of the newscast that Josie had watched when she woke up: Dallas Jones telling viewers about the mysterious Woodsman.

Josie found Heather sitting at a booth in the dining area and slid into the seat across from her. The bright orange vinyl banquette bowed under Josie's weight. Her palm touched something sticky. She was relieved when she turned her hand over and saw a smudge of what looked like maple syrup. A quick sniff confirmed it. A wet wipe appeared under her nose. "Here," said Heather. "It's antibacterial. I always carry them."

Thanking her, Josie scrubbed at the syrup. "Thanks for meeting with me."

"I'm here to shake down some of these truckers," said Heather. "About a missing woman. Might as well have breakfast." She pushed a pile of foil-wrapped sandwiches toward Josie. Each one oozed grease onto the table. "You have high cholesterol?"

"What?" said Josie, poking around until she found something labeled bacon, egg, and cheese. "No."

"You will after you eat that." Heather pushed a paper cup of coffee over, together with several creamers, sugar packets and a stirrer. She gestured to the nearest television. "You're here because of that, aren't you? The Woodsman."

Josie started dumping creamer into the cup. "That reporter? Dallas Jones? He likes to dig. It's only a matter of time before he finds out about your cases and tries to connect them to ours and this mythical Woodsman."

Heather nodded and opened a breakfast sandwich that appeared to be sausage, egg, and cheese on a bagel. "He won't have to try. They are connected to the Woodsman."

TWENTY-THREE

A burning sensation started in the pit of Josie's stomach. She pushed the coffee away. "What are you talking about? Heather, the Woodsman is a kids' story. It's folklore. He's not real."

"Didn't say he was," Heather said. "But Josie, these kids in Montour and Lenore Counties? They went into the woods looking for this guy."

Josie had never thought about the story beyond the fact that it had scared the hell out of Harris. "I didn't realize the story of the Woodsman came from outside Denton. I just knew it was circulating among elementary school students in the city."

Heather took a big bite of her sandwich. "Who knows where it came from. Hell, it probably started on the damn internet like everything does now. I'm just telling you that when we caught these two cases, this story about the Woodsman was the impetus for the kids to go into the woods."

"Where else have you heard about the Woodsman?" Josie asked, hating herself for using valuable investigative time on some kind of twisted fairy tale. Then again, she wanted to know whatever there was to know about him—or whoever was lurking in the woods hurting children—before the press got their hands on the information and drove the entire city into a panic.

"Not much, really. I thought with the first case that it was a one-off kind of thing. Something the local kids were kicking around, but then when we caught the second case it was clear that it wasn't confined to one area. Have you looked on social media?"

The burning in Josie's stomach intensified. "It's a hashtag?"

"It wasn't trending until today, but there's a smattering of posts about it, mostly from people in Pennsylvania. It's like a challenge. Two kids go into the woods after dark looking for the Woodsman. If both of them survive, they win the challenge."

This was not the lore that Josie had heard from Harris or even from the Patchett family. "What do you mean, if both of them survive?"

Heather took another bite of her sandwich, bits of scrambled egg falling onto the table. Josie waited for her to finish chewing. "The legend of the Woodsman, as I've heard it, is that two kids go into the woods and only one comes out. If both kids survive, you win. You beat him."

"That's not what I've been hearing," said Josie. "How old were the kids who went in?"

"Teenagers," Heather answered. She polished off her sandwich and started wiping both hands with a wet wipe. "What have you heard?"

"The Woodsman takes you and you never see your mom again—that's the gist of it."

Heather picked up her own cup of coffee and slugged some of it down. She grimaced as she set the cup back onto the table. "That'll give you an ulcer. Anyway, you're hearing this stuff from elementary kids. It makes sense that the lore would be more complex among teenagers. You know how these things are —they evolve. The story can only be repeated by so many people before kids start adding their own twists on it."

Josie looked over at the nearest television. Dallas Jones had been replaced by the meteorologist giving a weather report. "This isn't real, Heather."

"No," she agreed, tearing three sugar packets and dumping them into her coffee. "But someone is attacking and killing kids in wooded areas. Montour County, Lenore County, and now your county."

Josie mapped the locations out in her head. They were all relatively close to one another, each place only one to three hours from the others. "Tell me about the cases."

"The first one was in Lenore County. Seventeen-year-old male, Mark Canva and a sixteen-year-old female, Amanda Chavez went into the woods together around eleven thirty on a Saturday night. They told a few friends they were going to spend the night in the woods to see if they could find the Woodsman. The next morning Amanda's parents saw she hadn't slept in her bed. Tried calling her. No answer. Mark and Amanda were dating, so Amanda's parents tried Mark next. Nothing. They called the county sheriff to report Amanda missing. Amanda's phone was still on and had a charge, so they pinged it. Took some searching since the ping only gave them a three-mile radius to work with but they found her body in the woods. Her head was smashed in. Autopsy confirmed blunt force trauma to the head as the cause of death. No sign of sexual assault. Three hours later, they found Mark wandering around the woods about six miles away. He was in shock. We thought he was catatonic or something, but after a couple of days in the hospital he started talking."

In spite of the dread she was feeling, Josie's stomach growled. Heather pushed the bacon, egg, and cheese sandwich closer. "They're not the worst thing I've ever had."

Reluctantly, Josie opened it, taking a tentative bite. It was cold but her stomach clamored for more. "What did Mark Canva say when he started talking?"

"They were walking around in the woods. It was an area behind some old, abandoned church. No residences for miles. No roads for miles."

"How many miles are we talking?" asked Josie.

"Maybe ten miles north to south and about seven or eight east to west? They went in closest to the southwest corner. Parked by the church. Mark said they had flashlights with them. We recovered one of them. They also had their phones, like I said. He thinks it was about two thirty in the morning, a little after, when they heard something. Amanda got scared. He said it was probably deer. They huddled by a tree for a while. Didn't hear anything else so they kept going. Couple of minutes later, he says someone attacked Amanda. At least he thinks that's what happened. He said she tripped and went down. Her flashlight rolled away. He only saw her feet and then someone came at him from behind. A man."

"He saw the guy, then," Josie said. She ate the last bit of the breakfast sandwich and pulled her coffee toward her once more.

"No, it was too dark. He just thinks it was a man because of the guy's strength. Mark is six foot two, over two hundred pounds. He said the guy knocked him down, kicked him in the back."

Josie poured two sugar packets into her coffee and stirred. "Did Mark have any visible injuries?"

"Some bruising on his back," said Heather.

"What happened after he got knocked down?"

"Mark says the guy kept kicking him, so he ran. He was trying to find help but lost both his flashlight and his phone. Then he tried to go back to check on Amanda but he couldn't find her. That's why he was wandering around when we found him. To be honest, I think his biggest injury is the guilt he feels that he couldn't protect her—or even find his way back to her once he got away from the attacker."

"You don't think he did it?"

Heather looked at the television. Kayleigh Patchett's face was back on the screen. "That was my first thought and I've got no proof that he didn't, but my gut tells me he told the truth about what happened."

Josie sipped her coffee. It might take a layer of tissue from the inside of her stomach, but it wasn't the worst she'd ever tasted. "What about the scene?"

"It was a mess. It started pouring rain the next morning while we were searching. If there was anything there, it got destroyed."

"You said Amanda Chavez died from a blow to the head?"

"Her head was smashed in. Almost like something fell on her. The ME thinks that she was in a prone position when she was struck."

"She fell or was knocked down and then struck," Josie said. "Any idea with what?"

"A big rock. We found what we believe was the murder weapon but with the rain, most of the blood and tissue were washed from it. But this guy had to be big to wield this thing."

"What about the other case?" Josie asked. "In Montour County?"

Heather pawed through the pile of breakfast sandwiches between them before pushing them away. "Same thing. Two kids go into the woods. Only one comes out. Two girls. Sarah McArthur and Dawn Angels. Sixteen and fifteen. They were having a sleepover at Sarah's house and decided to sneak out in the middle of the night and take a walk in the woods." She motioned to the television which was showing footage of the line searches. "She lived in an area like that. Home out in the middle of nowhere. Forest all around. These two didn't bring flashlights, only Sarah's phone. We know from the GPS on the phone that they were out there for about three hours before anything happened. The younger one, Dawn, says that Sarah got her foot stuck in a hole and she couldn't get her out. They were going to call 911 but the flashlight app ran the battery all the way down, especially while they were trying to get Sarah's foot out. Dawn said it was some kind of rope or wire or something. A cable, maybe, inside the hole. They couldn't get her loose. Dawn left her there to go back to the house and get help."

"She got lost."

"Well, yeah, but she did eventually find her way back to the house, near dawn. Sarah's parents called 911. They pinged the phone. Found Sarah about two miles from the house, no longer stuck, no cable, rope, or wire to be found. She was face down with a fracture to the back of her skull. Autopsy confirmed manner of death as blunt force trauma, same as the other case. No sign of sexual assault."

Josie swirled the dregs of her coffee around in the bottom of the cup. "He struck her from behind."

"Looks that way. We also think that the place she was found is not where she got stuck. We couldn't pinpoint that location. It was dark when the kids went out. We did line searches of the area, but we didn't find much. We could not locate the place she got her foot stuck—or anything that it may have gotten stuck in. But Dawn was right."

"What do you mean?"

Heather leaned forward, putting her elbows on top of the table. "Sarah McArthur was wearing sweatpants and sneakers. Around her ankle were ligature marks. Thin."

Josie's heart fluttered. "She got caught in a snare trap."

"We think so," said Heather. "But without the trap, we can't prove it or trace it back to the person who put it out there. It's not even trapping season."

"Coyote is legal all year round," Josie said, echoing Morris Lauber. "Can you send me the crime scene photos?"

Heather raised a brow. "I can. You think your case is connected?"

"I don't know," Josie said. "But we found something out

there where Kayleigh was taken. It looks like a trap to me. Something made out of leaves and sticks. Not a snare or a foothold trap, but some sort of trap. It was in a heap when we located it. Our Evidence Response Team is trying to reconstruct it. Plus, we followed Kayleigh's scent to a cabin. Remote. Owned by a guy who did time on a charge of unlawful restraint of a young woman. His dad used to trap. Taught him. His dad is dead but he's got his dad's trapping equipment in his house. He also has a friend who is licensed and traps, and that friend uses this guy's property often."

Heather's spine straightened. "Really?"

"Yes, but we didn't take any of the trapping stuff into evidence because we couldn't prove any link between the traps and Kayleigh's disappearance."

"But this could be our guy," said Heather.

"Maybe."

"Any snare traps in his cabin?"

"No," said Josie. "Footholds."

"Shit." Heather sighed. "I can't get a warrant based on the fact that we think one of our cases involved a snare trap and some guy in your jurisdiction has foothold traps in his home—even with Kayleigh's scent being inside the cabin. This sure sounds like it could be him, though. I mean, in your case, the kids went into the woods during the day. Were they doing the challenge?"

Josie slugged down the last of the coffee. "No. Kayleigh wanted to prove to her little sister that the Woodsman wasn't real. Heather, this guy lives pretty close to the Patchett house. It's not out of the realm of possibility that he either ran into Kayleigh or stalked her—but these other kids? Montour and Lenore Counties are hours away from one another. How would he have known that these kids were going to be in the woods in the middle of the night?"

"He's hunting," Heather said. "You have to understand,

these aren't the first or only kids to go traipsing through the woods at night in either of these counties. They're just the only ones who ran into this guy."

Josie thought about the kids who had gotten lost in the woods throughout Denton in the last six months. None of them had told the police that they'd been looking for the Woodsman, but it couldn't be a coincidence that a rash of incidents involving kids getting lost in the woods coincided with the lore of the Woodsman infiltrating schools.

Heather continued, "We're talking about kids who live in mostly rural areas with not much to do. This Woodsman bullshit is all some of them are talking about. Then there is the social media aspect. Lots of these kids post that they're going into the woods. It's not that hard to figure out where they are because none of them know how to protect themselves on the internet. If you post a video of yourself standing in front of your damn house—with the house number visible—and you're wearing a shirt with your school name on it, it's not going to be hard to figure out which area you're in. Some of these kids even post where they're going into the woods. Really, all this guy would need to do is check the Woodsman hashtag on Instagram any given weekend and he'd have a pretty good idea where to lay his traps."

To Josie's knowledge, the search of Henry Thomas's phone had not turned up any social media accounts although it was possible he'd had a burner phone at some point. They'd searched his property and vehicles and not found one, but that didn't mean he didn't have other ways to search social media. The ERT was still examining his laptop.

"Where to lay his traps," Josie echoed. "You said in the Chavez case, she was prone when a large rock hit her in the head, right?"

"Yeah."

"What kind of rock? Was it flat?"

"Sort of, yeah."

"You find any large sticks nearby?" Josie asked.

Heather laughed. "It was the forest. So yeah. What are you thinking?"

"Could Amanda Chavez have tripped a deadfall trap?"

A deadfall trap was a primitive trap that usually involved using sticks to prop up a large rock or log. There were other, more modern tools available to use instead of sticks, but the concept was the same: a large, deadly item was propped up and beneath it was a bait stick or bait string of some kind where the trapper would leave some kind of food. When an animal touched or bumped the bait stick or string, it triggered the mechanism and the rock or log fell directly onto them, killing them. They were typically used on small to medium-sized animals. Building a deadfall trap that would kill or at least injure a human being would be a challenge, though not impossible.

Heather thought about this. Slowly, her eyes narrowed. "I don't know. Maybe. It would be really hard to make a deadfall large enough to take down a person. It would have had to be modified for her height."

"Or the killer set up an additional element. A trip wire that would make her fall, positioning her head under the deadfall trap."

Heather shook her head. "I don't know. There wasn't enough found at that scene to support the idea of a deadfall trap. If he did set one, then he took some stuff from the scene when he left. This is getting complicated."

"Complicated? It sounds absurd. We're theorizing that there is a man who wanders around various patches of forest in all different locations in the middle of the night, setting traps for kids. He can't possibly know when or where these kids are going to be in the woods but he somehow manages to trap them and kill them—and in your two cases, in the middle of the night."

Heather sat back. Her eyes wandered around the truck stop. People coming and going, most stopping at the coffee kiosk. No one paid any attention to them. "I hate to say this but we've both seen stranger things."

"Yeah."

"If you're right, and if all three cases are connected, we're talking about a serial killer. If you're right about your suspect—the guy in the cabin—we have to figure out a way to connect him to my cases."

"I'll send you what we've got on him," Josie said. "Maybe you can try to put him near one of your scenes in the hours before or after the crimes. You send me your crime scene photos. Maps of the two areas, as well. I'll look everything over and see if anything stands out."

"You got it, Quinn." Heather took out her phone and checked the time. "I better get moving. Have to show this photo to some truckers. I've got a whole bunch of other stops to hit after this one. I'll get that stuff to you today or tomorrow. I'll do my best to keep the Woodsman piece of it out of the press, but I can't make any promises."

"I know," said Josie. She stood up and glanced at the crowd of people near the coffee, gauging whether or not it was worth her effort to get a cup for the road.

"Quinn," Heather said. "You know, if you're right about all this, that means Kayleigh Patchett is already dead. You just haven't found her body."

The breakfast sandwich sat like a grease-soaked brick in her stomach. "Yeah, I know. Two go in, only one comes out."

TWENTY-FOUR

Now they say my name everywhere. A reporter has uncovered me. He's seen me for what I am. Now, when parents talk to their children, they'll no longer have the luxury of being secretly dismissive. Their reassurances will be empty. They'll lose sleep. They'll talk with other parents about how to approach the subject of me. They'll decide the safest thing is to keep their children out of the woods for now.

But they can't keep them all away.

TWENTY-FIVE

Josie dodged the press as she entered the stationhouse through the back. As was their habit when the police department caught a big case, they were camped out in the municipal lot, hoping to get a comment from the officers going in and out for their shifts. Josie pushed her way through the throng of reporters, calling out "no comment" like a broken record. Dallas Jones was not in attendance, but half of the other reporters' questions had to do with the Woodsman.

Once inside, she breathed a sigh of relief. In the second-floor great room, Noah and Gretchen sat at their desks, typing at their keyboards. They both looked haggard even as they greeted Josie with smiles. Chief Chitwood stood in front of a freestanding corkboard that Josie had never seen before. On one side of it was an aerial map someone had pieced together of the area between the Patchetts' home and Thomas's cabin. On the other side of it was a tentative time-line of events.

"Quinn," said the Chief. "You're late. You were supposed to be here at eight."

Josie drew up beside the Chief. "I was meeting with Detective Heather Loughlin from the state police. I think we've got a situation on our hands."

Noah and Gretchen stopped typing and looked over. The Chief folded his arms over his thin chest and gazed down at her, a scowl on his face. "You could have done that by phone and saved us all some time. You don't think Kayleigh Patchett's abduction counts as a 'situation'?"

"Okay then, we've got an aggravating factor to add to our already existing situation," she said.

"No one likes a smartass," the Chief snapped.

"Now that's just not true," Josie said.

Gretchen's chair squeaked as she rocked back in it. "Don't wind him up. Just tell us what Heather said."

Josie recapped the conversation she'd had with Heather Loughlin, watching as their faces grew more distressed with each word. When she finished, the Chief swiped a hand over his balding head. He let out a groan. "This stupid Woodsman. You've got to be kidding me. This is not a real thing."

Noah said, "Whether or not the killer thinks of himself as the Woodsman, the legend is very real. Clearly, because kids are going out looking for him."

"You're going to have to say something," said Gretchen. "To the press."

"I'm not feeding into this horseshit," the Chief insisted. "The story is irrelevant. It has no bearing on our investigation. We're looking for a man. A real man."

"Then say that," Josie told him. "Or work with Amber to come up with something close to it. They're not going to stop asking questions about it, and it's only a matter of time before the press connects Heather's cases to Kayleigh's and it will be a feeding frenzy."

"Quinn is right," Gretchen agreed. "This is just the sort of thing that people will eat up. It will be viral on social media in no time. Next thing you know, we've got national news coverage. We don't need that kind of noise while we're trying to find Kayleigh Patchett."

The Chief was uncharacteristically quiet. After a moment, he said, "Fine. I'll talk with Amber when she gets here. We'll hold a press conference. But you three—well, not you, Palmer, because I want you to go home and sleep—Fraley and Quinn, you have to stay on this. We need to work every lead, every angle."

"Let's start here." Josie turned and studied the map. Based on the handwriting marking the Patchett home, the approximate location where Savannah had been found, the location of the blood and trap evidence, and Thomas's cabin, it appeared the Chief had made it himself. Josie traced the path from the Patchett home to where the blood had been found to Thomas's cabin. "Have we accurately determined how many miles this is?"

The Chief said, "Kayleigh was three miles from home when she was taken. That's really far, at least for her eight-year-old sister. Why did she take Savannah out so far?"

Noah said, "Both sisters are pretty athletic. Could be that three miles didn't seem far for them."

The Chief nodded. "Maybe. Look here, though. From where Kayleigh was taken, it was another three miles on foot to Thomas's cabin."

Noah got up and came to the board. "That's a long way to force someone through the woods. Unless he carried her?"

From her desk, Gretchen said, "If he had a gun, it would be easy."

"Henry Thomas doesn't have any guns," said the Chief. "He's not allowed to have them with his conviction. Even if he had one illegally—which I would not put past him—the searches turned up nothing."

"If Kayleigh was trying to protect Savannah, she would walk with him, gun or no gun," said Josie.

"That's true," Noah said.

"From speaking to Savannah, it seems that Kayleigh was very protective of her," Josie said. "So imagine it: you're out in the woods with your little sister for the sole purpose of proving that the Woodsman isn't real. You encounter a man. He threatens you, injures you. You're bleeding. Your little sister is nearby. What would you do?"

"Everything I could to lead him away from her," said Noah.

Gretchen stood and walked over. She pointed at the thumbtack that marked where the blood had been found. "Did he injure her, or did that thing you found do it?" She looked at Josie. "The trap."

"Did Hummel type the blood that was found out there?" Josie asked.

"It was the same type as Kayleigh's," the Chief answered. "We sent it off to the state lab to have DNA analysis run on it, but it looks like it's hers."

Josie nodded, feeling a pit in her stomach. "Did Hummel find anything when he processed the trap?"

"No," said the Chief. "You were right. It was vines, sticks, twigs, leaves. That sort of thing. Except for the piece of blue cloth. He also found blood on that. Same type as Kayleigh's. The parents weren't sure whether she had a blue sweatshirt or not, but as you know from when you talked with her, Savannah confirmed that Kayleigh does and that she was wearing it while they were out."

"It has to be hers," Noah said.

"She was injured by the trap then," said Josie. "Savannah heard a noise, some kind of crashing. It would make sense that Kayleigh somehow tripped it and got injured."

Noah said, "But she called out to Savannah 'He's got me,' which means he must have been waiting there near the trap. What I don't understand is that if Henry Thomas is some kind of serial killer, why would he take someone so close to his home and invite so much attention to himself?"

Gretchen sighed and ran a hand through her hair. "We don't know that Henry Thomas is a serial killer. Here's what we can say with certainty. Kayleigh and Savannah went into the woods behind their house. They got separated. Kayleigh was injured by this apparatus which we believe might be a trap. Savannah heard a noise and saw a man wearing a yellow shirt and blue jeans. We found blue jeans but no yellow shirts in Henry Thomas's cabin. Kayleigh told Savannah to run because 'he's got me.' Savannah ran away." She pointed to the thumbtack that represented the approximate location where Josie and Luke had found the girl. "She hid here. In the meantime, whoever this 'he' is marches Kayleigh from where we found her blood all the way up, across this road, to the top of the mountain, and here to Thomas's cabin. We know she made it that far because Blue followed her scent there."

Noah folded his arms over his chest. "So the assumption is that Henry Thomas did one of three things: killed her and disposed of her body, is holding her somewhere not on his own property, or he contacted someone else to come take her away—dead or alive."

"Thomas doesn't have her," said Gretchen. "Either he buried her body somewhere we haven't checked yet or someone took her in a vehicle from Thomas's driveway. Whether that was Thomas or someone else, we don't know."

"Are we looking at an accomplice?" asked Noah.

TWENTY-SIX

A silence fell over the room. When none of them spoke, Noah tried to answer his own question. "But if Henry Thomas did this and he's got an accomplice, who is it? All of his associates check out, even Morris Lauber."

"We're not necessarily looking for an accomplice," said the Chief, gesturing to the timeline. "Thomas would have had plenty of time to take her somewhere else and dispose of her. I'm going to have line searches conducted here." He pointed to the wooded area across the road from Thomas's driveway. "It would have been easy for him to walk down his driveway, cross the road, go into the woods here and bury her somewhere."

"Or he drove her body somewhere and buried it," Noah said.

"If that's what Thomas did, the ERT would have found evidence of his movements in his Toyota's GPS report," Josie said. "Did Hummel send that over?"

Noah sighed and returned to his desk, fishing out a small stack of pages. He handed it to Josie. "Thomas told the truth about his movements. What time he went out and what time he got home. He didn't leave after that."

"The El Camino truly doesn't start or drive?" asked Josie, paging through the report. She remembered Noah saying the Montour County case had taken place three weeks ago. Each vehicle was different in terms of what its GPS system retained. Some went back months, some only went back days. Their warrant had only asked for Henry Thomas's movements on Saturday, but the download went back a week. Not far enough to know if he'd been in Montour County when Sarah McArthur and Dawn Angels had been in the woods.

"One of the first things I asked Hummel about was the El Camino," said Noah. "No. It's missing its torque converter. I had Hummel check it out, and we also had one of our mechanics come and take a look at it. I wanted to make sure that Thomas wasn't putting us on—telling us it didn't drive and then using it to commit crimes since it isn't equipped with GPS. Without the torque converter, there's no way that Thomas was driving it around. In fact, there was so little to be found in and on both vehicles, Hummel's got to return them tomorrow."

"Wait a minute," Josie said. "What's a torque converter?"

"It's this small, round device that is bolted to the engine's flywheel. It's got four parts: a pump, turbine, stator and clutch—"

"You lost me at flywheel, Fraley," Gretchen said.

Noah laughed. "It's located between the engine and the transmission."

"Okay," Gretchen said. "Keep going."

"Basically, it uses fluid to transfer power from the engine to the transmission."

"It makes the car go," said the Chief. "And Thomas's El Camino doesn't have one."

Noah added, "And we did not find one anywhere on his premises, although if he wanted to install one himself, it would take a couple of hours. It's not something he could just pop in and out easily or quickly to get the El Camino on the road."

"This is why we looked at Thomas's associates," said Gretchen. "If we stick with the idea that he's the one who took Kayleigh and then he needed to get rid of her, but couldn't do it himself, he'd need someone to come get her—or to help him dispose of her body."

"Hummel processed Morris Lauber's truck," said Josie, tossing the GPS report onto her desk.

"He found no evidence linking the truck to Kayleigh Patchett," Gretchen said.

Josie asked, "What did his GPS show?"

"He was nowhere near Thomas's cabin Saturday," said Gretchen.

"Also, there were no phone calls or texts between the two of them on Saturday," said Noah. "We're still waiting for Thomas's phone records from his carrier to make sure we can see anything he might have deleted, but it doesn't look promising."

Gretchen said, "Morris let us look at his phone. There was nothing between him and Henry on his phone either. I was going to prepare a warrant but without being able to place him near the scene or produce any evidence that he could be involved, I don't think a judge will grant it. If the two of them communicated, we'll get it from Thomas's phone records."

"What about Morris Lauber's girlfriend?" asked Josie.

"We talked with her at length," said Noah. "She was extremely cooperative. Pretty unhappy with Morris. She said she's tried to get him to stop hanging around with Henry for some time, but he keeps going back out of some misguided loyalty to Henry's late father. Anyway, she was at work at Sublime Cupcakes all day, from eight a.m. to eight p.m. Her car was in the parking lot. We pulled video. It didn't move, so there's no way that Morris Lauber could have taken it while she was at work, driven it to Thomas's cabin, taken Kayleigh Patchett off his hands and done something with her."

"We're back to Thomas acting alone," Josie muttered. "What about his laptop? Could he somehow have communicated with someone through that? Hummel had a chance to look at it. Did he get anything?"

"There was a lot of porn," said Gretchen. "Not much else."

"Social media?"

Gretchen shook her head. "No accounts."

Josie turned back to the board, this time studying the timeline.

7:00 a.m. Henry Thomas wakes up

8:00 a.m. Shelly and Dave Patchett wake up

8:13—8:52 a.m. Henry Thomas eats at the Denton Diner (confirmed by surveillance footage)

9:02 a.m. parents arrive at grocery store (confirmed by surveillance footage)

9:53 a.m. parents leave grocery store (confirmed by surveillance footage)

10:00—10:15 a.m. parents arrive home

11:30 a.m. parents begin to search for Kayleigh and Savannah

11:33 a.m. parents contact neighbor south of them (confirmed by neighbor's phone)

11:37 a.m. parents contact neighbor north of them (confirmed by neighbor's phone)

2:30 p.m. (approximately) Neighbor four houses to the south reports Shelly Patchett in their yard (confirmed by neighbor's statement)

2:47 p.m. first 911 call from Shelly Patchett

3:05 p.m. first units respond

3:30 p.m. K-9 search begins

5:45 p.m. Savannah Patchett found

8:10 p.m. second K-9 search begins

11:30 p.m. K-9 search concludes at Henry Thomas's cabin

Josie said, "We don't actually know when Kayleigh was taken. If it was after her parents were already out looking for them, between 11:30 a.m. and 2:47 p.m., wouldn't they have found both girls?"

"Or heard Kayleigh's shouts when she was being abducted?" added Gretchen.

Noah said, "Or, if she was taken before the parents started looking, sometime between 8:45 a.m. and 11:30 a.m., leaving Savannah alone in the woods, then wouldn't Savannah have heard them calling for them?"

Josie shook her head. "She heard us calling and she didn't come out."

"But she would have come out for her parents," said Gretchen.

The Chief used a finger to circle the area Savannah was found. "This is three miles out from the back of their house and almost a full mile to the north. How far did the parents spread themselves? Or did they only look south?"

Josie pointed to a house almost two miles south of where Savannah was found. "We know that Mrs. Patchett was in this neighbor's yard around 2:30 p.m."

Gretchen frowned. "Still, that leaves a lot of time for them to have been in the woods searching. We have no idea where the husband was all that time. It's hard to believe the parents were out there before the kidnapping took place and heard nothing. Even if they were out there afterward, they searched for a long time before they called 911 and still didn't find Savannah?"

"Seems suspicious to me, too," said the Chief. "Maybe we need to have a longer chat with them, but first, get the GPS coordinates for their vehicles. We know Kayleigh was walked over the mountain to the Thomas cabin and then disappeared. If one or both of them had something to do with this, then their GPS would put them out by that cabin. I want phone records, too."

Noah said, "I thought we were looking at Thomas as a serial killer? You think the parents did something to Kayleigh on purpose? This is all a big sham? The press? The search? What about the cases the state police are working on?"

The Chief said, "We have to worry about *our* case. Just because Thomas seems like a good suspect doesn't mean he did this. We should never try to make the evidence fit what we think happened. We have to look at everything."

Noah frowned. "But the parents?"

Gretchen said, "Come on, Fraley. You've been at this long enough to know that parents are prime suspects. The Patchetts had a lot of issues with Kayleigh. Maybe it wasn't intentional or thought out, but we can't ignore the possibility that they might have had a hand in whatever happened to her. We can't focus too hard on Thomas until we've eliminated them completely."

Noah put his hands up in concession. "I know that. I do. I'm just playing devil's advocate."

Like Mett, Josie thought instantly. She didn't miss the fact that both the Chief and Gretchen glanced back at his empty desk.

"Which means we need to keep barking up every tree," the Chief said. "We've exhausted the Thomas angle for now—at least until some of our evidence gets processed by the state police lab. I've got a unit out by his place around the clock. They've been instructed to follow him if he leaves. Can't see shit from the end of his driveway but if he makes any other kind of move, we'll know about it. I've still got patrols out in the area. There are volunteer searches going on, working their way outward in concentric circles from the Patchett home. If Kayleigh is buried in the woods somewhere that hasn't already been searched, there's a chance someone might notice a freshly dug grave."

Josie said, "Have we gotten anywhere with Kayleigh's phone records? From her carrier?"

"Not yet," said Gretchen. "But I called three times asking them to expedite it and trying to impress upon them that a girl's life might hang in the balance."

"What does that leave us with?" said Noah.

"Kayleigh," Josie said. "I still want to talk to her best friend, Olivia. See if we can track down the guy in the hidden photos on Kayleigh's phone."

"Speaking of that guy," said Gretchen. "Morris Lauber said that he saw teenagers come onto Henry Thomas's property more than once. Pulling some daredevil shit, trying to get close to the burial grounds."

"Right," Josie said. "Lauber said that Henry would go outside and get rid of them. Maybe we should ask Henry if he's seen the mystery boy."

The Chief looked around at them. "Palmer, you go home and get some sleep. Fraley and Quinn, you two get to work on the Patchetts and Kayleigh's friends."

"Sir," Gretchen said quietly. "I know this isn't the best time to bring it up."

He waved a hand in the air. Two circles of pink appeared on his acne-pitted cheeks. "I know, I know. We're down a man and I haven't hired anyone to replace Mett. I'm your fourth man right now. You got that? I'll go over to Thomas's cabin and ask about the teenagers. I'd like to get a read on this asshole myself."

Noah said, "We appreciate that, Chief, but as a long-term solution—"

The Chief cut Noah off with a yell. "I'm not hiring

someone today, Fraley! We've got a case to solve. A kid to find. I know you've seen the damn stack of résumés on my desk. The three of you are so damn nosy. I'll get to it when I get to it. Now let's get to work!"

TWENTY-SEVEN

Josie and Noah prepared the warrants for the Patchetts' phone records as well as the three vehicles registered in their names. Once the warrants were sent over to the cell phone carrier, they called Hummel and asked him to meet them at the Patchett household so that the family's vehicles could be impounded. Shelly stood at the front door, Savannah wrapped around her with her face buried in her mother's stomach while Dave paced back and forth between two of the vehicles, complaining loudly that they weren't doing enough to find Kayleigh. Josie and Noah assured him that this was merely protocol and that their entire staff was working around the clock to locate his daughter. He was not convinced.

"I'm going to hire my own private investigator!" he shouted at them as they got back into their vehicles to leave. "And I'm going to get a lawyer, too, and sue you all for not doing your jobs!"

Noah shook his head as he pulled onto the road and headed back into town, toward Timber Creek restaurant. "You sure Olivia Wilcox is working today?" he asked.

"Yeah," Josie said. "I called ahead of time and spoke with

the manager. He said she would be there after school from four to ten."

Even though Olivia was underage, her parents did not need to be present or even notified that they were going to speak with her, since they weren't questioning her as a suspect. In fact, Josie preferred to talk to Olivia away from her parents. In her experience, there were always things that teenagers would talk about without their parents present that they'd never admit to while they were there.

Noah said, "Did you actually sleep last night?"

Josie thought of Harris curled up beside her on the couch. At some point during the night, Misty had gotten them both off to bed, but Josie had no memory of it at all. "I did, actually. By the way, Misty and Harris stayed over last night. You'll be going off shift before me. They might still be there. I told Misty they could stay as long as they want."

"Of course," Noah said. "Did something happen?"

Josie recounted the conversation she'd had with Harris, still feeling sick to her stomach at how much fear he held in his little body and how powerless she had felt to reassure him. "Noah, I had no idea what to say to him."

"It sounds like you handled it well," he replied.

"I guess," she muttered. She turned her gaze to the window, watching the trees recede and more dense residential areas come into view as they reached the central part of the city. "It's this stupid Woodsman story. I feel like if he hadn't already been dealing with that for so long, then he wouldn't be so afraid now. Sure, he might see this on the news and be upset and scared, but the Woodsman thing has just amplified everything."

"I know," Noah said. "It's unfortunate, especially since he isn't the only kid affected by it. I mean, the whole reason Kayleigh took Savannah into the woods was to prove to her that this man or creature or whatever wasn't real."

"It might as well be real though," said Josie. "If Heather's cases are connected to Kayleigh's, then for all intents and purposes, he is real. A serial killer targeting kids, Noah. This is the world we'd be bringing a child into. Do you ever think about that?"

"Of course I do. With this job? Can't help it."

Josie looked at his profile. "It doesn't scare you?"

"It terrifies me."

She didn't speak. She couldn't push the words out: *then what are we doing?*

She turned back to the window, watching the city's central business district pass by. A moment later, one of Noah's hands closed over hers, squeezing.

"Knowing something bad might happen isn't a good reason not to have a baby, Josie. Something bad might always happen, whether we have a kid or not. Hell, something bad is happening in lots of places as we speak. That is the reality of the world. We still have to live." When she didn't respond, he added, "No regrets, right?"

She swallowed and turned to offer him a weak smile.

Another two blocks flashed by her window. He said, "You have a session with Dr. Rosetti tomorrow, right? You should talk to her about this."

"In the morning. I wasn't going to go to that," Josie said. "The case—"

"You need to go, Josie. It's fifty minutes. Gretchen and I can hold down the fort."

"I can reschedule," she insisted.

"No," he said firmly. "You haven't been sleeping. You need to go to these sessions."

Josie was trying to muster a protest when the Timber Creek restaurant came into view. Noah released her hands and made a right into the parking lot. It was a sprawling, one-story building that was made to look like a faux log cabin from the outside. It was early, before the dinner rush, and the parking lot was nearly empty. The perfect time to question the staff, Josie thought. Large wood carvings of bears and wolves lined the front entrance. They passed through a vestibule. The host station sat directly in front of the doors inside the restaurant and there stood Olivia Wilcox, her long red hair pulled back and twisted into a neat bun. She pasted on a smile for them. "Hello," she said in an overly cheerful voice. "Welcome to Timber Creek. Will there be two of you today?"

On closer inspection, Josie saw that her eyes were red-rimmed and puffy. She and Noah offered their credentials. Noah made the introductions. Before he could go any further, Olivia started backing away from the station. "I'll go get my manager."

Josie said, "That's fine, but we're mainly here to talk to you, Olivia."

She brought her hands up, curling them together into her chest. Her eyes darted back and forth between them. "Me?" she asked weakly. "Why me?"

Noah said, "I'm sure you've seen the news, Olivia. Kayleigh Patchett was abducted on Saturday. Part of our investigation is speaking to the people closest to her."

Josie said, "Her mom said you two are best friends."

"Yeah," she muttered. "Kayleigh and I are best friends. I guess. Don't you, like, need my parents to be here to talk to me?"

"Olivia, you're not in any trouble," said Noah. "So no. Would you feel better if we called them?"

The color drained from her face. "God, no." She looked down at her feet. "It's just that I really don't—I kind of don't feel well. I—"

Josie glanced over at Noah and said, "Olivia, you know what? We do need to talk to your manager and maybe a couple of other people here who know Kayleigh. This might go a whole lot faster if Lieutenant Fraley and I split up. If you could tell

Lieutenant Fraley where to find your manager, he could take care of that interview while you and I chat here."

"Sure," she said. She pointed to the left of the host station and gave him instructions. Even with Noah out of view, Olivia's skin was still pale, her hands still fisted and pressed into her sternum.

Josie said, "When was the last time you saw Kayleigh?"

"In person? School on Friday."

"When's the last time you talked with her?"

"Friday night. Her parents had taken her phone to punish her but they let her have it just to call me so she could ask me to cover her shift."

This matched up with the call history on Kayleigh's phone. "What did you talk about?"

"She asked me to take her shift today because she had softball practice. She hates softball but her parents make her play."

Josie smiled. "Yeah, that's the impression I've gotten."

Olivia still wouldn't look at Josie but some of the color had returned to her face. She picked up a dry-erase marker from the host station and pulled the cap off.

"Kayleigh's parents said that she's restricted from having social media accounts. It seems like it would be pretty hard to survive high school without any social media."

"I mean, some kids don't have it."

"Does Kayleigh really not have social media?" asked Josie.

"She doesn't. She's never had her own accounts."

"You won't be getting her in trouble, Olivia. You can tell the truth. This is important."

Olivia glanced toward the front doors, as if wishing someone would come in and put a stop to the questioning. "She really doesn't. Her parents are super strict about it."

"But her phone isn't the only place she can log in to the apps," Josie pointed out.

Olivia said nothing.

"Did Kayleigh ever use your phone to log in to any of them?"

"No."

"Olivia."

"She didn't use my phone, okay? She doesn't have social media. Her parents would kill her. They think, like, she's going to get groomed by some pervert on the internet or whatever. There were always things she pushed back on like not wanting to play sports, but social media wasn't one of them."

"Olivia, was Kayleigh dating anyone?"

She clicked the cap back onto the marker. Keeping her eyes on the laminated map of tables at her fingertips, she said, "No."

Josie took her phone out and brought up a picture of the mystery boyfriend from Kayleigh's phone. She placed the phone on top of the table map, directly in Olivia's line of sight. "Do you know who this boy is?"

Olivia's top teeth scraped over her bottom lip. The marker cap came off again, then back on. "No."

Josie left the photo in front of her. "This picture was in a secret vault app on Kayleigh's phone. In fact, there were about a half-dozen photos in that vault of him and of the two of them together. They looked pretty cozy, pretty close. We know that the photos were taken in the last year. She never talked to you about him?"

Olivia looked away from the phone, teeth scraping her bottom lip again. She twisted the marker cap around and around. "She said she was seeing some older guy, okay? But I didn't believe her. No one did."

"Who's no one?" asked Josie.

"Like here at work and at school. She kept bragging and bragging about her older boyfriend but—I don't know—we just didn't believe her. It just seemed like something she said so she could feel better."

"Feel better about what?"

The marker cap spun off and bounced onto the floor. Josie picked it up and handed it back to Olivia. Her fingers trembled. It took three tries for her to get it back onto the marker. When she looked back at Josie, her eyes were glassy with tears.

"Olivia?" Josie said.

Her face crumpled. A sob erupted from deep in her chest. She pushed her way past Josie and ran out the front door.

TWENTY-EIGHT

Josie raced after Olivia, slamming through the double doors and nearly knocking down a couple on their way in. She mumbled an apology and searched the area outside until she saw Olivia hurrying down the block, clutching her stomach with one hand and wiping at her eyes with the other.

Catching up to her, Josie said, "Olivia, please. Stop."

Olivia held onto the top of the nearest parking meter with one hand while the other pressed against her belly. "I'm going to be sick."

Josie drew closer. "Take some deep breaths."

Her body heaved and she bent as if to vomit, but nothing came out. Josie leaned over and spoke softly in her ear. "Olivia, I need you to calm down. You're going to be okay."

Olivia turned her face toward Josie. Tears rolled down her cheeks. "Sure, *I* am, but what about Kayleigh? She's my best friend and she's missing, and you want me to talk shit on her."

Josie found a tissue in one of her pockets and handed it to Olivia. "I'm not asking you to talk shit about your friend, Olivia, I promise you that. Come on, let's stand up. Why don't you come with me? There's a little coffee shop around the corner.

We can sit down. Have a cup of coffee. We'll talk. That's all I'm asking right now, one cup of coffee."

Olivia straightened. Josie followed suit. She watched as Olivia dabbed at her cheeks and sucked in a deep, shuddering breath. "I can't," she said. "I have to work. I'm probably already in trouble."

Josie took out her phone. "No. I'll make sure you're not. I'll text my colleague and have him tell your manager that I needed to talk with you on official police business and that you'll be back as soon as we're finished."

Josie sent the text as they walked the two blocks to Perk O'Latte. It wasn't Komorrah's but it would do for now. Josie let Olivia order whatever she wanted and then they found a table in the very back of the shop, away from the other patrons. They sat across from one another. Olivia had ordered a chocolate croissant and now she picked the flaky outside away with nails bitten to the quick. She had calmed down considerably but Josie gave her another moment, taking a long sip of her coffee. Compared to the truck stop coffee, it was the best thing she'd ever tasted. "Olivia, what did you mean when you said that no one believed Kayleigh had a boyfriend? That she made him up to feel better?"

"Do we have to talk about that? I feel bad enough even admitting to it or having thought it. God, I'm a terrible friend."

"Well, this is your opportunity to be a good friend to Kayleigh by answering all my questions."

Olivia peeled another piece of dough from her croissant. "That sounds like something dumb an adult would say to get me to spill my guts."

"Fair enough," Josie said. "But I really do need to know what you know, Olivia. I'm sorry if it's difficult to talk about. What did Kayleigh want to feel better about?"

She shrugged. "I don't know. About herself, I guess. School

is shitty, you know? Like, I don't mind it but it's tough for Kayleigh."

"Is she being bullied?" asked Josie.

Olivia shook her head. "No, it's not like that. It's just that, well, she hates softball, right? She's wanted to quit for ages, but her parents absolutely will not let her. She thought if she started playing like crap—the way she did with soccer and volleyball—that they'd let her quit, but they're totally obsessed with sports. It's like, if she doesn't play at least one sport, she's worthless or something."

Josie thought of the text messages between Kayleigh and Braelyn from softball. "Once she started playing badly on purpose but had to stay on the team, the other girls got angry with her."

Olivia met Josie's eyes briefly. "Yeah. I mean, they're a really good team. They almost went to state last year. If Kayleigh hadn't played so badly, they probably would have. So the other girls, like, hate her."

"Couldn't the coach throw her off the team? Or bench her?"

Olivia laughed drily. It was the most natural and least nervous she'd been since Josie had met her. "Have you met her dad? He totally bullied the coach into keeping her on and giving her at least some field time, which made everyone else even more angry, and guess who they took it out on?"

"Kayleigh."

"Yep. It was a shame. I told her she should just play. Like why screw over all the other girls on the team because her parents were being douchey?"

"What did Kayleigh say when you told her just to play?"

Olivia went back to peeling flakes from her croissant. "She said she didn't want her parents to have the satisfaction. I told her she was being stubborn and only hurting herself, but she didn't care."

"The girls on the softball team were unhappy with her,"

Josie said. "That's fair. Was she having problems with anyone else?"

"I don't know. At the beginning of the year, she was friends with a bunch of other girls. I'm not friends with them because we don't take any of the same classes, but Kayleigh was in some after-school club with a bunch of them. Some writing club or something. A couple of months into school she said they started ghosting her. One of those girls is in her English class and she had some beef with her about some assignment and things got ugly. Then she started talking about this boyfriend. I think it made her feel better about herself, like she had something on all those girls who were mean to her. I didn't think she was for real about it."

"You never saw her with this guy?" Josie asked. She tapped her password back into her phone and his photo appeared again. She slid it across the table.

Olivia didn't look at it. "No. I never did."

Josie wasn't sure she believed the girl, but she couldn't force her to tell the truth. "You said she talked about him. What did she say about him?"

Olivia shrugged again. "I don't know. Just that he was, like, older and stuff. He had a car. He thought she was awesome and called her brilliant."

"Did she ever mention his name?"

Olivia shook her head.

"Never? Not even to you?"

"No."

"Olivia, we know that Kayleigh was seeing this boy for at least a year. You said yourself that she talked about him a lot."

Olivia broke through the center of the croissant and pressed her forefinger into the gooey chocolate center. The filling clung to her finger, dangling in a sugary string as she lifted her hand. Using a napkin, she caught it and wiped her skin clean.

Josie tried again. "Olivia, this is really important. It could be the key to finding Kayleigh. All I'm asking for is a name. A name that I will find sooner or later through our investigation. It would be very helpful if you saved me all that digging and told me right now. I'm sure I don't have to tell you that your best friend's life may hang in the balance."

Looking everywhere but at Josie, she muttered, "His name is J.J. But that's all I know. I don't know his last name. She never told me."

"Thank you," said Josie. "That's very helpful. Any idea what that stands for?"

"No."

"Does J.J. go to your school?"

"No. He's older than that. That's why they had to keep it a big secret. That's what she said. Everyone at school just thought that was her way of getting out of ever having to prove that he was real."

"Did she ever say where he lived? How they met? Anything like that?"

"No. I mean, I'm pretty sure he lives in Denton, but I don't know. She didn't tell me how they met."

"Did she say how old he was exactly?" Josie asked.

"Like, twenty? I think that's what she said. It wasn't so old that it was, like, gross but old enough so he would seem cool to other girls at school, I guess."

"Kayleigh plays softball and belongs to at least one after-school club. She also works at the restaurant a few days a week. When would she have time to see him? Her parents are pretty strict."

Olivia rolled her eyes. "The strictest. I don't know. Like I said, I really thought she made him up. I didn't want to ask her about it because I felt bad for her. I thought I would just let her have it. She seemed so happy, and she hadn't really been happy in months."

Josie said, "Her parents told us she had been sneaking out at night. Do you know anything about that?"

Olivia used her fingertips to push the flakes of her croissant into its gooey center, as if trying to put it back together. "No. She never told me."

"Did you or Kayleigh or any of your other friends ever go out to the burial fields near Herron Road?"

"What?" Olivia's nose scrunched in disgust. "You mean Murder Mountain?"

TWENTY-NINE

A chill enveloped Josie. She thought of the place where so many innocent girls had perished, where so many lives had been destroyed, including hers. It had taken years for her to recover from what had happened there, both personally and professionally. Were Denton's teenagers really calling it by some flippant nickname?

"What?" she choked out.

Olivia didn't look up from her failed croissant repair. "I'm sorry. I know it's really horrible but that's what all the kids call it. Murder Mountain. I haven't been there. I wouldn't." Josie saw goosebumps erupt all over her bare arms. "All those girls died up there. It's really messed up. I don't think it's funny or cool. It's sad. Anyway, I know lots of kids from school who go there. They like to go at night 'cause they think it's haunted or something."

Josie concentrated on her breathing, willing her mind to stay focused on the Kayleigh Patchett case. Pushing away thoughts of the time she'd spent at the burial grounds, she asked, "Had Kayleigh ever gone there?"

Olivia covered the shredded croissant with a napkin. "I don't know."

Josie took her phone and scrolled through a few more photos until she found a photo of Henry Thomas that Noah had pulled from his personnel file at the city park. She showed it to Olivia. "Have you ever seen this man before?"

There was no flicker of recognition in Olivia's eyes. Only a blank stare. "I don't think so but he's, like, really old." She let out an embarrassed laugh as she looked from the photo to Josie's face. "Sorry. You're probably closer in age to him than me. I don't mean to say you're old. Just that to me, 'cause I'm not even eighteen yet, he seems old."

Josie smiled. "It's fine. I knew what you meant. You've never seen him before? Are you sure?"

"Yeah. I mean, he's kind of good-looking for an older guy. I feel like I'd remember if I saw him before, and I don't." An idea occurred to her. Her eyebrows lifted. "Oh God. Is he the one who took Kayleigh?"

Josie put the photo away. "We don't know who took Kayleigh, but we know that he lives near where she went missing, that's all." Before Olivia could ask more questions about Henry Thomas, Josie changed direction. "Do you know where Kayleigh got her drugs?"

Olivia's eyes bulged. Her teeth bit into her lower lip and then released it. She gave a short cough before saying, "What?"

Josie put both hands up in a gesture of surrender. "I'm a police officer, Olivia. I know kids do drugs. I see it every day. You're not going to get anyone in trouble right now—including yourself—by telling me the truth. We found Kayleigh's stash of weed in her room. Did you know about it?"

"No. I mean, yes. I mean, I know that she smokes weed but it's only because her parents are so crazy, and she needs to relax. I don't smoke with her though. I don't even know where she gets it."

"You're saying you have no idea where she got it from?"

"No."

Josie put both hands on the table. "Olivia, right now, at this precise moment, you could tell me that you bought it for her and the two of you smoke it every day together and I wouldn't care. I'm not interested in busting you over some petty drug stuff. I'm interested in finding out what happened to Kayleigh. Now. Today. So let's try this again. Who does Kayleigh buy her weed from?"

Olivia met her eyes. "I am for real serious when I tell you I don't know. I really don't."

"Does she get it from J.J.? Her older boyfriend?"

"I don't know," Olivia insisted. "I've been with her when she's smoked it and yeah, a couple of times, I smoked with her, okay? But I don't know where she gets it. I don't really want to know."

"Why not?"

Now she looked away again. With a sigh, she said, "For reasons like this! I don't want to get into trouble. I want to go to college. The school counselor thinks I have a really good chance of getting into some schools in California. That's where I want to move. It's warm and beautiful and celebrities live there. But mostly, I just want to get out of here."

There was a note of hysteria in her voice on the word "here." Josie said, "Okay, okay. Fair enough. I believe you. Just one more question for you right now. Was Kayleigh having trouble with anyone else recently? Besides the softball team and the girls at school?"

"No. Mostly everyone just ignores her."

Josie's phone chirped. A text from Noah. He was finished with his questioning. Olivia was visibly relieved when Josie told her that she could go back to work. Outside the coffee shop, Josie watched her sprint down the pavement and through the doors of the Timber Creek restaurant, almost bumping into Noah's chest as he emerged.

In the car, Josie used her phone to log in to social media, starting with Instagram, which, along with Snapchat, she knew was quite popular among teens. She found Olivia Wilcox's account fairly quickly. It was set to public. Josie scrolled through her list of followers and then the list of people she followed, hoping to see any username that could be associated with Kayleigh Patchett. There were a couple of spam accounts with usernames that were seemingly random combinations of letters and numbers that Olivia followed. Teenagers usually had their main Instagram account which their parents were aware of and on which they posted photos of benign things like sports games, family outings and school dances. For the stuff they didn't want their parents to see, they simply created a spam account, or a Finsta—fake Instagram account. It was a different Instagram account that almost always had the word spam right in its name. It was always set to private and usually had a smaller number of followers. Josie took screenshots of the spam usernames. Later, she would see if there was a way to connect any of them to Kayleigh and get a warrant for their records.

Noah sat in the driver's seat watching her, the car idling. He answered a text on his phone. "Gretchen's at the stationhouse to relieve me. You get something good?"

"I'm not sure." She told him about her conversation with Olivia. "She's lying about something."

"You think she's lying that Kayleigh had social media?"

Josie nodded. "Yes. This kid has gone to great lengths to undermine her parents' plan for her to continue playing softball. She's snuck out of the house. She's been smoking weed without her parents knowing at all. She had erotic novels hidden in her nightstand. She read smut on this story app on her phone—until her parents found out. Why wouldn't she have social media?"

"With Kayleigh missing, why would Olivia lie about her using her phone to log in to her social media accounts?"

"I don't know." She looked at her husband. Even in her tired and stressed state, she couldn't help but admire the lines of his face, his hazel eyes, and his thick brown hair. "What did you get? Anything?"

"Nothing immediately helpful," he said. "But one of the cooks has seen the secret boyfriend—or J.J. as we can call him now."

Josie sat up straighter. "Are you serious?"

He smiled. "Don't get too excited. He couldn't give me much that would help us find him, except that he sometimes picked Kayleigh up behind the restaurant after her shifts. That's why he saw them. He hangs out the back door to smoke. They never even noticed he was there. Anyway, the kid pulls up, waits. Kayleigh comes around the side of the building, gets in, they leave."

"The car," Josie said.

"A black four-door sedan. Maybe a Mitsubishi or a Hyundai."

"Plate number?"

"No. He didn't notice. Didn't think it was important. I asked the manager to pull any footage of the parking lots for as far as it goes back but he's not on there."

Josie looked around at the various businesses that had external surveillance as well as the traffic cams. "Gretchen and I can cross-check the last three or four of Kayleigh's shifts with the camera footage nearby and see if we can spot the car via some other establishment's security footage."

Noah grimaced. "That could take a while, but it might be worth it."

THIRTY

I'm so close to them and yet they don't hear me. I knew they would be here. It never fails. They don't see me. But they're talking about me. Teenagers, fearless, drinking in the woods. Talking about me. They still don't think I'm real. Not truly. I wait and watch and listen. It's too risky to grab one of them here. Too many witnesses. I am at a disadvantage. I have to be patient and hope that one—or more—will delve deeper into my territory. I have to be patient. Drunk teenagers do stupid things. It's only a matter of time before one of them wanders into my darkness. Studying them, I have some hopes for which of them it might be, some preferences, but even if I don't get my wish, I will get my kill.

Patience.

THIRTY-ONE

Josie and Gretchen didn't find the car. By the time Josie went home to get some sleep, they were no closer to finding Kayleigh Patchett's secret boyfriend. They were no closer to finding Kayleigh either. Misty, Harris, and Pepper had gone home so there was only Trout to keep Josie company through the night. As usual, sleep was difficult. This time, the memories of Mettner's death were interspersed with a dream in which Josie chased a man through the woods. He was pursuing Kayleigh Patchett. Josie could see the girl ahead, running for her life, but couldn't seem to catch up. Then her foot got caught in a snare trap and Josie woke to the sounds of screams echoing in her head.

She went to see Dr. Rosetti the next morning.

It didn't help. She felt a slight relief at having unburdened herself to her therapist but on the whole, she was still every bit as exhausted and stressed as she had been when she'd tried to go to sleep the night before. In the car, she checked her phone to see a message from Noah telling her to meet him at Denton East High School in the back of parking lot A. She got there in under ten minutes, heart whipping into a frenzy as she wondered if it was a lead or something worse. Parking lot A was on the side of the football field which backed up to the woods. When she pulled in, the lot was mostly full. The last few parking lanes, closest to the forest, were empty save for a small white pickup truck. Standing around it were Noah, two uniformed officers, and a blonde woman in her forties who looked very distressed.

Josie parked a few spaces away and jogged over. On closer inspection, the woman's blue eyes were red-rimmed from crying. She wore a pair of pajama pants and a white blouse, the buttons of which were crooked, as if she'd hurried to put it on. She pushed her short hair around on her head, making it stand up on one side, and regarded Josie with a hopeful look.

"Detective Quinn," said Noah. "This is Pam Hicks."

"My child is missing," Pam said.

"I'm sorry to hear that," Josie said.

Noah quickly filled her in. "Brody's a junior here. Mrs. Hicks went to wake him for school this morning, but he wasn't in his bed. She tried calling his phone, but it went to voicemail—"

"His battery must have run out. He would never send me to voicemail. He wouldn't do that," she said. "We have a rule. No matter where he is or what he's doing, he always picks up when I call. When he didn't pick up, I came here because I thought maybe he got up before me and came to school. Sometimes he does that so he can use the weight room. If he's lifting weights, he won't look at his phone."

"But he's not here?" asked Josie.

Noah said, "His truck is here."

"I drove through the lots and found it," Pam explained. "I thought, 'oh good, he's in the weight room. When he's done, he'll call me.' I was almost home when I got an automated call from the school saying my child was not in attendance today. I turned right around. Marched into the office to find out what was going on, but no one has seen Brody today. He never reported to his homeroom."

Noah twirled a hand to indicate the overhead lights in the parking lot. "No cameras out here, so we have no idea when he arrived in his truck. I'm waiting for dispatch to ping his phone."

"When is the last time you saw him?" Josie asked Pam.

She hugged herself tightly. "Last night, around ten. He was watching TV. I told him I was going to bed. I was supposed to have a big meeting at work today and I wanted to get some extra rest." Tears glistened in her eyes. "I don't—I don't know where he is and he's a good boy. He wouldn't make me worry like this."

Josie said, "Would you have heard him if he'd left your home last night to go somewhere?"

Pam shook her head. "No, no. I sleep with a fan on. I wouldn't have heard him."

"Does anyone else live with you and Brody?" asked Noah.

"No, it's just us. His dad died when he was thirteen."

Josie asked, "Does Brody have social media? Have you checked it?"

Three vertical lines appeared on her forehead. "Checked it? For what?"

"To see if he posted anything about going somewhere," Josie explained.

"Oh, um, I didn't look, but..." With trembling fingers, she reached into the purse slung over her shoulder and took out her phone. Tapping a passcode into it, she brought up Instagram and found his account. She turned the screen toward Josie. Brody's profile photo showed a stocky teenage boy with a mop of curly brown hair and a wide smile. He was dressed in his football uniform, his helmet in one hand, the stadium lights bright behind him. Josie held out her hand. "May I?"

Pam relinquished the phone. Noah moved closer so that he could look over Josie's shoulder.

Josie noted the username. She checked the stories first.

There was one that had been posted around eleven thirty the night before but all it consisted of was a black screen. Had he been here last night? In the woods? As if reading her mind, Noah said, "We can always get the GPS from the truck to confirm what time he arrived in the parking lot."

Pam watched them closely but didn't speak.

Josie scrolled through some of Brody's posts. The most recent post was from Saturday afternoon—around three thirty p.m., just about the time that Josie, Luke, and Blue had begun their first search for the Patchett girls. In it, Brody held the phone high over his head and away from him so that the camera revealed him standing in the field of flowers on top of what Olivia had dubbed "Murder Mountain." The caption read: *Not afraid of a little murder* followed by the hashtag #murdermountain. There were twenty-nine likes and a half-dozen comments, most of them saying he was cool or badass or simply saying "damn" while one person said, "not cool, bro."

Josie felt a flush of irrational anger and tried to push it down, reminding herself that these teenagers had no real concept of what had taken place on that mountain—and she sincerely hoped they never would. She wouldn't wish that kind of knowledge on anyone. Ever in tune with Josie's emotions, Noah rested a hand on her lower back. His touch instantly quelled some of her anger.

"Do you see something?" Pam asked. "Did he post something?"

There were various photos of Brody with his teammates on and off the football field as well as additional selfies—most of them taken in the forest wearing hunting gear and posing with his kills: a six-point deer, a turkey, and a pheasant.

Noah said, "Brody likes to hunt?"

"My brother takes him. Always has. Like I said, his dad died when he was thirteen, so having a male in his life has been a good thing, I think."

The captions of Brody's posts bore this out, mentioning frequently how much he enjoyed hunting with his uncle. This was not unusual. In many areas of Central Pennsylvania, entire school districts closed for the opening of deer season. Many teens took hunting safety courses and got their licenses, going hunting with older members of their families who were also lifelong hunters. Josie knew for a fact that a lot of families hunted out of practicality. A large enough deer could feed a small family for an entire season. For some families, if they didn't get anything hunting, they didn't eat.

"Is there anything on there?" Pam asked. "Do you see anything from this morning?"

"I don't see anything on this account," Josie said. "Does he have other social media accounts?"

Pam took her phone back and stared at the screen. "Oh, I mean, I think he's got something called Snapchat. He's always going on about 'snaps' but I don't have that, so I can't show you his account."

It wouldn't do them much good in the moment without a warrant anyway, Josie thought, since that particular app deleted most everything rather quickly.

Pam dropped her phone back into her purse. "Can you find my son?"

Josie said, "We're going to do everything we can."

Noah's phone buzzed. He answered it, turning away from them momentarily as he carried on a murmured conversation.

Josie continued the questioning. "Does Brody ever come out here, to this area?"

Again, the lines appeared on Pam's forehead. "Here? You mean the school?"

Josie motioned toward the woods. "Behind the football field, back there, is a place called the Stacks. Do you know it?"

Still, she looked confused.

"Did you grow up here in Denton?"

A slow shake of her head.

Noah came back, pocketing his phone. "Last place it pinged was over by the Stacks."

"What is the Stacks?" asked Pam.

"There's an area in the woods where a number of large, flat rocks fell, stacked on top of one another," Noah explained. "Looks like a giant stack of jagged pancakes. East Denton high-schoolers have been hanging out there for decades."

"For what?" asked Pam, eyes wide.

Josie and Noah exchanged a look. She said, "Usually to drink, Mrs. Hicks. Does Brody drink, that you know of?"

Her fingers twitched over the top two buttons of her blouse. "What? No! He's sixteen!"

When they didn't respond, she added, "He's on the football team. He's an A student. He wouldn't do that."

"Okay," Noah said, not bothering to argue with her. "We're still going to have a look back there since dispatch told me his phone pinged in that area last night."

"I'll come with you!" Pam said, lunging forward and clutching Noah's arm.

Without missing a beat, he patted one of her hands and steered her toward a uniformed officer. "Mrs. Hicks, I'm going to ask you to go inside with one of my colleagues so they can get some more information from you for our reports."

Before she could protest, the uniformed officers stepped forward. One of them began guiding her toward the school building. Josie called the other one back. His name tag read *Conlen*. Josie had met him last year when he joined the Denton PD in his rookie year. He was young, earnest, and very thorough. "Go to the main office," Josie said. "They'll have a list of every student who did not show up for school today. Get them to call each student's family until they find the student who isn't at home."

"You think this Hicks kid went into the woods with a friend," Conlen said.

Josie nodded. "We'll need to contact that friend's parents and get their cell phone number so we can use it to try to locate them. If Hicks is out here, so are they."

I hope, she added silently.

"Consider it done," said Conlen.

Noah stood beside her as she watched Conlen jog toward the school building. "You think this is another one," he said. "These kids doing this stupid Woodsman challenge. Two go in and only one comes out."

"I hope it's not," Josie said. "But if it is, we need to be prepared. If there is another kid out here we should be searching for, I want to know sooner rather than later."

"We've had a unit outside Henry Thomas's driveway since Sunday."

"But we don't have eyes on his cabin," Josie pointed out. "He could easily have left his cabin and come here on foot. How would we even know?"

"Shit," Noah said. "The reports said that he's only left to go to work at the city park. He leaves his house at six thirty a.m. and gets home around three thirty p.m. He's probably at work now, but I can get someone to go talk to him."

"You can," Josie said, thinking of Thomas's smug demeanor in the interrogation room the night after Kayleigh Patchett was abducted. "But if he's behind this, whatever damage he meant to do is already done."

Noah made the call anyway. Hanging up, he said, "It's still a hike from his place to down here. Miles. In the dark."

"But not impossible," Josie said. "If this is what we think it is and if it was Thomas."

"If this is what we think it is," Noah said, "how would the perpetrator know that these kids were going into the woods? Here, in Montour, in Lenore? Anywhere?"

"I don't know," Josie said. "Social media? Stalking? Luck? Some combination of the three? I mean, in this case, if you grew up on this side of the city, you know that kids hang out in the Stacks. All you'd have to do is come from the other direction and lurk."

"I'm going to call in some more units to help us search," Noah said.

THIRTY-TWO

Ten minutes later, they had another patrol unit—Brennan and Dougherty—and together, they set off toward the woods. They spread out as they reached the Stacks. Josie hadn't been there in a few years—not since another case of a missing child—but it looked much the same. Part of the base of the mountain was just a rock face. Slabs of it had broken off and fallen flat, one atop another, almost like pancakes, just as Noah had said. It formed a large platform that teenagers in Denton had been frequenting for ages. The thick canopy of foliage overhead made the space so dark it looked like evening. Even the mid-morning sun didn't penetrate it. They picked their way through discarded beer cans, liquor bottles, condoms, and food wrappers.

"This place is disgusting," Noah groused. "When we used to hang back here, we kept it cleaned up."

"We'll have to start sending more patrols back here during the night," Josie said.

Brennan laughed. "That won't stop 'em."

Noah knelt next to a natural depression in the stone floor and used a stick to poke at the charred wood and ash where there had clearly been a small fire. "True. It never has before.

This is pretty recent. There were kids out here last night. Why would they be out here after what happened to Kayleigh? That damn reporter has done nothing but talk about the Woodsman for over twenty-four hours. There is no way these kids don't know about that story."

"'Cause kids are dumb, Lieutenant," Dougherty offered.

Josie looked around, feeling a chill in spite of the warm May temperature. "We are talking about the same teenagers who do dumb online challenges that get them killed and injured, like eating laundry detergent pods. Why wouldn't they be out here, hoping to see the mysterious Woodsman? That's exactly what the kids in Montour and Lenore Counties did."

Noah stood and shook his head. "It's a joke to them."

Josie sighed. "Yes, but also they think they're invincible."

Brennan took his hat off and wiped at his brow. "Where did this kid's phone ping?"

Noah stood and pointed east. "About a mile that way."

Brennan started to trudge in that direction with Dougherty in tow.

"We'll have to climb to get to the top of the rock face," Josie said. "There's a spot over there with some natural handholds."

Dougherty groaned. "You've got to be kidding me."

Josie and Noah walked along the rock face, looking for the break in the stone that was filled with dirt and protruding tree roots. "You could go around," she said. "But it will take a lot longer."

Brennan followed them. "Come on, don't be a wimp. You think this kid we're looking for took the long way around? He's on the football team."

"Here," Noah said. He reached inside a three-foot-wide crevice and grabbed onto a gnarled tree root. He pulled at it and the two above it. Satisfied they were secure, he hoisted himself up, climbing to the top of the ridge in seconds. Josie followed suit, Brennan at her heels. Moments later, Dougherty appeared, sweating and red-faced.

Noah pulled up the GPS map on his phone, where he'd marked the location that Brody Hicks's phone had last pinged. He led the way while the rest of them spread out, following slightly behind him, panning the area for any evidence of Brody or his phone. When they reached the area the phone had last pinged, they stopped to catch their breath. Here the foliage overhead was less dense. Sunlight warmed Josie's neck. She'd taken off her jacket and tied it around her waist, but her polo shirt was soaked with perspiration between her shoulder blades.

"What now?" asked Dougherty.

"We keep looking," Josie said. "This isn't an exact science. Plus, if the phone ran out of battery or Brody Hicks turned it off, and he kept going, we wouldn't find it—or him—here."

Brennan said, "This kid could literally be anywhere by now. We need a bigger search team. Maybe the K-9 unit. The dog could use the kid's truck to scent him."

Noah wiped sweat from his brow. "Yeah, we should call Luke. We tried finding this kid using his phone and he's not here. At this point, we're wasting valuable time."

Josie's phone buzzed in her pocket. She took it out and found a message from Officer Conlen. Her breath quickened. "Wait. We've got the identity of the second student."

"What second student?" said Dougherty.

Noah said, "The other student who didn't turn up at school today but isn't at home either."

"Felicia Evans," Josie said. "A junior. Same class as Brody Hicks and Kayleigh Patchett. She was reported absent today. Her parents usually leave before she gets up for school so they didn't see her this morning. The mother got the automated call reporting the absence and left Felicia a voicemail, figuring she was just sick in bed. Dad just went home to check on her and she's not there. Conlen called dispatch to have them ping her phone. I've got the coordinates. It's about a mile and a half from here, closer to the old textile mill."

"Let's go," said Noah.

They moved more quickly this time, with Josie in the lead. Her heart galloped in her chest. With every step they took, Josie felt dread envelop her. They were nearly to the spot where Felicia's phone had last given a signal when a figure emerged from between two black walnut trees ahead of them and to Josie's left.

Josie saw only a shadow before Brennan started shouting. His weapon was drawn. "Hands up! Denton PD. Get your hands up. Now!"

Dougherty drew his weapon as well and trained it on the figure.

Brennan called, "Step out slowly with your hands up."

Brody Hicks emerged. He wore a Denton East football hoodie and blue jeans, streaked with blood. His hair was in disarray. A red smudge marred his pale cheek. He lifted his hands. They were slick with blood.

"Oh shit," said Brennan.

Josie moved closer to him, keeping herself out of range of the other officers' weapons. "Brody, stop right there."

From this close, she could see tears streaming down his cheeks and tremors in his hands. He froze in place. His eyes darted from her to his hands, and he thrust them toward her, as if imploring her to look.

"Brody," Josie said. "Are you hurt?"

He looked down at himself, eyes going wide, as if he was only just realizing that he was covered in blood. "It's not mine. It's not mine."

Noah said, "Brody? Whose blood is that?"

"You have to help," he said, voice high and squeaky. "You have to help her. I found her—I found her, like... bleeding. I tried to help her but..." His voice dropped to a whisper.

Josie took another step forward, straining to hear him.

Dougherty said, "We need to check him for weapons, Detective."

"She's dead. I'm pretty sure she's dead."

Josie said, "Who's dead, Brody?"

He squeezed his eyes shut. Hands still extended, his arms shook. "Felicia."

THIRTY-THREE

A halo of blood circled Felicia Evans's head, staining her blonde hair and mixing with the dirt beneath her body. Her glassy brown eyes stared upward at the sky, visible in a break between the trees. Aside from all the blood, she looked like she'd simply laid down for a nap. Her legs lay straight. Josie watched from behind a strip of crime scene tape as Officer Hummel took a photo of the bloody palm print on her jeans, above her left knee. One of her hands rested loosely across her stomach and the other was thrown to the side, palm upward. Her phone was inches away. Next, Hummel took a photo of the two bloody fingerprints on her throat, where her pulse would have been. Josie already knew that the ERT wouldn't find a weapon anywhere near her body.

Behind her, a branch snapped. She turned to see Noah returning from the nearest road where they'd staged various vehicles, including ambulances and the vehicles of the Evidence Response Team, and now, Josie was certain, the press.

"Did you get in touch with her parents?" Josie asked.

Noah nodded, features dark. "They came to the school. I

talked with them. Made a tentative ID using her driver's license."

Josie felt the sadness rolling off him in waves. Even after so many years on the job, the death notifications never got any easier, especially when the victim was a young person. She moved closer to him, nudging her elbow against his.

He cleared his throat. "Dougherty's with them. He'll make sure they get home. Make sure they've got someone to be with them."

"Where's Brody Hicks right now?"

After calling for backup, Noah and Dougherty had gotten Brody out to the nearest road and into the back of an ambulance while Josie and Brennan located Felicia Evans's body. It was not far from where they'd encountered Brody. Since it was abundantly clear that Felicia was already deceased, they'd sealed off the scene and waited for the Evidence Response Team to arrive.

"At the hospital," Noah said. "His mother went with him."

"Did he say anything else?"

"No. He's just crying."

"My God." Josie looked back at Felicia, struck by how something so gruesome could happen in a place so beautiful and peaceful. "What do you think?"

"About Hicks? I don't know. You see a kid hysterical like that and you wonder: is he hysterical because he's innocent and he just saw a dead body, or is he hysterical because he killed her?"

More branches snapped behind them. Josie turned and saw the signature silver-blonde hair of the county medical examiner, Dr. Anya Feist, moving among the trees.

"Hicks was on the mountain where Kayleigh was taken on the day of her abduction," Josie said. "He's an experienced hunter, comfortable in the woods, but if this wasn't his first time killing someone, I don't think he'd be that upset."

"Plus, he's only sixteen," Noah said.

She shot him a look. "You know what Mett would say."

"His age doesn't mean he's not a killer. I know. I guess then to eliminate Hicks we have to consider whether what we saw out here was real or an Oscar-worthy acting performance."

"We can also check his alibi and his vehicle's GPS for the dates of Detective Loughlin's cases in Montour and Lenore Counties. We should ask his mother for permission to search his truck. See if there's any evidence that Kayleigh was in it. What about Henry Thomas? Did anyone check on him?"

Anya emerged into the clearing, lugging her equipment with her. She greeted them with a nod and then dropped her things beside Hummel's equipment station. Josie watched as she pulled on a Tyvek suit over her clothes.

Noah said, "The Chief tracked him down at the city park. It was just like you said: he had no idea what the Chief was talking about and said he was home sleeping last night."

"We can't prove otherwise," Josie muttered.

"It's pretty ballsy of him to do this right in his own backyard when he knows damn well he's under suspicion for Kayleigh's abduction," Noah said.

"He probably gets off on it," Josie said. "This is all a game to him."

"Well, he's winning," Noah said. "And I don't like it at all."

Anya appeared beside him, a strained smile on her face. "Detectives. Hate meeting you like this. What've we got here?"

Noah said, "Two teenagers in the woods. Overnight, we believe. This morning we found the male walking around, covered in blood. He says it belongs to the female. Felicia Evans, age sixteen." He pointed toward the teen. "He said he tried to help her. We located her here."

"That's all we know," said Josie. "For now."

Anya pulled on her skull cap. "We'll start with that, then.

Why don't you two get suited up? Looks like Hummel's about done."

He wasn't nearly done. They waited another hour, sweating in their Tyvek suits, while the ERT cleared the scene for Anya to have a look at the body. She started out by taking her own photos.

"The ME in Lenore County called me about a case a lot like this," said Anya as she worked. "He's a friend of mine."

Josie and Noah looked at one another. He raised a brow. They hadn't discussed Detective Heather Loughlin's cases with Anya at all.

She stowed her camera and squatted next to Felicia's head, probing at her eyelids. Noah watched over her shoulder while Josie stood on the other side of the body. "Two teenagers in the woods, male and female. The male survived. The female did not, and—" She paused, putting her face inches from the pool of blood surrounding Felicia Evans's head. "She died from blunt force trauma to the head. A rock, probably. Just like this girl."

She sat back on her haunches and looked around. "Weapon?"

"We didn't find anything," Josie said. "Neither did Hummel."

Noah said, "So if it was a rock, he took it with him."

"I should be able to tell you something about the wound on the back of her head once I get her on the table."

Anya stood up and arched her back, stretching. Then she moved down toward Felicia's midsection. Her bootie-covered foot slipped on a small patch of trampled purple wildflowers. Noah was close enough to reach out and snag her elbow before she went head over feet. Her cheeks flushed as she thanked him.

"You guys," she muttered. "Always coming to my rescue."

From the catch in her voice, Josie knew she was referencing the case that had resulted in Mettner's death. It had involved some ugly elements of Anya's past, including her abusive ex-husband. Josie knew she blamed herself for Mettner's death even though it had not been her fault.

"Doc," Noah said softly.

When Anya looked at him, tears shone in her eyes. Her voice was throaty. "One of the last murder scenes I attended was with Mett. I'm sorry. It's just a little... it's harder than I thought."

"We know," Josie said. "We're here with you. We'll get through this together."

Anya took a bracing breath and knelt near Felicia's waist. "Back to work."

She tugged lightly at Felicia's hand, trying to pry it from where it rested over her abdomen, but it was fixed in place. "She's in full rigor. Don't ask me about time of death. The best estimate I can give you right now under these conditions, without taking her internal temperature and making my calculations, would be that she died within the last six to twelve hours."

While Dr. Feist continued to look over Felicia Evans's body, Josie took a closer look at the area. There was no sign of any traps. No sticks carved, bent, or split in such a way that could be used for a deadfall trap. No heap of leaves, twigs and coiled vines. Nothing hanging from the trees overhead. Had the killer simply attacked Felicia? Was this a departure from his MO? Was this not the work of the same person after all? Were they trying too hard to force all the cases into a pattern? Maybe it had been a simple disagreement between Brody Hicks and Felicia Evans. They didn't even know what type of relationship the two had had. They might have been dating. Domestic violence among teenagers was on the rise. Was Felicia Evans's death a horrible coincidence?

Josie's gut told her that it wasn't.

She knelt down across from Anya and pointed to Felicia's feet, both clad in sneakers. "I'd like to look at her ankles."

The three of them gathered at Felicia's feet. Josie had to contort her body, her cheek almost pressed into the dirt to see the backs of Felicia's sneakers. The pull tab of the right shoe was crushed down and in, as if she'd put the sneaker on in a rush. "This one," Josie said.

She sat back up and watched as Anya folded back the cuff of Felicia's jeans, revealing a sporty white sock, its elastic band soaked in blood. Anya said, "Lieutenant Fraley, get me my camera."

Noah found it and handed it to her. She snapped some photos. Then she said, "Josie, would you mind?"

Carefully, Josie hooked one gloved finger inside the sock's elastic and pulled it down.

"Would you look at that," said Anya, rapidly snapping photos.

A thin ligature mark marred Felicia's skin.

Noah gave a low whistle.

"What do you think that's from?" asked Anya.

Josie said, "A snare trap."

THIRTY-FOUR

Dr. Ahmed Nashat, the attending physician at Denton Memorial Hospital's emergency department, emerged from behind one of the curtained treatment areas and strode toward Josie and Noah, who waited at the nurses' station. Behind him trailed Pam Hicks, looking haggard but calmer than she had earlier. Dr. Nashat smiled at them. "I have Mrs. Hicks's permission to tell you that her son is just fine. He's a bit dehydrated. We were worried about shock. He's been getting oxygen and fluids. We gave him something to calm him down as he was quite distraught when he arrived."

"I brought him a change of clothes," said Pam. "One of your officers took the clothes he was wearing. They said it was evidence. Brody told me that a young lady—" Here she lowered her voice to a whisper even though the medical staff rushing to and fro around them weren't paying attention. "She died out there. Is that true?"

"I'm afraid that it is," Josie said.

Pam closed her eyes and tilted her head back to the ceiling. After several deep breaths, she looked at them again. "I had hoped maybe he was wrong. That maybe she survived, even though there was so much blood."

"Is he able to speak with us?" asked Noah.

"Yes. But only for a short while. I don't want him upset again just when I have to take him home."

"We'll try to keep it brief," Josie said.

Pam turned and motioned for them to follow her. They crowded in behind the curtain that surrounded Brody's gurney. He was asleep on his back, a sheet pulled up to his chin, its edge clutched in both of his meaty hands. Although someone, likely his mother, had made a valiant effort to clean him up, blood still stained his cuticles. A cannula fed oxygen into his nostrils. His dark hair looked as though it had been wet and slicked to the side. He looked smaller than he had in the woods. Pam touched his shoulder gently, whispering into his ear. One of his fists nearly made contact with her face when he startled awake. Josie recognized the blind terror in his eyes as he transitioned from sleep to waking. His mind was still in those woods, reliving whatever terror he'd found there.

Pam recovered well from his unexpected thrashing, jumping back, waiting a few seconds, and then approaching him again, gentle as ever. Josie watched the fog of his nightmare clear with each word Pam whispered into his ear. After two slow blinks, he focused on Josie and Noah.

In a quiet voice, Brody said, "Did you find her?"

"Yes," said Noah.

He fisted his hands under his chin again. "Do her parents know?"

"Yes," Noah repeated.

A tear slid down Brody's cheek. Pam reached over and stroked his hair away from his face.

"Brody," Josie said. "We know you've been through a lot. We can do a longer interview later, but for now we just need to know what happened out there."

Another tear rolled down his cheek. "I don't know," he said. "I don't know what happened."

Pam used the sleeve of her shirt to wipe away his tear. Brody seemed oblivious to her presence.

Noah said, "Let's just start with last night. The last time you saw your mom. At home."

He unclenched his fists, gathered up some more of his sheet and clenched them again, holding them lower this time, at his chest. "Oh, that's easy. I was watching TV and she came into the living room to say goodnight."

"What time was that?" asked Josie.

He looked toward Pam. She said, "You don't remember, honey?"

"I don't know. I just know that when the news came on, I was going to go to bed but one of my buddies on the team texted me. He said a bunch of people were going to the Stacks. He wanted me to come."

"The news comes on at eleven," Noah said. "Was it still on when you left for the Stacks?"

Brody nodded. He darted a glance at Pam. She said, "You tell them the truth, Brody. You already came clean with me, and we'll deal with it accordingly when all this is over. Now you tell the police."

There was the beginning of an eye-roll that was swiftly aborted. Then Brody looked back at Josie and Noah. "Yeah, I left for the Stacks while the news was still on. I remember because they were showing Kayleigh's face. Again. And I didn't want to go to the Stacks because this girl just got abducted from the woods, and while the Stacks isn't deep in the woods, it's still in the woods."

"Then why did you go?" asked Josie.

"My buddy said there'd be at least ten of us and I figured there was safety in numbers. Plus, the guys from the team who were going are big dudes. I figured if that Woodsman guy came up on us at the Stacks, we could handle him."

Noah said, "Were there ten people there?"

"More like fifteen. I never saw it so crowded." Another glance at Pam. "Not that I go there much."

She gave him a severe look. "Don't lie, Brody."

"I'm not lying, Mom. I don't go there a lot. Some kids go a few times a week. The last time I went was weeks ago."

Josie said, "We're going to need you to write down the names of everyone who was there."

His eyes widened. "You want me to rat out every person there?"

Noah said, "Felicia Evans is dead."

Shame colored his cheeks red.

"What did you do at the Stacks last night?" asked Josie.

"We hung out and talked. Some people were drinking and doing other stuff."

"Other stuff?" said Pam. "What does that mean?"

His hands relaxed, now resting on his chest. He turned them palms up. "Mom, please."

"You told me about the drinking but not the other stuff."

"Because I don't do it. It's weed, mostly. I think other kids do other drugs but me and my friends drink. One of the guys on the team has an older brother who gets us beer."

Josie asked, "Did Kayleigh Patchett ever hang out there?"

He shook his head. "I never saw her there."

"Do you know her?" asked Noah.

"She's in my English class but I don't know her. I've never talked to her. Felicia knew her. They seemed like they were friends, but then sometime earlier in the year they stopped talking. There was some kind of beef but I don't know exactly what it was about. I think it had to do with some story-writing contest or something for English class. A couple of people asked her about it last night but she said it was nothing. 'Stupid shit,' she called it. Wouldn't talk about it. I think she felt bad because Kayleigh got taken."

"When you were at the Stacks last night, Kayleigh was the topic of conversation?"

Brody looked to Pam, who nodded for him to answer. "Well, yeah. It was a pretty big deal. A girl from our school abducted? It's all anyone could talk about—in school and out. A lot of kids there knew her better than me. Like, people don't usually drink at the Stacks during the week but people were so freaked out by her kidnapping. Anyway, everyone was talking about her and... what happened, especially 'cause the news keeps saying that the Woodsman took her. We all thought that was some dumb story."

Josie stopped herself from blurting out that it *was* a dumb story.

"A few people there, especially the girls, were really freaked out. One girl got so freaked out, she left. Mostly though, everyone thought it was a big joke."

"That Kayleigh was abducted, or that the Woodsman took her?" Josie asked.

"The Woodsman thing. I mean, we all know some pervert took her. Or at least, that's what everyone thought last night." He tugged the edge of the sheet back up, covering his chin.

"Had you heard about the Woodsman before Kayleigh Patchett was abducted?" asked Noah.

"Yeah. A little. It was going around school, but no one really took it seriously. That's what I'm telling you. Last night? Going into the woods? It was a joke!"

Josie said, "You and Felicia Evans went into the woods as a joke?"

"No, I mean everyone thought the story of the Woodsman was a joke. It turned into this dare or challenge or whatever. Kind of like the Murder Mountain challenge."

The words grated over Josie's already exposed nerves, but

she tried not to show it. "You did that challenge, didn't you?"

"No. Yes. Sort of. I did go up there to do the challenge, but it didn't really count because it wasn't overnight."

"How did you get up there?" asked Noah.

"Kelleher Road," Brody answered. "There's an access road. It's chained but I just parked on the road and walked up."

Josie took out her phone and pulled up a photo of Henry Thomas. "Do you know this man?"

Brody's face remained blank. "No. Who is he?"

"He lives near there," Josie said. "On Herron Road. The other side of the fields. He's had trouble with teenagers coming onto his property trying to get to the burial grounds."

The sheet lowered to his neck. "I never saw him. I didn't know anyone lived up there. That's creepy."

Noah asked, "What time did you go up there on Saturday?"

Pam frowned.

"I don't know. I don't remember. During the day sometime."

"How long were you up there?" asked Josie.

"I thought you were here to talk about what happened last night," said Pam. "Why are you asking him about Saturday?"

"Kayleigh Patchett was abducted sometime during the day on Saturday near the burial grounds," Noah explained. "We'd like to know if Brody saw anything."

Josie addressed Brody. "Maybe it didn't seem like it was important then."

"I didn't see anything," he said.

"If you wouldn't mind, Mrs. Hicks, we'd like to have a look at Brody's truck as well as his phone."

Brody said, "That officer who met us here took my phone. My clothes, too. Said they needed to be 'processed' or something."

Pam narrowed her eyes. "You think my son had something to do with that Patchett girl going missing, don't you?"

"Brody was in the area at the time of the abduction," Josie

said. "We can't ignore that. It's standard procedure to look closely at anyone who was in the vicinity."

Pam moved closer to her son, putting one hand on his shoulder. "My Brody is a good boy. He would never hurt anyone."

Noah looked at Brody. "Let's move on to last night. You were at the Stacks. It was dark, after eleven thirty p.m. You and several other students from Denton East were drinking. You started discussing Kayleigh's abduction and the story of the Woodsman. There was some kind of dare. What exactly was the dare?"

"A couple of guys said that one of us should spend the night in the woods."

"For what?" asked Pam. "Brody, really."

"Mom, I'm sorry. I didn't think that the Woodsman was real! I told you that!" Turning back to Josie and Noah, he continued, "I said I'd do it because I wasn't afraid of the woods or some child's story about a guy lurking in the woods. Then someone said that it had to be two people because I could just say I was going into the woods and wait for everyone to leave and then go home. No one wanted to go with me. I thought that was going to be it but then Felicia volunteered."

"Are you and Felicia dating?" asked Noah.

"No. I mean, not really. We just started getting closer the last few months. I thought maybe she was into me. I liked her. I was trying to work up the nerve to ask her out before the end of the year. Then she volunteered to go into the woods with me—overnight! I thought it was my chance, but then—"

He broke off, a sob rising in his throat. Fresh tears streamed down his cheeks. He clamped his mouth shut, as if trying to hold in his cries. What came out was a long, high-pitched keening noise. Pam perched on the edge of the bed and wrapped her arms around him, pulling his head to her chest and stroking his hair.

Josie and Noah waited a few moments for him to compose

himself. Finally, he disentangled himself from his mother, leaving a wet imprint of his face on her shirt. Using the edge of the sheet to wipe his cheeks, he started to speak again. This time the words came rapidly, as if he was afraid if he slowed or stopped, he wouldn't be able to begin again. "I told her all we had to do was find a good place to hunker down for the night. A sort of shelter. Somewhere kind of comfortable and we could just stay there, and once it started to get light, we'd be able to leave. We used our phones as flashlights. So we started walking, trying to find any kind of shelter. She was worried about finding our way back in the morning, but I told her not to worry 'cause we could just use the GPS and it would be light out.

"We finally found a place at the base of a pine tree that was kind of covered and we got under there. We were talking and we both got really tired. We lay down next to each other and kind of, like, cuddled, I guess. It got cold at night. She kept saying she heard something, but I told her it was probably just some animal. I mean, we were in the woods! I told her we'd be fine where we were. Eventually we both fell asleep and then I woke up later—I checked my phone and it was like after four thirty—and she was gone. I thought maybe she got up to pee or something. I waited about a half hour to see if she'd come back but she didn't. It started to get lighter. I texted her because I thought she'd ditched me, but she didn't respond. Then I was worried she got up to pee and got lost 'cause it had been dark. I started trying to find her. I thought I heard her crying or calling me or something. I heard something like that. I kept searching."

"Why didn't you call for help?" Pam said.

He didn't look at her. "Because I didn't want to get her in trouble for being out in the woods all night doing some dumb challenge. Felicia's really smart. She's like one of the smartest girls in school. Plus, my phone died."

"How long did it take you to find her?" asked Josie.

"I don't know. It felt like hours. I saw her there—" He

choked up again.

Pam patted his shoulder. "Deep breaths."

He nodded, sucking in several long breaths before resuming his story. "I found her laying there. Her head—her head didn't look right. I tried to wake her up, to help her. I didn't mean to make a mess but there was so much blood. I got it on me. I tried to feel her pulse, but I couldn't. I kind of freaked out. Like, blacked out."

Pam raised a brow. "What do you mean, blacked out?"

"I can't remember anything after that until we got here. I remember finding her, trying to help her. Blood everywhere. Then I was here in the hospital."

"Brody," Noah said. "You're doing great. We only have a few more questions. I know this is a difficult question, but we need to know: did you and Felicia have sexual intercourse last night?"

"What? No. No. It wasn't like that. We just talked."

"Okay," Josie said. "When you found Felicia, do you remember seeing anything unusual at the scene?"

"Like what?"

"A snare trap, maybe," said Noah. "Something like that?"

"No. I didn't see anything. Why would there be a snare? It's not even trapping season. Well, I guess coyote, but that's it."

"Do you trap?" asked Josie.

"No. My uncle does. I've seen him do it but I've never tried it. I don't have my license. I prefer hunting."

Josie took out her phone and pulled up a photo of Kayleigh's secret boyfriend. She showed it to Brody. "Do you know this person?"

He stared at it, brow furrowing. "I can't see his face. You have a picture of his face?"

"This is the best photo we have," Josie said.

"I don't know him. Who is he?"

Noah said, "Someone named J.J. That name ring a bell?"

"No."

Josie gave it one last try. "We believe that Kayleigh was dating this guy. Did you ever hear anything around school or at the Stacks about her boyfriend?"

"Nah, no one talked about her till she was taken. I didn't know she was seeing someone but then again, I didn't talk to her. Felicia might—" He broke off.

A heavy silence filled the tiny space. Brody choked out, "I'm sorry. I'm so sorry."

Pam moved back in to hug him again. Noah said, "I think that's enough for today. You did great, Brody. Mrs. Hicks, we'll be in touch about his truck."

Josie handed Pam a business card. She and Noah turned to leave.

"Hey," Brody called after them. "Does this mean the Woodsman is real?"

Josie turned back. It seemed like such a meaningless distinction now. What had started out as a stupid story wending its way through area schools was now, for all intents and purposes, real. There was a man in the woods trapping, abducting, and killing kids.

Again, Josie was torn about what to say. She was fairly certain that Brody Hicks was not behind the killings here or in the other counties or Kayleigh's abduction, although they would still investigate him. What she saw before her was a young man traumatized by finding the body of his crush savagely murdered. She didn't want to scare him more or say something he'd pass on to his friends that would burn like wildfire through the schools and make it to the press, causing a frenzy. She also didn't want to lie.

Noah saved her the trouble. "Brody, the Woodsman is just a stupid kids' story, but the person who killed Felicia is real and we're going to do everything we can to find him and make sure he pays for what he did."

THIRTY-FIVE

There have always been rules. Bring as little as possible to each hunt and leave as little as possible at each scene. My arms ache from carrying the stone miles away from where I used it to smash the girl's head in. However, it's a good pain. Satisfying. Exhilarating. As I roll the stone down an embankment into a stream, I think of the satisfying sound it made when it hit her skull. Of course, nothing was more satisfying than the look of shock and horror on her face in those final moments. Sometimes those last moments are too messy, too fast for me to enjoy, but I'm getting better at this.

Evolving as my legend grows.

THIRTY-SIX

Denton PD's impound lot also doubled as their evidence processing station. Most of the evidence they collected was sent off to the state police lab, but there were many things that Hummel and his team were able to do in-house. These things took place in a nondescript cinderblock building located in a remote part of North Denton. It was on a gated lot, and Josie had to show her credentials to the officer in the guard booth before she was admitted. She drove past a row of cars and found a spot next to the Chief's car. The garage bay doors were closed, as usual, their windows covered with white laminate so that no one could see inside. She walked past them and knocked on the blue door. A moment later, it swung open. Noah smiled at her.

"Everyone's here," he said as she stepped past him into a small office area. With no one around, he pulled her in for a quick kiss. "You get any sleep?"

"Yeah," she lied. Surely, two hours still counted as sleep.

After leaving Brody Hicks and his mother at the hospital the afternoon before, Noah had gone home to rest. Gretchen had replaced him. She and Josie spent the rest of the evening chasing down leads until Noah came back in to send Josie home. Even though it had been late, she'd taken Trout for a lengthy walk and then played with him, hoping that she'd wear them both out. But once in bed, she lay awake, a demonic carousel of thoughts keeping her from sleep. Most had to do with the Kayleigh Patchett case and the new Felicia Evans case and whether they were related, but when she finally did begin drifting off to sleep, memories of Mett's death crowded her mind, making it impossible to rest.

Noah gave her a look that said he didn't believe her, but he didn't push it. Releasing her, he said, "Everyone's back here. Come on."

They walked through the office and into the larger evidence processing room. Chief Chitwood and Gretchen stood in the center of the room, sipping coffee. On one of the empty stainless-steel tables lining the walls, Josie spied a cupholder from Komorrah's with one cup of coffee left in it. Noah said, "That's yours."

"Thanks," she said. "Why are we meeting here?"

Across the room sat Officer Chan working at a different table, her gloved hands trying to piece together the trap-like thing they'd found during the line search behind the Patchett home. Several sticks were laid out side by side. Most had vines coiled around them though they were loose and broken. Next to those was a pile of leaves and the sharpened pieces they'd recovered.

The Chief said, "The damn press. Can't get away from them. They've swarmed the stationhouse but they never think to come out here and even if they did, they'd be locked out."

Gretchen said, "Hummel has some updates. He's in the garage now. He said he'd be right in."

Josie took a sip of her coffee and crossed the room so she could peer over Chan's shoulder. "Getting anywhere?"

Chan sighed. "No. I don't know what this thing was supposed to be. I've looked up every type of trap I could find on the internet and didn't see anything similar. Most traps are made of metal or use paracord or chains or something." She flicked a finger against a loose piece of vine. "Whoever made this? I don't know what they expected to catch with it. From what's here, it wouldn't hold a squirrel and the only animal it's legal to trap right now is coyote. No way is this flimsy thing holding a coyote."

Gretchen came over and stood next to Josie. "I think we can assume that the person who built it—whatever it is—and put it out in the woods wasn't concerned with what's legal."

Josie said, "Paracord, metal pieces, cable—all those things can be traced or processed for evidence. This stuff can't. I think that's why he used it." She thought of the ligature on Felicia Evans's ankle. She'd caught it in something and yet, there was no trap left behind. "Or there were pieces that could be processed, and he took them with him."

"Maybe that's why I'm having trouble reconstructing it," Chan said. "I'll keep trying to reconstruct it keeping in mind that I'm missing pieces."

"Do what you can," Josie said. She touched Chan's shoulder. "I appreciate it."

Josie walked over to the window that overlooked the garage bays and saw that both of them were occupied. Brody Hicks's truck, which they'd impounded the night before, sat in one bay. In the other was a sedan.

Josie said, "Is that one of the Patchetts' vehicles?"

"Yes," said Officer Chan. "We processed the truck with the plow on it and the minivan earlier. They'll be returned tomorrow. We had that one left but with the murder, we wanted to get that truck processed sooner so the sedan has to wait. Hummel will be in soon to talk about the truck."

The Chief said, "Let's do this briefing before we send Palmer home for some sleep. First things first, the line searches conducted in the woods across from Henry Thomas's cabin turned up nothing. No signs of Kayleigh Patchett. No freshly dug graves or overturned dirt. Palmer, what do you have?"

Gretchen said, "I checked in with both Amber and Sergeant Lamay before I came over here. They tell me that the tip line is more of a hindrance than a help. It's been days and we haven't had one viable lead. Amber said it rang late into the night and then started again this morning. It's kids making jokes. Mostly about the Woodsman. They think this is funny."

"Guess my press conference didn't do any good," The Chief replied.

"Teenagers don't watch that stuff," said Noah. "This is such a joke to them that it got Felicia Evans killed."

The Chief rubbed at his scalp. "I can't shut the tip line down, though. Speaking of teenagers, Palmer, you and Quinn talked with the other kids who were at the Stacks the night Brody Hicks and Felicia Evans went into the woods, right?"

Josie and Gretchen had spent their entire evening tracking down each teenager that Brody Hicks said was at the Stacks and interviewing them. "Most of them were uncooperative," Josie said. "None would admit to drinking or drug use."

"None of them heard or saw anything," Gretchen said. "And we were able to verify using their phones' GPS and interviewing parents that they were all home by one a.m."

"You show them the photos of J.J.?" asked the Chief. "Kayleigh's secret boyfriend?"

"No recognition," Josie replied. "But it's hard to identify someone when all you can see is their profile."

Noah said, "Has anyone interviewed the school staff yet? Maybe one of them can identify him."

The Chief shook his head. "I talked to them. No one recognized him. There was no kid named J.J. in the school. Or who had gone to school there recently."

"All this effort to find him and he could be a dead end," Noah grumbled.

"Or he could break the case wide open," Gretchen said.

It was exactly something Mett would have said. "We can't ignore him," said the Chief. "I know that Henry Thomas looks best for these crimes, but we can't prove that he's behind them. Either that's because we don't have enough evidence against him yet, or it's because someone else took Kayleigh Patchett and killed Felicia Evans."

Gretchen sighed. "Unless the hair we found in Thomas's cabin comes back as belonging to Kayleigh, we might never be able to prove that he did anything—even if he did."

The Chief turned to Chan. "Where are we with those results, Chan?"

Without looking up from the mess of leaves and sticks before her, she said, "The state lab is still working on it. Believe me, the moment we know, you'll know."

The Chief said, "Quinn. What do you make of this Hicks kid? He was close enough to the area Kayleigh was taken that he could have done it."

Noah added, "And he was out there long enough to have taken her. Hummel pulled the GPS from his truck and sent it over last night. The report doesn't go back far enough to tell us where he was when the Montour and Lenore County murders went down, but he was up on Kelleher Road near the burial grounds from eleven thirty in the morning until about three thirty in the afternoon. Plenty of time to have taken Kayleigh."

Josie said, "But he used the access road, which is nowhere near Henry Thomas's driveway, and Blue followed Kayleigh's scent to Thomas's driveway. She was there. The GPS from Hicks's truck doesn't put him near Thomas's cabin, does it?"

"No," Noah admitted.

"Dogs can be wrong," said the Chief. "Hicks is still on our list. What else is outstanding?"

"Kayleigh Patchett's phone records," Josie said. "We should have had them by now—even without them being expedited."

"We got them," Gretchen said. "This morning. Early. I looked through them already. There's not much."

"You've got to be kidding me," Josie said, trying not to look visibly defeated. "No calls or texts or anything to someone who might be the boyfriend? Or even a burner phone?"

Gretchen shook her head. "What you saw on her phone is basically what you get."

Josie said, "How in the hell was she communicating with this guy? We searched her laptop. I searched her room—thoroughly. If she had another phone, we would have found it."

"Through her friends, maybe?" Noah suggested. "Olivia?"

Josie shook her head. "No. Olivia thought that Kayleigh was making this guy up."

"Maybe she lied," said the Chief.

"No." Josie thought about how upset Olivia had become when the subject of the boyfriend came up. How she had fled the restaurant in tears, wracked with guilt that she had thought all along Kayleigh had made up the boyfriend. "She may have lied about other things but not that. I'm telling you, we're missing something. She had to have a way of communicating with this guy."

"Social media?" asked Noah.

"No. I checked through all of Olivia's followers and people she follows, and couldn't connect Kayleigh to any of them. It seems that Kayleigh really didn't have social media." Josie looked at Gretchen. "Wait. You said 'basically.' The contents on the phone were *basically* what was in the records. Did you find something?"

Gretchen slugged down the rest of her coffee and threw the empty cup into the nearest trash bin. "I don't think it's relevant. It's just the only thing that was not on the phone. There were texts between her and Felicia Evans. They'd been deleted from her phone. They were from the fall. The records from the cell phone carrier only tell us when the messages occurred and how many were sent and received. We can't see the content."

The door to the garage bays banged open and Hummel stepped through it, carrying two evidence bags. "Thanks for coming," he said. "We're still working on a ton of stuff, but I thought you guys might want these." He froze and looked around. "I didn't need all of you. Is something going on?"

"They're trying to avoid the press," Chan said over her shoulder.

Hummel laughed. "Oh yeah. Chief, I guess your press conference yesterday about the Woodsman just threw more fuel on the fire."

The Chief raised a bushy brow. "You think you can do better, Hummel?"

Gretchen rolled her eyes. "Don't wind him up. For the love of God."

Quickly, Noah said, "What did you bring us?"

Hummel handed him the two bags. "The phones belonging to Felicia Evans and Brody Hicks. I checked mainly to see if either of them had taken video or photos the night they were in the woods. Sometimes you get lucky, but not in this case. Thought you guys might want to take a closer look at them. Maybe there's something that will stand out to you that doesn't to me."

Gretchen said, "What about the Evans scene? Anything we need to know about?"

"There wasn't much to work with," Hummel said. "No murder weapon. No ligatures. Outdoor scene. The Hicks kid trampled all over it. But her sneaker—the one on her right foot?"

"The ankle with the ligature mark," said Josie.

"Yeah. I think the killer took her sneaker off and put it back on."

Josie thought about how the pull tab had been dented

downward and in. "He had to do it to get the snare from her ankle."

"Yeah, probably," Hummel said. "I pulled some DNA from the sneaker. Sweat, most likely."

A stillness fell over the room and Josie could feel it filling with their collective excitement. It could blow the case wide open if they could match the DNA found on Felicia Evans's sneaker to someone.

The Chief said, "I'll call the lab about getting things expedited."

Josie resisted the urge to point out that they were still waiting on the expedited DNA results from Henry Thomas's cabin. She knew it was beyond the Chief's control. She just hoped no one else died or was abducted in the time it took them to get the results.

THIRTY-SEVEN

Josie's lower back ached. She had been at her desk hunched over Felicia Evans's phone for an hour. She shifted in her chair, trying to appease the spasm knotting its way across her back. Across from her, Noah leaned back as far as his chair would allow, studying Brody Hicks's phone. With a sigh, he threw it onto his desk. "There's nothing here. You got anything?"

"Not yet," Josie said.

She'd started with Felicia's texts, since they already knew that she'd been in contact with Kayleigh, but Felicia hadn't saved any of them. In fact, Kayleigh wasn't even a contact in her phone. It probably didn't matter. Gretchen was right: it was irrelevant that the two had been in contact. They went to the same school. Of course they'd had contact. Plus, Josie knew from Brody and Olivia that there'd been some "beef" between the girls early in the year that had to do with something academic.

"I think this might be a waste of time," Josie muttered.

Noah stretched his arms, lacing his hands together behind his head. "What else have we got? We're pretty much in a holding pattern until the state lab sends back the DNA results."

Josie swiped through pages and pages of apps. She opened Instagram and quickly scrolled through Felicia's posts. The most recent one was of Felicia and four other girls, all wearing formal dresses, standing on a front lawn. There were various hashtags to indicate that it was a prom. Josie remembered that prom had only been about a week before Kayleigh was abducted. She'd been relieved, especially after last year's prom night, that there hadn't been any serious crimes that night, other than the run-of-the-mill underage drinking. Although Kayleigh didn't have social media, there hadn't been any prom photos on her phone. Had she not gone to the prom? It would make sense that if her boyfriend was around twenty years old as Olivia had said, and out of high school, she might not have wanted to bring him to the prom, even though the age of consent in Pennsylvania was sixteen. More likely, Kayleigh hadn't wanted her parents to know she was dating an older guy. Had she not gone to the prom because of that, or because her parents had punished her for some transgression? They seemed to have an endless list.

Felicia's feed offered nothing of note. Josie went into her private messages. There were dozens. The most recent exchange was between her and another girl who had been at the Stacks the night Felicia and Brody went into the woods. Josie and Gretchen had interviewed the girl, who had denied any drinking or drug use among the kids at the Stacks. But here in Felicia's private messages, she promised there would be plenty of beer, liquor, and weed and that the whole event would be "lit." Felicia was reluctant to go.

Everyone's just going to be talking about Kayleigh, she had messaged. *It's too sad. What if she's dead?*

So what? The girl had typed back. *I thought you'd be happy about that especially after all the bullshit she put you through in the fall.*

OMG how can you say that??? Are you serious? I'd never be happy anyone died. Definitely not Kayleigh. Yeah we had a problem but I never wanted anything bad to happen to her. She's really talented and smart. I feel so horrible. I just want her to be ok.

You're a weirdo. She threatened you!!! Or did you forget that? I hope you still have the screenshots.

She didn't threaten me. Her fictional boyfriend did. It's just sad. There's a lot more to what happened than anyone knows, Felicia wrote back. *I'm just saying that Kayleigh doesn't deserve this and I hope she's ok. This whole situation is making me cry 24/7. I don't want to go to the Stacks rn and listen to everyone talk about it like it's some big joke. Maybe another time.*

Oh come on. Don't be a buzzkill. Everyone's going to blow off steam because they're freaked out too. Besides, Brody will be there. Morgan told me he likes you. This could be your chance.

The chat went on with Brody Hicks's presence the deciding factor in Felicia going to the Stacks that night. Josie's heart felt heavy. Two high school kids with crushes just doing what high school kids do, and it had ended in unimaginable tragedy.

Josie closed out Instagram and opened Felicia's photo gallery, punching the icon for her folder of screenshots. She had to go back to November to find what Felicia's friend had referenced. She had, in fact, kept the screenshots. Or at least some of them. Back then, Kayleigh had been a contact in Felicia's phone, named simply KP.

KP: *You won't get away with this.*

Felicia: *Leave me alone. It's over.*

KP: *This will never be over until you tell everyone the truth.*

Felicia: *Leave me alone. I'm going to block you.*

KP: *You know I have proof that you stole my SJ story. You and I both know you blatantly took it and passed it off as your own. You can't just accept that award. That's my award. My story.*

Felicia: *You can't prove anything.*

KP: *Of course I can. I wrote that story months ago. I have receipts. Plus my boyfriend read it right after I put it up. He can confirm I wrote it.*

Felicia: *Your imaginary boyfriend? Be real.*

KP: *He is real and he knows what you did.*

Felicia: *You can't prove it was an SJ story. You'd have to tell your parents what you've been writing. I read the other stuff you wrote. You're sick. You can delete them but I've got screenshots. Who do you think people will believe?*

KP: *If you won't tell the truth, my boyfriend says he'll kill you.*

Felicia sent a row of laughing emojis and then: *Bye, bitch.*

KP: *He would do anything for me. He wouldn't think twice about making you pay. Better watch your back.*

Felicia: *Whatever. Blocking you now.*

Clearly, Kayleigh had deleted the exchange from her phone so that her parents wouldn't see it.

"You got something?" asked Noah.

"Texts between Kayleigh and Felicia. Screenshots."

She stood up and walked over to his desk, handing him Felicia's phone.

"Kayleigh's boyfriend was going to kill Felicia?" Noah said. "That's quite a threat for a grown man to make against a teenage girl. It's also creepy as hell. Maybe finding this guy isn't a waste of time after all. What's an SJ story?"

"Not sure," Josie said. "Kayleigh was part of an after-school writing club. It could be related to that. Felicia was in it as well."

Even as she said the words, something nagged at her. Something just out of reach of her consciousness.

Noah started swiping through the gallery. "I don't see screenshots of the stories that Felicia mentions. The ones she said were sick."

"I didn't get that far." She watched as he methodically swiped through the entire screenshot gallery. It took long enough that Josie's back started to hurt from standing. There was nothing. He went back to the screenshotted text messages. "Doesn't seem like Felicia felt threatened. She blew this off."

"She thought the boyfriend was made up, just like everyone else did."

Josie's desk phone rang. She circled back to her desk and snatched up the receiver. "Quinn."

Sergeant Dan Lamay said, "We've got two sets of parents down here in the lobby looking for updates, and they're not exactly getting along so well."

"I'll be right there."

THIRTY-EIGHT

Josie heard shouts as she pushed open the stairwell door on the first floor with Noah at her heels. Two uniformed officers raced down the hall toward the lobby. Josie and Noah followed, hurrying their pace. The door swung open and she recognized Dave Patchett's voice. "You think we don't know how it feels?"

Josie caught the door before it swung shut. She bypassed the small reception area where Lamay sat, separated from the rest of the lobby by a tall desk, and pushed through the second door into the main area reserved for visitors. The two uniformed officers had separated the couples. The Patchetts stood on the left, another couple on the right. Behind her, Noah whispered, "That's Sasha and Jeremy Evans. Felicia's parents."

Sasha and Jeremy Evans were thinner, taller, and more smartly dressed than Dave and Shelly Patchett. Even in jeans and casual shirts, both of them looked fresher and more put-together than the Patchetts, although Sasha's bloodshot eyes and swollen face told another story. Maybe the stress of the ongoing search for Kayleigh was getting to the Patchetts. Dave looked like he hadn't bathed at all. Shelly wore sweatpants and a soccer mom T-shirt that was torn beneath the right armpit.

Sasha pointed a finger in Dave's direction. Her voice shook with grief. "You have no idea how this feels. Our daughter is dead."

Weakly, Shelly replied, "Our daughter could be dead, too. Please. We didn't mean anything. We're sorry for your loss."

"No, you're not," Sasha hissed.

Jeremy put a hand on her shoulder. His voice betrayed the utter exhaustion and defeat beneath the surface of his calm demeanor. "Sasha, please."

"They're not!" she said, voice high-pitched. "Kayleigh hated Felicia because she was more talented, better liked, and she wasn't a liar!"

Dave surged forward, and the uniformed officer stepped directly into his path, blocking him. "Are we really going to do this again now? Over a stupid story? Our daughter is missing!"

Shelly said, "Dave."

Sasha said, "At least she might still be alive! Our baby is dead! She didn't deserve this. She didn't. She was good, not like your—"

Dave lunged toward them, but the uniformed officer held him back.

Noah said, "Let's get the Evanses into the conference room."

Dave shouted over him. "What the hell are you talking about? Are you trying to say Kayleigh deserves to die? Why? Because of some stupid shit she did in English class? Are you serious, lady? She apologized for that. We punished her. Why are you bringing up this old shit? It's got nothing to do with what's happening now."

"It's not fair! Our baby should still be here!" Sasha snarled as the other officer ushered her and Jeremy out of the lobby.

"And our Kayleigh shouldn't?" Dave hollered after them.

Shelly's voice was barely a whisper. "That doesn't—that's got nothing to do with Kayleigh."

The door slammed behind the other couple. Noah said, "I'll handle the Evans parents."

Josie nodded as he disappeared behind them, leaving her alone in the lobby with the Patchetts and the uniformed officer. Dave paced back and forth, pushing a hand through his hair. His face was flushed. Sweat gleamed along his forehead. Shelly quietly wiped tears from her cheeks.

Josie said, "Let me get a room ready and we can sit down and talk."

Shelly said, "We heard that a young woman had been found dead. We didn't know—we thought it might be Kayleigh. No one had called us. We heard, from other parents, that it was Felicia, but we had no way of confirming that, so we came here to find out if it was true or not. I needed to know. I needed to hear it from someone official that it wasn't Kayleigh. Then we saw Felicia's parents. We didn't expect them. I know it's just terrible, but we were relieved that it wasn't Kayleigh."

Josie said, "I think any parent would be relieved to find out that it wasn't their child who had been killed."

Dave stopped pacing but his face was even ruddier than before. "Is it the same guy? Did the same guy who took Kayleigh kill Felicia?"

"We don't know that for sure," Josie said. "We believe that it was the same man, but we have no proof. Not yet."

Dave pointed a finger at Josie. "What the hell are you doing? Where is Kayleigh? Why haven't you found her yet? You found Felicia! Why not our daughter? You're all just standing around with your thumbs up your asses while our daughter— while Kayleigh—you aren't even looking for her!"

"Mr. Patchett, we're doing everything we can," Josie said. "We're waiting for evidence to be processed and we're following up on some leads. Believe me, this department is working around the clock to locate Kayleigh."

The uniformed officer watched Dave carefully as he glared

at Josie. "This Woodsman is out there kidnapping and killing kids and you're all just sitting on your asses."

Josie worked hard to maintain her composure. "Mr. and Mrs. Patchett," she said, casting about for some way to change the subject, to distract Dave so that maybe he would calm down. "We found some text messages between Kayleigh and Felicia on Felicia's phone. There was some dispute over a story. It seems like you and Felicia's parents were also arguing about it."

"We weren't," Shelly said. "I don't even know why they had to bring it up. It was resolved."

"Can you tell me what happened?"

Dave said, "Good lord. You're really something, you know that? Wasting our time asking dumb questions when you could be looking for our daughter. I'm sick and tired of hearing about this damn story. No one cares! It doesn't matter! Why don't you just do your fucking jobs!"

With that, he stormed out of the station. Josie silently scolded herself. She'd done the exact opposite of defusing the situation. She'd dealt with hotheads like Dave Patchett before, but it had never gone so badly. Either the stress of the case or her sleep deprivation, or both, were starting to get to her. She tried to reset and refocus.

Shelly watched her husband go, eyes wide with shock. When she turned back to Josie, her cheeks were colored with embarrassment. "I'm sorry," she muttered. "He's just—"

"A father whose daughter is missing?" Josie filled in. "It's fine. Mrs. Patchett, I know that some of the things we ask seem strange and irrelevant but in investigations like these, we never know what might lead to something useful. In the texts that Kayleigh sent to Felicia, she was extremely upset." Josie stopped short of telling Shelly that Kayleigh had used the threat of her boyfriend to make Felicia pay for stealing her story.

Shelly cleared her throat. She glanced at the front doors, as if expecting her husband to burst back in, but only the uniformed officer stood there, as if guarding the entrance. "Everyone was upset. Us most of all. We didn't think we raised a child who would lie on such a grand scale."

"What do you mean?"

Shelly twisted her purse strap in her hands. "There was a writing contest at school. All the girls in the after-school club submitted a story. The winner of the writing award would be guaranteed a slot at Denton University's Youth Summer Writing Program. It was a big deal. Kind of like when I was young, we had Governor's School. Do you remember that?"

For years, the Commonwealth of Pennsylvania's governor's office had sponsored summer programs in various subjects where specially chosen students from all over the state could join. They went away for several weeks each summer, like they were going away to college, and they worked on their craft. Josie had never been interested in them, but she remembered how prestigious they were, how hard they were to get into, and how much other students at her high school coveted spots. "Yes," Josie said. "I remember."

"Sasha—Felicia's mom—went to the Governor's School for the Arts when she was in high school. She's a pharmaceutical rep now, but whatever. Anyway, the Governor's School for the Arts was discontinued in 2005, but Denton University hosts something very similar each year—for young writers."

"Did Kayleigh want to go?" asked Josie.

"Yes. After she joined that after-school club she got it into her head that she should go. We told her that she needed to focus on softball. She should let someone who had been inter-ested in writing for longer try for the spot. She said she was interested in stories. She's always said that, but we've never seen any stories. Plus, her English grades have never been that great.

Dave didn't even want her to join that after-school club, but Kayleigh promised she'd try harder at softball if we let her. Somehow, she convinced him. Huge mistake. Like I said, the students submitted stories and when the teacher saw the submissions, she realized that both Kayleigh and Felicia had submitted the exact same story. The teacher confronted them. Both girls said it was their original story. There was really no way to tell whose story it was but let's face it, aside from that club, Kayleigh doesn't write even though she claims she always wanted to. We had already told her not to enter."

Josie thought about the texts between the girls. Felicia had borderline admitted to stealing the story. "Did you ask Kayleigh if she had written the story?"

Shelly looked surprised. "Why would we do that? It wasn't her story."

"How did you know that it wasn't hers?" asked Josie, now feeling like she was going out on a limb. For her purposes, it didn't matter at all whose story it was, it only mattered that Kayleigh had told Felicia that her boyfriend would kill her for taking it and passing it off as her own.

Shelly's gaze swept the floor. "Sometimes with your kids you have to be brutally honest. This is going to sound harsh to you, but it's the truth. That story was too good to be Kayleigh's. Felicia insisted she had written it. Felicia's mom had gone to Governor's School. She said that Felicia always wrote stories, since she was a little girl. It was clear to everyone that Felicia had written it."

"What was the story about?" asked Josie.

Shelly waved a hand in the air. "I don't remember that well. Evidently it was a fantasy story."

"In these messages between the girls, Kayleigh says it was her 'SJ' story. Does that mean anything to you?"

"No. I don't know what that means."

"Felicia won the award, didn't she? As well as the spot in the program?"

"Yes," said Shelly. More tears slid down her face. "Now she won't even be able to go."

THIRTY-NINE

Josie stopped in the first-floor breakroom after Shelly Patchett left. The coffee pot had one cup left in it, but it was thick and smelled scorched. Josie turned the coffeemaker off and took the pot to the sink to rinse it out. She was mentally calculating which would take longer—cleaning it and brewing a new pot or walking down to Komorrah's, when Noah walked in. "There you are," he said. "Everything go okay?"

Josie used a sponge to scrub the bottom of the coffee pot. Flakes of burnt coffee came off its glass surface. "Dave Patchett thinks we're incompetent and lazy but other than that, I suppose."

She told him about her conversation with Shelly.

He leaned against the doorway, crossing his arms over his chest. "Interesting."

"What did the Evanses want?"

"They just had a lot of questions about how this works—a murder investigation. They also spent a lot of time complaining about the Patchetts. I think it was easier to focus on them than the loss of their daughter. They were upset that Kayleigh had accused Felicia of plagiarism, even though from the text exchange between the two girls you showed me upstairs, it looks like Kayleigh was right."

"And her own parents didn't even believe her," Josie said.

"Pretty sad," Noah agreed.

"Did you happen to ask them what an SJ story was?"

"They didn't know. Maybe it has something to do with the after-school program. I'm not sure it really matters."

Josie got the last of the scorched coffee remnants out of the pot and started rinsing the soap from it. "I guess it doesn't. What really matters is trying to locate this boyfriend. Especially since he made threats, according to Kayleigh."

Josie filled the coffee pot up with fresh water and dumped it into the reservoir. "It's just strange to me that Kayleigh had proof and didn't use it. Even Felicia basically admitted that Kayleigh had the proof."

"Felicia bluffed on having screenshotted her other stories."

"If those stories were sick, like Felicia said, then it wasn't for school."

"Right," Noah said, crossing the room and opening the overhead cabinet next to Josie. He fished out the coffee and handed it to Josie. "They had to be somewhere that Felicia could access them and screenshot them. Where would—"

Josie froze midway through scooping coffee into the filter. "An app! Noah, the story Felicia stole—all of Kayleigh's stories —were on an app. I can't believe I didn't notice."

"Notice what?"

"They've both got the same app on their phones: StoryJot. The Patchetts told me it was an app where Kayleigh could read fan fiction from her favorite video games. An app that allows for fan fiction would be an app where users could both read stories and write their own. The content must be user-generated. The SJ story. It has to be StoryJot. Kayleigh uploaded a story to the app and Felicia stole it and passed it off as her own. Can you get

Kayleigh's phone from the evidence locker and meet me at my desk?"

"Of course."

Josie abandoned the coffee, her adrenaline driving her back up the stairs to her desk, where Felicia's phone waited. The StoryJot logo danced across the screen as the app opened.

It took a couple of minutes for her to familiarize herself with it. It was not user-friendly. By the time Noah arrived with Kayleigh's phone, she had found the menu.

"This app has a messaging feature."

Noah wheeled his chair over to her desk and plopped into it, watching over her shoulder as she accessed Felicia's messages via the app. There were no personal messages, only messages from the app itself promoting particular stories and encouraging her to upload content. Evidently there was a ranking system according to how engaged you were on the app. Felicia had the lowest ranking, which meant she only read stories and hadn't uploaded any of her own.

Noah handed her Kayleigh's phone. "Try hers instead."

Kayleigh had been far more active on StoryJot. Her ranking was high. She'd read thousands of stories by other users and uploaded almost one hundred of her own. Her private mailbox was filled. The messages appeared in the app more like conversations and were listed by the name of the user she'd been messaging with. They were ranked according to the person she messaged with the most—that person receiving five stars after their name and the conversation sitting in the top of the inbox.

"Look, the user Kayleigh messaged the most is someone named Ajax2733." Josie held the phone closer to Noah. "Look at Kayleigh's username. AshesLove887."

"That's got to be the boyfriend," Noah said. "Maybe his name is Ash? Ash's Love. As in his love interest." He pointed to her username. "Looks like she changed it about a year ago."

Josie tapped it to see Kayleigh's profile. A note beneath it read "modified" with a date that was mid-May of last year. She clicked to see the history. "She used to be StoryGirl887. So she met him and changed her username."

"Let's look at the messages," said Noah.

Josie went back into the messaging feature and opened the conversation between Kayleigh and Ajax2733. The most recent messages were at the top, but she decided to start from the beginning, scrolling back until her thumb ached.

"Wow," said Noah. "These two were in constant contact."

Josie shook her head. "This was pretty smart though, on Kayleigh's part, since her parents are so strict, and on the boyfriend's part, too. Even though the age of consent here is sixteen, he's still dating a minor. Rather than having a trail of texts or social media messages, which are the first thing that anyone would check—her parents and us—he keeps the contact here in a story app."

"Kind of like how pedophiles use gaming systems to chat with and message with kids," Noah pointed out.

Josie finally came to the beginning of the messages. Ajax2733 had initiated contact, leaving Kayleigh a message that said:

> *I've read everything on your profile. I can't get enough. I hope you'll be uploading new content soon. You're brilliant. Your command of language is impressive and your fearlessness in tackling taboo subjects leaves me wanting more. Forever your fan, Ajax*

"Does he know at this point that Kayleigh is a minor?" asked Noah. "What kind of information about users is available?"

"He wouldn't have known that. Users can only upload avatars. Geographic location is optional, but Kayleigh's was listed as here in Denton. Other than that, all they can share is a few lines as a bio, but from what I gleaned from a brief look at this app before you came up is that most users simply designate whether they're a reader, writer, or both, and the subjects they like to read or write about."

"But her original username had the words 'Story' and 'Girl' in it," Noah said. "I wonder what taboo subject she wrote about."

"Not really the point," said Josie, scrolling through several more messages. For a month Ajax and Kayleigh exchanged messages solely about Kayleigh's stories, with Ajax going into great detail about what he loved and why. From the conversations, it appeared that Kayleigh wrote about sex a lot which probably explained Ajax's sudden and fervent interest. At some point, they decided to meet.

Ajax: *I don't want to make you uncomfortable, and feel free to say no, but your stories really turn me on. I'd love to meet.*

Kayleigh: *I was hoping you would ask. Of course I want to meet you.*

Ajax: *I feel so connected to you. I need to see you in person.*

Kayleigh: *What if I am a disappointment in person? Most people seem to think I am.*

Ajax: *Then most people are assholes. I don't know how anyone could know what's in your amazing mind and think you are disappointing.*

They set up a meeting time, after one of Kayleigh's shifts at Timber Creek, at the same coffee shop that Josie and Olivia had gone to. Josie looked at the date of the proposed meet-up. It was nearly a year ago. There wouldn't be any security camera footage now. After agreeing to meet, there was a lull. Kayleigh messaged him but he didn't message back. After four attempts to re-establish contact with him, he finally answered.

> Kayleigh: *I knew it. I was a disappointment to you in person. You could at least grow a spine and just say so instead of ghosting me.*

> Ajax: *That's not true at all. You were anything but a disappointment. You were everything I hoped for and more in person. I can't stop thinking about you. I want to see you all the time, but you must realize that things are complicated. We live in different worlds. We're too different for this to work in the real world. At least, for now.*

Then came lengthy conversations on the subject of whether or not they should see one another again although rather than saying that Kayleigh was sixteen, Ajax continued to say that she was "too different."

Noah gave a low whistle. "This guy really knew what he was doing."

"Classic grooming," Josie said. "Clearly, Kayleigh's got self-esteem issues. She puts him on notice of that immediately, telling him she's a disappointment to most people. He's laying it on thick though with the 'you're everything I hoped for and more' and 'I can't stop thinking about you.'"

"I think the only thing he missed was 'you're so special,'" Noah grumbled.

Josie sighed. "I'm sure if we scroll long enough that'll be here, too."

"He seems like he's trying to break it off so she'll be even more inclined to want to be with him. Forbidden love. Except this guy is so careful, he won't ever explicitly say that she's a minor. They're just 'different.'"

"Exactly." Josie scrolled through more messages. Eventually, they decided to return to their original app-based relationship where he read her stories and they discussed them. In the weeks after that, Kayleigh offered him story after story and finally, he messaged to say that he couldn't resist her and agreed to see her under certain conditions.

Ajax: *We have to keep this secret. Everything. Even the fact that we talk about stories.*

Kayleigh: *Even that? Why?*

Ajax: *If you want to do this, really do this, I need you to not ask questions. Don't you want to be together?*

Kayleigh: *Of course. More than anything. These last weeks have been hell not being able to see you.*

Ajax: *Then everything is a secret. For now. I promise this protects us both. You have to agree to do everything I ask.*

Kayleigh: *Fine. I promise.*

Ajax: *All of our communication should be here, on SJ. No texts or calls or emails or social media or anything like that. Just here. Do you promise?*

Kayleigh: *Promise. When can I see you?*

Another meeting was set up. Kayleigh was to meet him on a city street after one of her shifts. Most of the messages after that were about stories. Every so often, Kayleigh would message something like, "last night was amazing," but Ajax would turn the conversation back to something she'd written. There was a spat once she changed her username. He was afraid people would ask questions, but Kayleigh insisted that no one who knew her even knew she was active on the app. There were messages setting up meetings and dates and late-night trysts. Then more exchanges about her stories. Ajax started editing them for her and Kayleigh began writing less about sex and more about other things, culminating in a short story called "Bumper Cars," which, based on Ajax's notes, was about two sisters on a family vacation where one got left behind at the bumper cars. Later, she began dabbling in fantasy stories, writing a story about two sisters poised to inherit a magical kingdom from their parents.

"They're talking here about the story Felicia took," Josie said. "Based on these exchanges, I'd say that Kayleigh did write it."

Reading along with her, Noah said, "Yeah, these are intense editing notes."

"This doesn't help us, though." Josie kept going until she found the messages where Kayleigh told Ajax about the plagiarism, including the drama that had taken place in school, and the fact that Kayleigh's parents didn't believe her and never even considered that she could have written something good enough to earn a spot at a writing program. Ajax was supportive and consoling and offered several lessons on copyright law until Kayleigh said she was going to use their messages and her upload history on StoryJot to prove that she had written the story.

Ajax turned downright mean at that point. *You cannot use these messages or anything from StoryJot. You cannot show them to your parents or anyone else. If you do, it's over between us.*

Kayleigh: *Are you serious? I thought you were on my side. It's literally the only way that I can prove that I'm telling the truth and that Felicia stole my story!*

Ajax: *If you show anyone your account on this app, we are over. If anyone comes asking me about it, or your story, I will tell them I don't know you.*

Kayleigh: *Who even are you right now? Why are you acting like this? You're the one who told me all that stuff about copyrights. It's my story! I can prove it! You can help me prove it!*

Ajax: *At what cost? Let's be frank. If people found out about us, I could get in serious trouble. You know that. You've always known that. That's why I didn't want to be together in the first place.*

Kayleigh: *That's not what you said. You said we were too different.*

Ajax: *I was right. We must be too different if you can't understand where I am coming from with this. You're talking about one story. I'm talking about my life.*

Kayleigh: *I'm talking about my life, too. That award and the summer program could change my life.*

Ajax: *You can always write more stories. You can go to college. This one thing isn't going to change anything for you but if you expose me, my life is completely over. If you really love me, you can sacrifice this one story for me. There are other ways to make Felicia pay.*

Like what? Kayleigh had written. *What other ways? Wait, I know! What if I wrote a story so good and so big that it went viral? Then she couldn't steal it from me.*

Don't be a child, Ajax had responded. *That's not even possible. There are other ways.*

"Here we go," Noah said, an edge of excitement to his voice.

But Ajax never offered any other ways. He didn't threaten Felicia or say he would kill her. He didn't say anything at all. "He's too smart," Josie said. "He'd never make threats in writing. Not after going to so much trouble to keep his relationship with Kayleigh secret."

"Then we've got to find this guy and talk to him. Let's prepare a warrant for StoryJot and see if we can get user information or an IP address over the phone."

"That could take forever," Josie said. "If we can get the IP address right away, we could probably track him down, as long as he's not using any sophisticated program to block or hide it."

"Even if we have to wait, it could still help us find this guy. What if the DNA from Felicia's body comes back and it's not Henry Thomas?" Noah said. "What if we're wrong about him, and this Ajax is the person we need to be looking for? We'll already have this in the works."

Josie explored the app. "True. I'm just saying with some of these online outfits, trying to get any human on the line is frustrating. This one is popular but it's not that popular. Remember when we tried to get information out of that review website on the Collins case? It was almost impossible."

"That was a website," Noah pointed out. "This is an app with tens of thousands of users. Someone out there is running it. They've got to have a legal department. We just have to find it."

"They don't even have a customer service number. They

want you to fill out this 'contact us' form and wait five to seven days for an answer, even for legal inquiries!"

Noah stood and wheeled his chair back to his own desk to write the warrant. Josie looked up to see him grinning at her. "What?" she said.

"You always find ways around that sort of thing. Just do what you do."

FORTY

I'm right under their noses and they don't see me. So much care has been taken to make sure that the police would not capture me and yet, they seem to know nothing. Just yesterday, the Chief of Police was on television attempting to discredit me, saying that I'm not real. I certainly showed him. Yet, even with my latest kill, the news reports spend more time asking questions and speculating about the investigation than reporting anything at all. At least they are still talking about me. The entire city is in my grip. Fear is a haze that thickens the Denton air. The police can say what they wish.

I will not be denied.

FORTY-ONE

It took twenty-four hours to get the information they needed from StoryJot. Josie did an internet deep dive on the app and its founder. Lucky for her, it was a US-based company. The founder was from California, so she searched the state's corporation database to find an address and phone number for the company so they could serve the warrant before she went home to sleep—or not—for the night. Thursday morning, at the stationhouse, Noah waited until mid-morning due to the time difference to call them to follow up, impressing upon their legal department that getting the information about user Ajax2733 might very well be a matter of life and death. By mid-afternoon, after Noah made several more calls, StoryJot released the IP address to them by phone. The subscriber information would take longer. Josie's heart raced as she punched the IP into a database. Sometimes the IP address search could give them a fairly specific location and other times, the area it belonged to was too wide to be of any use. Relief sent her heartbeat ticking upward even more when she got the results—an address. She read off the address as she entered it into a separate database. "This IP address is coming from Romig's," she said.

"The bar?" Noah said. He circled the collective desks to look over her shoulder. She could smell a whiff of his cologne and coffee on his breath.

"Yeah." She pulled up a map and pointed to its location.

"That's pretty damn close to where Felicia Evans's body was found. I think there are apartments over the top of that bar."

"I'll call the owner and find out," said Josie. "I know him from a few cases. He's a good guy."

Fifteen minutes later, she pumped a fist into the air. "Got him! Asher Jackson Jenks. Twenty years old."

"Let's go."

While Noah drove, Josie used the Mobile Data Terminal to pull up a driver's license photo for Asher Jackson Jenks. It was difficult to tell if it was the same person they'd seen in the photos from Kayleigh's phone, but he had shaggy brown hair. His eyes were a dull blue. He had no criminal record and he'd lived over Romig's bar since he was eighteen. Romig's was one of Denton's oldest bars, located on a strip of road about four miles from the Stacks. The owner had taken one of the two-story houses along the road and converted it into a bar. It had gray siding. The front door was now an emergency exit and a door along the side had been installed as the bar entrance. The windows on the first floor were blacked out. Wooden stairs had been affixed to two sides of the building, leading to the apartments on top.

Happy hour was just beginning. Music blared from the bar, so loud that the air around the building seemed to pulse. Noah cruised through the parking lot out front, which was packed with cars, and circled the building. The parking lot out back was even more crowded with vehicles. Josie spotted Asher Jenks's Subaru among them. It was blocked in by two other vehicles. Noah found a spot next to the dumpster and they got out. The stairs leading to the apartments trembled along with the bass of the song coming from inside the bar. Josie felt it through her feet and in her hands when she grabbed onto the railings.

Behind her, Noah said, "How does this guy sleep?"

At the top of the steps, Josie used a fist to pound against the door, hoping that if Asher was inside, he would hear it over the music. A long moment passed, and she pounded once more. She waited a beat longer and as she was about to try again, the door swung open. Asher Jenks stood before them in a Nirvana T-shirt, a pair of cargo shorts, and bare feet. A thin moustache clung to his upper lip. A line creased his forehead as he looked from Josie to Noah and back. He had to raise his voice to be heard over the music. "Who are you?"

They produced their credentials. He studied them for a moment and then pointed to the ground. "It's the bar."

"What?" said Noah.

"The noise violation," he said. "It's the bar. I'm not the owner or anything, I just rent this place."

Josie said, "We're not here for a noise violation. Are you Asher Jackson Jenks?"

One corner of his mouth lifted. "Are you middle-naming me? What kind of mom shit is that?"

"Are you Asher Jackson Jenks?" Noah repeated as if he hadn't spoken.

"Yeah, but everyone just calls me Ash."

"Not J.J.?" said Josie.

"You mean A.J.?"

"No," said Josie. She stopped and waved a hand around them. "Mr. Jenks, it's really difficult to talk with the noise from the bar. We'd like you to come with us to the Denton police station."

He pressed a hand to his chest. "Me? What for?"

Noah said, "We need to speak to you about Kayleigh Patchett."

"Who?"

Josie couldn't decide if he was being genuine or if he had rehearsed not reacting to Kayleigh's name. While he awaited their answer, he started cracking his knuckles.

"The teenage girl who was abducted over the weekend," Noah replied. "Right here in Denton."

"Is that the girl on the news?" he said.

Deflection, distraction. He was buying time, Josie thought. She said, "Mr. Jenks, please come with us."

More knuckle-cracking. He looked behind them, out at the parking lot. "I really don't think—"

"Now," Josie said.

He stared at her for a beat and then gave a half-shrug. "Sure, okay. But my car is blocked in."

Noah smiled. "We'll give you a ride."

"Uh, sure, okay. Let me get my shoes. Hang on."

FORTY-TWO

Unlike Henry Thomas, Asher Jenks was not at all relaxed inside the interview room, even after Josie and Noah offered him food and drink. He sat in the same chair that Thomas had occupied less than a week ago, legs spread, elbows resting on his thighs. This time, Josie could actually hear his knuckles cracking. Every few seconds, he shifted, turning the chair and pulling it up to the table, putting his elbows on top of it. Below the tabletop, his heels bobbed up and down. *Crack, crack, crack* went his knuckles. Josie sat next to him, Noah across from him. She read him his Miranda rights. When she asked if he understood them as she had read them, he said, "Whoa! Am I under arrest or something?"

"No," said Noah. "We're here to talk."

"Do I need a lawyer though?"

Josie said, "Do you think you need a lawyer?"

"I don't know. I was just at home chilling and you guys showed up and brought me here. I don't know what's going on."

"Would you like a lawyer?" Josie asked pointedly.

Crack, crack. He looked around the room, shifted in his

chair, and then met her eyes. "I haven't done anything wrong, so no."

Noah said, "Do you understand these rights as we've read them to you?"

"Yes," Asher said.

Noah pushed his phone across the table. A photo of Kayleigh Patchett filled the screen. "When is the last time you saw Kayleigh?" he asked.

Asher gave the photo a brief glance. *Crack, crack.* "On the news. I saw her on the news. You brought me here to talk about some kid who went missing?"

"She was abducted," Josie corrected. "Asher, we know that the two of you were seeing each other."

He narrowed his eyes and laughed. "Seeing each other? Did you guys get drunk at the bar before you came up to my place? Isn't this kid sixteen years old?"

Josie said, "You know exactly how old she is, Asher. We know that the two of you had some sort of relationship. We found photos of you on her phone."

He shook his head. *Crack, crack, crack.* "Nope. Not possible. I never met this kid in person. I'm sorry she's missing and all, but I don't know anything about that."

Josie looked over at Noah. The silent communication took only seconds. They wouldn't show him the photos. The truth was that there was nothing in any of those photos that could definitively prove that Asher was the person in them. Noah went for their ace. "We've got a year's worth of messages between you and Kayleigh on StoryJot, Asher. Or should we call you Ajax2733?"

He didn't respond this time. *Crack, crack.* He pushed the chair away from the table, all the way to the wall, and leaned back in it, lacing his fingers together across his stomach. Josie inched her chair closer to him. "Asher, I understand that you don't want to admit to having a relationship with a minor, but we already know that you were dating Kayleigh Patchett when she was abducted. You can lie to us as much as you want but right after I leave this room, I'm going to go to my desk and prepare some warrants. We're going to search your home, your car, your electronic devices—all of it. I think we both know what we're going to find, so let's cut the shit. Make this easy on yourself and start telling us the truth."

Crack, crack. He pushed his rear end back so that he was sitting up straighter. The back of his skull pressed into the wall.

Noah said, "Asher, what do you do for a living?"

Surprise at the change in questioning loosened his posture. He seemed relieved to find Noah looking at him from across the table. "I'm a T.A. at Denton U."

"A teaching assistant," Noah said, as if he were impressed. "Really? What's your major?"

"I'm a double major," he said. "English and Philosophy."

Josie said, "That pays the rent?"

He laughed, a little more relaxed now. "No. My student loans pay the rent. The T.A. gig feeds me. Also, I help out with cleaning down at the bar—after hours—and the owner takes some off my rent. It's already pretty cheap because of the noise."

"I guess the English major helped when you were editing Kayleigh's stories."

He hesitated, looking to Noah as if for help.

Josie said, "The longer you deny your relationship with her, the worse it looks for you, Ash."

No response.

Abruptly, Josie stood, her chair scraping the tile. She looked at Noah. "Lieutenant, I'll go prepare those warrants now."

She didn't look back, letting the door slam behind her. Slipping into the CCTV room next door, she watched as Noah sat in the chair she had just vacated. *Crack, crack, crack* went

Asher's knuckles. He lifted his chin toward the door. "Is she serious?"

Noah gave a slow nod. "I'm afraid so. That's the job. Listen, I don't want to be here any more than you do but I don't have a choice. She's right. We've got your messages from StoryJot, and even though there's nothing criminal about them—I mean, they're pretty benign, and even if they weren't, the age of consent in PA is sixteen, so you're all good there—we've still got to do our due diligence. Pretty young teenage girl goes missing? They've got us turning this whole city upside down. Gotta cross all of our 'T's and dot all of our 'I's, you know what I mean?"

Asher studied Noah, whose personality had transformed in a matter of seconds. From where Josie sat, he no longer resembled her husband. A smirk twitched on his lips. He spread his limbs, legs splayed—manspreading, Gretchen called it—one elbow over the back of his chair while his other arm rested on the table, spinning a pen around. He let a few seconds go by and then he said, "You remember that crazy case a while back? All those girls? Oh, maybe not. You were, what? Twelve at the time?"

"You mean, Murder Mountain?"

Noah nodded, kept the pen spinning. "Yeah, that's the one. Ever since that case, our boss is insane about missing persons, and you know, some other teenage girl was found dead in the woods Tuesday morning. Shit's been crazy lately."

Crack, crack. "So you guys are really going to look at all my stuff? My apartment? My car?"

"They'll probably start with your phone and any other devices you have—laptop, tablet, whatever. Go from there. But yeah, eventually they'll want a look at your apartment and car and all that. The whole city's on high alert, you know? We gotta check out everyone. It's like the process of elimination, you know? We talk to parents, neighbors, friends, classmates, teachers, anyone Kayleigh was dating. Find out what everyone knows, hope it will give us some direction. Now with this other girl getting killed…"

Noah sighed heavily and pulled his phone from his pocket. It appeared to be a monumental effort for him to punch in his passcode and pull up the photo of Felicia Evans. "You recognize her?"

Asher studied the photo and shook his head. "No."

Noah nodded and took his phone back. "She's the one who stole Kayleigh's story. Felicia."

No response.

"Must have been rough when that went down. Kayleigh seemed like she was pretty upset. She bend your ear a lot? My wife goes nonstop when something pisses her off."

Josie laughed. It was a lie but still, Noah's new persona was convincing.

"Listen," Asher said, lowering his voice, "I did help Kayleigh with her stuff, okay? She's actually a really good writer. Really advanced for her age. But we weren't dating. Kayleigh had a crush on me, I'll admit that, but we never crossed a line."

Josie thought back to the messages. If they were presented in a courtroom, could a defense attorney make the case that they didn't point to a sexual relationship? It would likely never come to that, since the age of consent was sixteen, except that Kayleigh had been fifteen when they started seeing one another. If a prosecutor wanted to make an issue out of that, they could, but the messages were too vague to prove anything.

"Oh, come on. Pretty girl like that?" Noah said, without missing a beat. "You're only what? Four years apart? That's nothing. Hell, I'm three years younger than my wife."

"But you're what? In your forties?"

Noah laughed. "Thirties! Damn, man. I didn't think I looked that bad."

Asher shook his head. "Sorry. Your thirties. My point is that you're an adult. Yeah, Kayleigh and I aren't that far apart in age and legally she can consent to a relationship but she's still in high school, you know? It doesn't look good for me."

"Okay," Noah said. "I get it. You don't want people to know you're dating a high-schooler."

Asher cracked his knuckles again, but he didn't deny it.

Noah kept spinning his pen as if he didn't have a care in the world. "All right. Well, like I said, due diligence and all. I've still got to ask you some questions. You okay with that?"

"Your crazy partner out there? Is she still gonna look at my shit?"

"Nothing I can do about that, my friend," Noah said with a sigh. "My advice? With these things, it's always best to answer everything truthfully the first time. Don't give us a reason to come back and knock on your door again." He waggled an eyebrow and gave a subtle nod toward the door. "You understand?"

Asher looked at the door, as if expecting to see Josie there. The kid clearly had an issue with women, which was probably why he was dating a teenage girl. "Yeah, yeah. I get it. What do you want to know?"

"When is the last time you saw Kayleigh Patchett?"

Crack, crack went his knuckles. "Uh, like, a week and a half ago? It was during the week. I picked her up from where she works, and we hung out. Her parents punished her for some shit, so we couldn't see each other for a while."

His answer lined up with the messages he and Kayleigh had exchanged on StoryJot.

"Has she ever been to your apartment?"

Asher shook his head. *Crack, crack.* "Come on, man."

"My colleagues are going to search your apartment. They'll find her DNA. What I want to know is will they find it because you were seeing her and had her over as a guest, or because you abducted her?"

Asher's spine straightened. "What? Are you kidding? I didn't abduct her! Yeah, she's been there a few times. To hang out, and she was free to come and go as she pleased."

"Okay, okay," said Noah. "That's good to know. Where were you on Saturday? From nine a.m. to five p.m.?"

"I was home. It was a Saturday. I went down to help set up the bar around one in the afternoon. You can confirm that with the bartender, Saundra. Saundra Fish."

"Good, good," said Noah. "How about overnight Monday into Tuesday?"

Asher's eyes narrowed. "What? I was home, asleep, like most normal people. What the hell kind of question is that?"

Noah changed track. "Let's talk about your place. We know we'll find evidence that Kayleigh's been there, so that won't be a surprise. What else are we going to find, Ash?"

"What do you mean?"

Noah smiled. "What will we find that you wouldn't want the police to find? Remember, telling the truth now helps you out and saves us multiple visits to you."

Asher sighed. "Shit, man. If I've got something I don't want you guys to find, then I'm fucked. You're going to find it anyway."

"So just tell me now."

"You gonna bust me over it?"

"Depends on what it is," Noah said. "But your cooperation in the search for Kayleigh will be noted."

Another sigh, this one heavier. "I've got some drugs, okay? Some ecstasy, a little Oxy, and weed. And some beer. I know I'm not twenty-one yet, but I live above a bar. Like I said, I help clean and set up. I see some things and I take them, okay?"

"You ever give weed to Kayleigh?"

"I'm not answering that."

Josie took that as a yes. Noah did as well but knew better

than to push, since Asher's posture had already tightened up. His knees knocked together, and his shoulders curled inward.

Moving on, Noah asked, "Ash, you ever do any hunting or trapping?"

Asher gave a nervous laugh. "You're all over the place, man. When I was in high school, I used to go with my dad. He was super into it, I wasn't. I was into books. He thought I was a pussy. That's why I left home right after high school. That's why I'm putting myself through college."

"You and Kayleigh connected over books," Noah said, bringing the questioning back to Kayleigh. "You both like reading and writing."

"Yeah," Asher said.

"From the messages we've got between you two on StoryJot, it seems like you're both pretty serious writers."

Asher shrugged. "Yeah, sure."

"It was pretty shitty when Felicia Evans stole Kayleigh's story. You knew she'd written it. You edited it, didn't you?"

"Several times, yeah."

"But you didn't want to come forward on Kayleigh's behalf."

"Well, at first I told her she had some recourse through copyright law, but the more I thought about it, I realized she was just a kid, you know? If she wanted to go that route, she'd need an attorney and to get one, her parents would have to hire one. The last thing I needed was those two psychos finding out about me. So yeah, I didn't want to come forward. It was a dumb high school contest. She could sacrifice one story to protect our relationsh—to help me out."

"It wasn't just a story, though," Noah said. "Was it? Felicia Evans was admitted to Denton University's Youth Summer Writing Program on the strength of that story."

Asher looked at his feet. His hands twirled around one another at warp speed. *Crack, crack, crack.*

Noah added, "As someone whose father didn't understand his facility with words or his ambition to be a writer, I'd think that you of all people would understand how devastating it must have been for Kayleigh. Not only was her story stolen but her spot in that program."

"Sure," he mumbled. "I was upset for her. Of course. I'm not a monster."

"Did you tell her there were other ways to make Felicia pay?"

Asher's gaze swept back up toward Noah. "Well, yeah, but I meant that she should try some other way to expose Felicia. Like going onto TikTok or something and making one of those viral videos. Showing how she'd posted the story on StoryJot months before Felicia turned it in at school. I didn't mind her using StoryJot as long as she didn't involve me. No one would have to know I edited for her that way. She could prove it was hers, probably by the timestamp on the app."

"You never suggested that you approach Felicia directly?"

"What? Hell, no. I told you, I wasn't getting involved."

"You and Kayleigh never discussed you carrying out some sort of revenge on Felicia Evans? Even if she didn't know who you were?"

"Are you crazy, man? No."

"You never said you'd kill Felicia Evans?" Noah said.

Asher's face twisted in disbelief. "What? No. I never said that."

"Not even privately to Kayleigh? Maybe in a postcoital flush? You know as well as I do, men will say anything right after sex."

Asher's cheeks flamed. "No. I did not say that. I would not say that, and I sure as hell wouldn't threaten anyone with violence, certainly not a teenage girl."

"Okay." Noah took his phone out one more time, scrolling

and swiping until he found a photo of Henry Thomas. He turned it toward Asher. "Last question. You know this guy?"

Asher stared at the photo, giving a slow blink. He cracked his knuckles once more. Josie counted four seconds. He recognized Henry Thomas, and by the nervous glance he shot at Noah, he knew that Noah knew. He licked his lips. *Crack, crack.* "Um, he looks familiar."

"Okay," said Noah. "Where have you seen him?"

Crack, crack, crack. "Oh, I remember. He lives up on Murder Mountain. He's got like some cabin or something up there. Creepy as hell. Some of my friends thought it would be cool to drive up there and check it out. People think it's haunted. Anyway, we drove up there once, saw this driveway and we thought that's how you got into the fields. I mean, the city planted this whole field of flowers, you know? We thought that was the entrance, but then this dude comes out of this little log cabin and starts screaming at us to get the hell off his property. I thought he was going to kill us."

"You know his name?"

Asher looked at the photo again. *Crack.* "No, man. I only saw him that one time with my buddies and we got the hell out of there. He wasn't exactly inviting us in for drinks."

Noah nodded and took his time standing up. "Great. I'll go see where we are with those warrants."

FORTY-THREE

By the time they were ready to execute the search warrants on Asher Jackson Jenks's apartment and vehicle, Noah had gone home to rest, replaced by Gretchen. While Hummel's team used a flatbed truck to impound Asher's Subaru, Josie and Gretchen searched his apartment. It was small, cramped, over-flowing with books, and it reeked of fried food and stale beer. In his bedside table were condoms and lubricant. There were long brown hairs on the pillow beside his and a nearly full bottle of women's bodywash in his bathroom, but other than that, there was no evidence that he had abducted or killed Kayleigh Patch-ett, or that he had killed Felicia Evans, in spite of his apart-ment's proximity to the scene of her death. There were no snare traps or blood evidence. They found the drugs that Asher had mentioned. Not enough to charge him for possession with intent to distribute, but damn close. Josie was certain that he was Kayleigh's supplier. They took his devices into custody for processing, but Josie doubted they'd find anything that would suggest he was a killer.

He was too careful.

The shifts rotated again, with Noah relieving her late that

night. She went home to Trout, again taking him for a long walk and initiating a lengthy play session with him, hoping to wear herself out as much as him, but sleep still wouldn't come. Her eyes burned. Her limbs ached. Even her stomach rebelled, burning with acid no matter how many antacids she consumed. In bed with Trout snoring happily beside her, she lay awake, staring at the silver moonlight streaming through the windows, turning the case over in her head.

She had the sense that Asher Jackson Jenks, aka Ajax, was lying about something but she didn't know what. He had a connection to Kayleigh, and by extension, Felicia Evans, which he'd admitted to, and he'd gone to great lengths to hide his association with Kayleigh even though their relationship was not illegal. That level of deviousness and cunning would serve him well if he wanted to kill. He had admitted to having hunted and trapped, although his assertion that he had no affinity for it was believable. Henry Thomas also had experience trapping, and he still regularly associated with Morris Lauber whose trapping license was current. Henry had trapping equipment in his home even though, according to the ERT, all they'd found were footholds that were old and rusted. He was older than Asher, more sophisticated, and he had a prior conviction—a proven history of violence. He had no connection to Kayleigh other than the fact that Blue had followed her scent into his cabin. Not that proving a connection was necessary. If Henry Thomas was some kind of serial killer who hunted and trapped kids in the woods, his run-in with Kayleigh could have been random. Ballsy to do it in broad daylight only miles from his own home, but it still could have been random.

Still, Denton PD couldn't prove that either Thomas or Asher had taken Kayleigh or killed Felicia. Even if the DNA from the hair found in Henry Thomas's cabin came back as belonging to Kayleigh, they'd have enough to arrest him, but there were still pieces missing—like Kayleigh's body, for one. If the cases in the other counties and Felicia Evans's murder were connected to Kayleigh's abduction—and Josie believed they were—then the pattern dictated that Kayleigh had been killed. Josie considered the cases in Lenore and Montour Counties. It was difficult not to take them into account, but the fact was that they were out of Denton PD's jurisdiction. Even if she could prove that either Thomas or Asher were in those counties on the dates of the murders, that didn't help her solve her own cases.

As if sensing the tension radiating from her body, Trout woke, wriggled his body closer to hers, and gave a heavy sigh. She patted his back. "Sorry, buddy. I'm keeping you up, I guess."

She lay awake for another hour before finally picking up her phone. There were no text updates, not that she'd expected any. She thought about messaging Gretchen, Noah, or the Chief, but she knew they'd all tell her the same thing: get some rest. Instead, she downloaded StoryJot and opened an account.

She found Ajax2733's profile and scrolled through some of his stories. There weren't many, less than a dozen. All were boring, rambling, filled with verbose and florid language and about nothing; just characters sitting around, navel-gazing. One story featured a male character in a café, contemplating an orange. Another, more interesting story told the tale of an older male mentoring his much younger lover on the subject of literary criticism. The others very nearly put Josie to sleep. She made a mental note to come back to them in the future as sleep aids. Then she found Kayleigh's profile. She had uploaded almost one hundred stories, though some of them were considered flash fiction—only a paragraph or two. They went back two years. Each story was ranked by how many views it had, together with ratings. All of her stories had four- or five-star ratings. Josie wondered if it ever bothered Asher that his girlfriend, still in high school, had higher ratings and far more readers than his own stories.

Josie read through some of the stories, sorting them from oldest to newest instead of how they were ranked. Kayleigh's early stuff was fairly juvenile and focused solely on sex. It was clear on reading them that she had never actually *had* sex. Some of them were comical, as if she was trying to emulate the erotica books Josie had found in her room. Later, she dabbled in fantasy, writing tales of faraway kingdoms in magical, made-up lands filled with knights, princesses, and dragons. Many were violent, featuring sword fights that led to characters being dismembered and slain in battle. The descriptions were overly graphic, but again, knowing what Josie knew about the human body and how it could be injured and killed, not particularly realistic. She wondered if those were the stories that Felicia had referred to as "sick." There was certainly an element of shock value in them, and she was sure that Shelly and Dave Patchett would be horrified, but there wasn't anything more gruesome than any teenager might find on television. Her fantasy stories also had sex scenes which became more realistic as time went on. Josie could trace the realism in Kayleigh's erotic writing from her first meeting with Asher, per their messages. It was after she began her relationship with him that she began to write more stories based in real life. "Bumper Cars," the story that Asher had praised so highly in his messages to her, showed a vast leap in both maturity and style. Reading across Kayleigh's work, Josie could see how she'd improved; how hard she must have worked on her craft.

How devastating it must have been to have her work stolen and then have no one believe her. Not even her parents.

Trout stirred beside her, kicking his legs out toward the empty side of the bed, and squirming until he was pressed against her hip. Josie stroked his side with one hand as she found the story that Felicia Evans had passed off as her own.

Kayleigh had titled it "Reign." It was another fantasy tale, set in a magical kingdom ruled by a king and queen who were grooming their twin daughters to take over their rule one day—taking on the mantle together so that the king and queen would never have to choose between them. In order to prepare them for their reign, the daughters were tasked with various challenges—casting a banishment spell, learning to play an instrument, finding a rare, mystical flower called a *Saintpaulia ionantha* that would protect the kingdom from marauders for one hundred years, taming a dragon, and then battling a mythical creature that had the ability to shapeshift into any animal. Each challenge became harder than the last until the sisters came together to insist that their parents teach them the practical aspects of ruling a kingdom instead of sending them on harrowing and exhausting quests.

Josie could see some parallels between the story and the Patchett girls. She wondered if the quests were a metaphor for sports. It would certainly make sense given Kayleigh's aversion to continuing to play softball when she had no interest in it. Regardless, the writing was advanced and engaging. The theme of the sisters leaning on one another and coming together was admirable. Josie could see why it had won Felicia Evans an award.

And now none of it mattered because Felicia was dead, and Kayleigh was most likely dead as well.

Kayleigh. Felicia. The story. The Woodsman. Henry Thomas. Asher Jackson Jenks. The kids in Montour and Lenore Counties. The traps.

The carousel went round and round in Josie's mind. She kept waiting for something to click into place. Sometimes that happened. Sometimes there was a pattern or a clue that had been there all along but without the right context, it seemed meaningless.

Sometimes, you just had to go with the cold, hard, factual evidence.

Josie lay back, resting her head on the pillow. As the thoughts circled again, a drowsiness threatened to overtake her, if only she would let it. It was like a bird fluttering nearby, afraid to land. Would she give it a place to perch? Some errant thought about the cases flitted through her mind, jolting her awake, scaring the bluebird of sleepiness away entirely. But when she tried to catch it, to remember it, she couldn't.

It was gone.

She let out a stream of expletives.

Trout rustled again. This time, his head popped up, ears pointed. A low growl emanated from his throat. "What is it, boy?" Josie whispered. She closed out of the StoryJot app and checked the security system app on her phone to see Noah at the front door, putting his key in the lock. "Daddy's home," she told Trout.

He jumped out of the bed. Seconds later, she heard his nails clicking along the steps. She listened as he and Noah went through the ritual they'd developed for whenever Noah arrived home from work—or anywhere. She heard Noah in the kitchen and then in the yard, letting Trout out and bringing him back inside, then opening and closing the fridge. Finally, he came up the steps. As he walked into the bedroom, he said, "Why are you still up?"

Josie looked at the clock beside her bed. She'd lost track of time. It was after three in the morning. "Couldn't sleep. Why are you home?"

"Chief sent me home. We're kind of at an impasse. We've questioned everyone and their mother, collected a shit-ton of evidence and now we're just waiting for something to break. He said I needed rest. Like you."

Trout hopped up onto the bed and curled up at Josie's feet. Noah started pulling off his clothes and dropping them into the hamper until he was wearing nothing but his boxers. Exhausted though she was, Josie couldn't help but admire him as he climbed into bed next to her, positioned on his side. "Josie," he said. "You can't keep going like this. Did you talk to Dr. Rosetti?"

"Of course I did," she said, eyes drawn to the puckered flesh at his right shoulder. She'd given him the scar when she shot him. It had been during the case that led them all to what the Denton teens now called "Murder Mountain." At the time, Josie hadn't known who to trust, and she'd been focused on saving a very damaged girl. She'd shot him and he'd covered for her, lied for her, proved himself to be on the side of justice no matter what it cost him. She'd almost forgiven herself for shooting him. He'd forgiven her the instant it happened.

"What did she say?" Noah asked.

"That I've got trauma on top of trauma on top of more trauma and that I'd barely begun to start processing my child-hood stuff, let alone Ray's death and my grandmother's murder, when Mettner died holding my hand. She thinks I would"— here she used air quotes— "'benefit' from a retreat."

"What kind of a retreat?"

Josie threw her hands in the air and let them fall back to her thighs, causing Trout's head to shoot up. Once he figured out there was nothing to be alarmed about, he rested it back on the bed with an admonishing huff. "I don't know," Josie said. "A retreat with some uber-famous psychologist or life coach or some shit like that. Like the kind where you go into the moun-tains with no electronics and chant, I guess. I didn't ask because I'm not going."

He reached across the bed and took her wrist in his hand. Instantly, she felt a warm wave of something pulse through her body. She was never quite sure what it was exactly—relief, comfort, relaxation, but his touch was a natural tension-reliever. "Why not?" he asked, pulling her toward him.

She moved into him, stretching out onto her side so they were facing one another. "Because the idea is stupid, don't you think? I've been seeing Dr. Rosetti for three years and we haven't scratched the surface of my trauma. A week in the woods is supposed to solve all my problems?"

Noah laughed softly. "I'm sure that's not what Dr. Rosetti was trying to sell you. If a week in the woods worked that well, we wouldn't need psychologists."

"Noah, please," Josie said.

He pushed a strand of her hair off her cheek. "Josie, all I'm saying is, why don't you find out more information before you reject this out of hand? Find out what it's about and why she recommends it in the first place. Then decide. She's gotten you this far, hasn't she?"

Josie touched his scar, gently trailing her fingernails over it. "What does that mean?"

"It means that I think she's helped you a lot even if you don't realize it. Even if you can't sleep right now. I think you should trust her. At least consider it."

She didn't respond, but she knew that he was right. He kissed her softly. She moaned. It had been days since they'd been in bed together. His mouth moved down to her neck. "Want me to clear your head?" he asked against her skin.

Josie laughed even as she felt desire and need wake deep inside her.

"It's been a few days. You think we could start trying for that baby again?"

She stiffened and he felt it. He lifted his head and met her eyes. "I'm sorry," he said. "I guess that's not sexy."

"No," she said. "It's not that."

He studied her face. "Tell me."

"I just—this case—these kids... I keep thinking about their parents. I mean, some of them are terrible. Well, maybe not terrible, but not great and I look at them and think, 'well, we'd do a better job than that, surely,' and then I see other parents who are fully invested in their kids, kind and caring and protective, and it's like they did everything they could to nurture and protect their children and sometimes none of it matters."

Noah adjusted his pillow under his head and then returned his hand to her body, resting it on her hip. She was grateful for the connection, for how intently he listened to her.

"What do you mean, none of it matters?"

"Sometimes those kids end up dead and their parents end up shattered and you can't stop that, Noah. You can try, but there are millions of ways to lose someone and for every way that you think you can prevent, there are two that you can't."

"That's true," he said.

Josie felt tears sting the backs of her eyes. She gave a little laugh and swatted his chest. "Aren't you supposed to be reassuring me?"

"I don't like empty reassurance," he said. "I think that part of life is being honest about things that are horribly but unequivocally true. Pretending they're not doesn't make them go away or make them less frightening."

"So what? We're supposed to bring a child into this world knowing that at any moment, no matter how hard we try to keep them safe, they could be taken from us?"

"Yes," Noah said. "Basically. Josie, any of us can be taken at any time. We keep going. We survive. We do the best we can with what we have."

A tear leaked from her eye and Noah wiped it away with the pad of his thumb.

"But a child, Noah," she squeaked.

He stared at her silently for a beat. "When you think about Harris, you have a lot of fear, don't you?"

"Yes," she said. "I'm terrified all the time that something will happen to him."

"But you love him."

"Of course."

"Which is stronger? Your fear or your love?"

Her answer was automatic. "My love for him."

He let that sink in.

"Boy," Josie said. "This 'no regrets' thing is hard as hell."

Noah laughed.

She had vowed, after Mettner's death, to live with no regrets, as he had, but it had seemed so much easier in theory, when she was locked in an embrace with Amber at Mettner's grave. In that moment she had felt emboldened and fearless, but the truth was that incorporating the philosophy into her daily life was painfully difficult.

"I know," Noah said. "But trying to live like that honors Mett, and that's the least we can do for him."

Josie wiggled closer to him, and he moved his hand up and down her back. She felt tense muscles in her shoulder blades loosen and some knot of apprehension deep inside her begin to unravel. "Okay," she said. "Clear my head."

His breath was hot in her ear. "You sure?"

She put her hand inside his boxer shorts. "Yes, it will help me sleep. I need sleep. My focus has been off. I feel like I'm in a fog. I need to be sharper. We've got a killer to catch."

His mouth moved back to her throat, planting small kisses along her collarbones. "I love it when you talk sexy."

Josie laughed but rolled onto her back to give his mouth better access to her skin. "That's enough talking, Lieutenant."

FORTY-FOUR

The next day, Friday, passed uneventfully with the team waiting on any news from the state police lab, dodging the press, and following up on useless tips that came in through the tip line. Josie's mind kept circling the hidden thought in her mind, waiting for it to show itself. Mentally, she reviewed everything she knew about each case, even the ones outside her jurisdiction, hoping something would jar her brain into revealing the slippery thought. No such luck.

By Saturday morning, Josie felt like she was repeating the same day as she and Noah returned to the stationhouse for the morning briefing. They sat at their desks while Gretchen moved around handing out fresh coffees. The Chief was at the corkboard, mumbling under his breath. Josie took a sip from her cup, delighted to find it was her new favorite, a flat blonde latte. Exhaustion still weighed on her, but her mind felt sharper, more focused, than it had in days. Whether that was from two nights spent with Noah or the few hours of deep sleep she'd gotten after each time they made love, it was difficult to say.

The Chief tapped his index finger against one of the new

pushpins. The map had been expanded to include the Stacks, the area where Felicia Evans's body was found just a few miles away, and Romig's. "Whether this killer is Henry Thomas or Asher Jackson Jenks, you know what we're missing?"

"A lot," said Gretchen, settling into her seat.

"The snare trap," said Josie. "In the Felicia Evans case."

"Exactly," The Chief said. "He's got to be keeping it somewhere, but we searched both their homes and their vehicles and we've got nothing."

Noah said, "Are we absolutely sure that none of the traps in Thomas's cabin marked as his dad's were snares?"

"They were all footholds," Gretchen said. She gave a shudder. "Coiled spring. Barbaric."

The foothold traps were made of metal jaws that snapped onto an animal's foot when tripped, much in the way mousetraps worked against mice. They were considered inhumane by a number of anti-fur groups. Often, animals would chew their own leg off rather than stay trapped. Some states had banned them although they were still legal in Pennsylvania.

The Chief sighed. "What this killer is doing to these kids is barbaric."

The stairwell door swished open, and Amber sailed in. Although she looked beautiful, as always, with a long, flowing maxi dress that complemented the auburn locks cascading down her back, Josie noticed the deep hollows beneath her eyes. She tossed her purse and tablet onto her desk and walked over to the television hanging on the wall. The remote was in a tray under it. She snatched it up, pointed it at the screen like a weapon, and clicked the power button. WYEP was in the middle of a breaking news alert. Dallas Jones stood in front of a state police barracks in Lenore County. The chyron beneath him read: *Serial Killer "The Woodsman" On the Loose.*

A collective groan went up in the room.

Josie took out her phone and sent Heather Loughlin a text.

Turn on the news.

Amber turned to them. "This is going to go national in a hot second. It doesn't matter now if the Woodsman is just some story or that the killer you're looking for is 'just a man.' In the eyes of the country, he's the same and he's a serial killer targeting children. Right now, his hunting ground is Denton. You need to be ready for the onslaught of press."

Josie's phone buzzed. Heather responded:

I wasn't the one who leaked this.

Gretchen pointed at the television. "How much does he know?"

Amber's voice went up an octave. "Enough! He knows enough to make your investigation extremely difficult from this point forward."

Noah said, "I think Gretchen is wondering whether or not Dallas Jones knows about the trapping aspect of this case. That this killer is using snares and potentially deadfall traps to capture these kids before he kills them."

"Yeah," said the Chief. "It would be great if we could keep that close to our vests. We don't need people or the press conducting their own investigations based on that information."

Amber looked back at the screen which was now a montage of scenes from the search for Kayleigh Patchett with the reporter talking over it. The volume was too low for Josie to make anything out. "I watched this once before I got here," said Amber. "He hasn't said anything about the trapping. He's mostly concerned with the stories going around schools and how these kids are doing some kind of 'challenge.'"

Josie texted Heather back.

Plug the leak if you can. We'd like to keep the traps out of the press.

She was about to put her phone away when it buzzed again. This time, it was a text from her twin sister, Trinity Payne, a nationally renowned journalist who lived and worked in New York City. She had her own show, *Unsolved Crimes with Trinity Payne*. The text read:

You have a new serial killer in Denton and didn't even call me????

Josie groaned and looked up from her phone to everyone staring at her. She waved it in the air. "It's already gone national. Trinity just texted me."

"Not good, people," said the Chief.

"If the damn lab would hurry up with our DNA results," Noah complained. "That would be helpful."

"I'll call them," the Chief said.

Before he could go to his office, the stairwell door swished open again. This time, Hummel strode in, a large brown evidence bag in his hands.

"Well," said Gretchen. "This must be good because we never see you up here."

"It better be good," the Chief said, his voice almost a shout. "We need a damn miracle."

Hummel gave a half-smile. "You need to pay me more if you want miracles. I've got a couple of things for you, though." He walked up to their desks, which had all been pushed together. A quick glance at Mettner's empty chair drained some of the color from his face. He moved around it to stand beside Josie and set the bag down. "I finished processing all of the Patchetts' devices and vehicles. Their devices were clean. The father watches porn on his phone. A couple of those 'barely legal' sites with eighteen- and nineteen-year-olds. I called a buddy of mine in the Internet Crimes Against Children task force to ask him about these sites, see if Dave Patchett is looking at child porn charges, but he said they were legal. Disgusting, but legal."

The Chief made a noise deep in his throat. "Do we need to be looking at Dave Patchett more closely?"

Hummel held up a finger. "Wait till you hear what else I've got. In terms of the Patchett vehicles, there wasn't much to work with. We know Kayleigh's been in them so finding her DNA isn't exactly a shocker. We did find plenty of unidentified prints on the plow truck, the minivan, and the sedan, most of which are not in AFIS."

"Most?" said the Chief. "That means you found something."

Hummel pushed a hand through his red hair. He looked around at each one of them. "On the hood of the Patchetts' sedan we found a partial handprint. It belongs to Henry Thomas."

"What?" Gretchen blurted out.

Hummel took his phone out and punched in his passcode. "I'll show you the photos but basically, it looks like he was maybe leaning against the hood, and he rested his hand on it."

Gretchen said, "The Patchetts have denied knowing him. He has denied knowing the Patchetts. We've found no connection between him and Kayleigh. How could he have left his handprint on the car?"

Hummel handed his phone to Josie, since she was closest. Sure enough, it showed a developed latent partial handprint on the hood of the Patchetts' sedan. The fingers stretched toward the windshield, so he had put his hand on the hood while facing the car.

"Kayleigh and Savannah have softball and soccer games in the city park," Josie said. "Thomas works there."

Hummel shook his head. "The GPS doesn't support that. It looks like Dave Patchett uses the sedan to go to work and come home but the records go back six months and it's never been near the city park."

Josie said, "What about before that? We don't know that it's never been at the park, just not in the last six months."

The Chief said, "We need to talk to the Patchetts about where Henry Thomas might have encountered that car."

"What's the theory here?" asked Noah. "That Thomas was stalking Kayleigh Patchett?"

"We just don't know yet, Fraley," the Chief said.

"There's one more thing you all need to see," Hummel said.

He took a pair of gloves from his pocket and snapped them on before reaching inside the evidence bag. From it, he pulled a large yellow zippered sweatshirt. He held it up for them to see. It was wrinkled and streaked with dirt.

Gretchen said, "A sweatshirt?"

"The man Savannah Patchett saw when Kayleigh was abducted was wearing yellow," Josie said. "Blue jeans and a yellow shirt or jacket or something. Hummel, where did you get that?"

"This was balled up and stuffed under the passenger's seat of Asher Jackson Jenks's car," Hummel announced.

"I'm pretty sure lots of people in this city own yellow sweatshirts," Noah said.

Hummel raised a brow at him. "You think I'd come here with some basic sweatshirt?" he pointed at the lapel. "It had blood on it. Right here. I typed it. It's the same blood type as Kayleigh Patchett's. I sent the rest in for DNA to see if it's really her blood. It's also got these weird holes in it." He poked a finger through a quarter-sized hole in the upper arm of the left sleeve, then the right. "But I'm not sure that's important."

Gretchen stood up. "Wait. You found a yellow sweatshirt with what might be Kayleigh's blood on it under the seat of Asher Jackson Jenks's car?"

"It might not be Kayleigh's blood," said Noah. "It's not enough to charge that kid. He might have the same blood type for all we know. We need the DNA to confirm that."

"Even so, someone go rattle Asher Jenks's cage," said the Chief. "Ask him about this."

The thought that had skittered across Josie's mind two nights before, when she almost fell asleep mulling over the case, danced through her brain again, but she couldn't hold it. It was like the flash of a mirror in the sun, a signal from far off. One second there, the next, gone. "Blue followed Kayleigh's scent to Henry Thomas's cabin," she said. "And Asher was in a relationship with her. He wouldn't need to trap her in the woods. He had regular access to her. What about the GPS reports from Asher's vehicle? Was he anywhere near the Patchett home or Henry Thomas's cabin on the day that Kayleigh was abducted?"

"No," Hummel said. "But we only looked at that one day. It doesn't mean he was never there."

Noah said, "He admitted to being up there at some point and having a run-in with Thomas."

"He was lying," Josie said.

Everyone looked at her. The Chief said, "About what, exactly?"

She sighed and rubbed her eyes with the heels of her palms. "I don't know. I just know he was lying when he talked about Thomas. Anyway, go on, Hummel. We were talking about the yellow sweatshirt."

"Look," Hummel said. "I never said this was the find of the century, just that we did find it. When the DNA comes back, we'll know more."

"When will that be?" Noah grumbled. "Next year? We're

still waiting on all the other stuff which was supposed to be expedited."

"I'll call the lab again," said the Chief. "In the meantime, Palmer, you go home. Fraley, you talk to this Asher kid about the sweatshirt. Quinn, you talk to the Patchetts about the handprint."

FORTY-FIVE

In a single day, I've had both a setback and a major achievement. I try to keep my focus solely on the good news: the press has finally discovered my other kills and connected them to my work here in Denton. They've branded me a serial killer. With just a few headlines and a handful of minute-long news spots, my myth has expanded and become a tale that will be told for years to come. It may even rival the story behind Murder Mountain. They'll never catch me. They'll never know the face behind the Woodsman, not really. The not knowing will make their obsession stronger.

It will make me stronger.

FORTY-SIX

Josie parked outside the city park and walked to the sports fields, dodging families, joggers, cyclists, and dog walkers. It had taken a few phone calls to learn that the Patchetts were there because Savannah had soccer practice. Josie found them quickly, as they were positioned quite some distance from the crowd of other parents. Dave Patchett stood, arms crossed over his chest, watching as Savannah ran through practice drills. Occasionally, he clapped and yelled encouragement to her, drawing appalled stares from the other parents. Josie wasn't sure if they were reacting to him that way because of his personality or because they thought it was odd that the Patchetts were there at all, given that Kayleigh had now been missing a week. Then again, even though one of their children was missing, they were still responsible for the other. Perhaps they just wanted Savannah to have some normalcy after the trauma she'd experienced. She was clearly very attached to Kayleigh. Maybe bringing her to soccer practice was a good distraction.

Shelly Patchett sat in a folding chair nearby, alone, her face hidden by sunglasses and a bucket hat. She waved as she saw Josie approaching. When she stood up to greet her, Josie noticed her legs were trembling. Dave jogged over, his face hopeful.

"I'm sorry," Josie said. "We don't have any news about Kayleigh."

Dave's face went tomato red in a matter of seconds. He managed to keep his voice low so as not to draw attention, but it dripped with menace. "What the fuck are you people doing? How dare you come here in the middle of my kid's soccer practice to tell me you've got nothing?"

"Dave," Shelly said. "Please. Enough."

He pointed an index finger at Josie's face. "I told you, I'm suing the shit out of you. Not just your department. You, personally."

Ignoring him, Josie said, "Our evidence response team processed your sedan, and we found a handprint on the hood that belongs to Henry Thomas."

"Who?" said Dave, his tone now more curious than angry.

Shelly took her sunglasses off and looked at him in disbelief. "Who? The man they think took Kayleigh!"

"Mr. and Mrs. Patchett, all we really know for sure is that our search dog followed Kayleigh's scent to Thomas's cabin. You both said you did not know him, and our investigation has confirmed that. We also found no connection between him and Kayleigh except now this handprint on the hood of your car."

"He was stalking her, then, right?" said Shelly.

"I'll fucking kill him," Dave snarled.

"Mr. Patchett, I'd advise against approaching him at all. In addition, I'd caution you that as a sworn officer of the law, I'm required to take all death threats seriously."

Shelly slapped his upper arm. "Shut up, Dave! Just shut up!"

He blinked at his wife. The flush of anger drained until his cheeks were bloodless. He turned his gaze to Josie. "Have you arrested him yet?"

"We can't arrest him because of the handprint," Josie explained. "It doesn't prove anything. What I need to know is if either of you remember coming into contact with him?"

They both shook their heads.

Josie turned and motioned around the park. Several feet away, the girls on the field had gathered around their coach. They had moved closer to where Josie stood with the Patchetts. She wondered if the coach had done it on purpose to try to eavesdrop on them. When Josie glared at him, he quickly turned to the girls and began shouting. "Remember," he said. "Next week, we play Danville and the week after that, we play Fairfield... I need you to give one hundred percent effort..."

"Henry Thomas works in this park," Josie said. "I know your family is here often for games and practices."

Shelly looked at Dave. "But we never bring the sedan. Dave uses it for work. We always come in the minivan. It's the only thing big enough for the girls' equipment and sometimes, after games, we take Savannah's friends out for lunch or dinner."

Josie said, "Are you telling me you've never had the sedan here? Not even on a day when maybe Shelly brought the kids in the minivan and Dave was late coming home from work? Maybe he arrived separately?"

The Patchetts looked at one another. "Well, I mean, I can't say never," Shelly said.

Savannah came running over. She threw herself at Shelly, wrapping her arms around her mother's waist.

Dave said, "I'm sure I've driven it here like that before, but I couldn't tell you when. Why would he have been messing with our car?"

"Who's messing with our car?" asked Savannah, her forehead creasing.

Shelly stroked her ponytail. "No one, sweetheart. The police took our cars to make sure they were okay, remember?"

Savannah stared at Josie, nodding.

"Well, good news," said Shelly with forced brightness in her tone. "They're fine! No one messed with them!"

Josie smiled at the girl. "Your mom's right. All your family's cars checked out."

"Are you still going to find Kayleigh?" Savannah asked, a small tremor in her voice.

"We're doing everything we can to find her," Josie said, feeling like a fraud. They were doing everything, but if they did find her, it would not be the outcome that Savannah was hoping for. "In fact, I've got to go talk to someone else right now."

She turned to go, feeling the stares of every parent and child there as she walked away. The coach gawked openly at her, and his words echoed in her mind, although she wasn't sure why. The team would play Danville next week and Fairfield after. Josie was trying to figure out the significance—why her brain had alighted on this, of all things—when she heard small footsteps running up behind her. Next, she felt a tug on her wrist. Savannah Patchett held fast to her. "Mrs. Police," she said.

Josie laughed. "My name is Detective Josie Quinn," she said. "But you can call me Josie."

Savannah tugged at Josie's arm until she squatted down so that the two of them were roughly face level. Savannah reached up behind her head and pulled at her ponytail, removing the scrunchie that held it in place. She folded it into Josie's palm. "When you find my sister, can you give this to her? It's my favorite. I want her to have it."

Josie felt a hairline fracture form in the protective shell she mentally donned each day on the job. She gave Savannah a smile she hoped wasn't wobbly and said, "Sure. Of course."

FORTY-SEVEN

Josie waved to the patrol unit parked outside of Henry Thomas's driveway as she pulled into it. The tires of her SUV bounced over the gravel, fighting for purchase as she punched the gas to make the climb up to the cabin. Trees closed in on either side, forming a green arch. The late-morning sun struggled to penetrate it. The area would be so beautiful if this mountain wasn't home to so many evil acts, if it had not hosted so many evil men. Did it attract them? Josie wondered. Like some kind of fucked-up siren song only violent psychopaths and deviants could hear? Or had it just been bad luck that a team of serial killers had operated there for decades, unchecked, leaving behind land that only Henry Thomas could stomach living on?

The roof of the cabin came into view first. Then its small porch and finally, the driveway, the backs of the two vehicles facing her. They sat in roughly the same places they'd been the night Josie had followed Blue and Luke here. This time, the hood of the El Camino was propped up. As she brought her own vehicle to a stop, Josie saw Henry Thomas peek his head around the hood and then disappear again.

Josie got out and walked over, studying the car. The last

time she'd seen it had been the night Kayleigh was abducted, under the cabin's exterior lights and the occasional strobe of the state police helicopter passing overhead. Now, in full daylight, she saw rust eating at the edges of its body and the bed, where leaves and pine needles gathered in the corners. Paint had faded in some places, been reapplied in others, and then only half removed so the entire thing was a patchwork of gray and white. The side mirror on the driver's side door was missing. About the only things that looked new were its rear bumper, brake lights, and tires. Not a speck of dirt or dust on any of those things. She supposed you had to start somewhere when it came to restoration.

Thomas didn't acknowledge her as she rounded the car to join him near the front. He was bare-chested again, wearing a pair of low-slung jeans that had more stains and tears on them than Josie could count. He stood on a large piece of cardboard while he fitted a drop cloth across the opening beneath the hood. As he worked, the scales of a large snake tattooed across his back rippled. A paint sprayer lay next to his feet, along with several rolls of tape.

She said, "What color are you painting it?"

Without looking at her, he said, "I know you didn't come here to talk to me about paint."

"You get yourself a torque converter for this?"

From his profile, she saw one corner of his mouth quirk. "Nope. It's on backorder. Now come on, I know you didn't come to talk to me about cars."

"That's not technically true," Josie said.

This earned her a glance. A lock of his black hair fell across one of his eyes and he pushed it aside.

"Mr. Thomas, when I interviewed you, you told me that you didn't know Kayleigh Patchett, that you had never seen her before."

He picked up a roll of tape and started taping off the head-lights. "That's right."

"We found a partial handprint on the hood of Kayleigh's parents' sedan that we were able to match to you. You want to explain to me how it got there?"

He sighed heavily. "I can't because I don't know the Patch-etts, and if you lined up one hundred cars and asked me which one was theirs, I couldn't tell you. What I do know, thanks to this kid going missing and your little investigation, is that they live just over the mountain, which means that we probably use the same grocery store, the same bank, the same urgent care, so there's a good chance that their car was in the same parking lot as my car at some point. Maybe I dropped something and when I leaned over to get it, I touched their car."

"Our search dog followed Kayleigh Patchett's scent here, Mr. Thomas. You're going to have to do better than that."

"The Patchett kid," he said. "She play sports? She ever drive her car over to the town park? I'm part of the clean-up crew there. That includes parking lots."

He stood up, twirling the roll of tape between his hands, and came within inches of her. She could smell his sweat, see the individual hairs on his chin that formed his five o'clock shadow. When he spoke, his breath washed over her face: meat, beer, and something else. Something sour. "Look, Detective, there are about a half-dozen ways I could have come into contact with that car, and none of them involve me kidnapping that Patchett kid."

Josie didn't move, keeping her posture straight and still, as if it didn't bother her in the least to have him invading her personal space. She'd be damned if she showed him just how much she wanted to recoil. "Is one of those half-dozen ways you stalking Kayleigh Patchett?"

He tipped his head back and laughed. Josie wanted to take the opportunity to move away from him, but she didn't. When he looked back at her and realized she was still waiting for an answer, he said, "No. I was not stalking that girl."

Josie took out her phone and pulled up a photo of Asher Jenks, one she'd pulled from his driver's license rather than the secretive pictures that Kayleigh had taken in profile. "You recognize this guy?" she asked Thomas.

"No," he said easily.

"He said he knew you."

There was no reaction, not even a micro expression indicating that he was lying. "Then he's lying or mistaken, Detective."

Josie put her phone back in her pocket. She was about to ask another question when they heard a vehicle gunning it up the driveway. Gravel spit in every direction, pinging off the underside of Josie's SUV as a red Dodge Challenger roared into view. Its driver turned it slightly to avoid hitting the back of the El Camino. Josie looked back at Henry Thomas and was surprised to see his normally serene expression change over to fear, then anger. She turned back to their visitor, a young man no older than twenty-five, with long, greasy brown hair, a patchy goatee and beady brown eyes which were locked on Josie's breasts. A sneer curled his lips and he started to nod—along to music or in appreciation of what he saw, she wasn't sure—until he noticed Henry Thomas's glare.

Thomas edged around Josie and strode over to the car. Josie watched the man's face as Thomas approached. He opened his mouth, lips forming what she was sure was a word beginning with H. Hey, hello, hi, Henry, maybe? He recognized Thomas. The word never made it across his tongue. He clamped his mouth shut quickly, his eyes widening.

Thomas waved the roll of tape at the man, yelling. "Who the hell are you? What are you doing up here? This is private property. If you want to visit Murder Mountain, find another way."

A momentary blip of confusion flashed over the driver's face. Then he looked back at Josie and seemed to come to some kind of understanding. He lifted a hand and waved it at Thomas. "I'm sorry, I'm sorry, man. I made a wrong turn. I-I'll just go now."

Thomas kicked the driver's side door and then spit into the open window. "Get off my property and don't come back!"

The kid couldn't throw the car into gear fast enough. More gravel turned up and hit Josie's vehicle as he made an awkward turn and raced back down the driveway. Josie studied the license plate, committing it to memory. A new thought took hold in her mind, this one not as shadowy as the one she'd been trying to pin down since the night before.

"Sorry about that," Thomas said, offering an uncharacteristic smile, as if they were on a date and they'd just been disturbed.

The coffee Josie had had earlier congealed in her stomach. "It's fine," she said. "I've got to go anyway."

On her way back down the driveway, she noticed the rows of purple wildflowers in the distance, growing beneath a giant oak.

FORTY-EIGHT

It's daytime. I don't usually operate during the day, but I couldn't help myself. Besides, who would even know that I'm here? Who would expect me to be here? Really, I've always been hidden in plain sight. Until now, it was never this much fun. I wait near the edge of the woods and watch her, alone in her yard. She's so small and thin, light on her feet. Agile. I feel a surge of pleasure pulse through my body thinking about how horrified her family would be if they knew that the feared Woodsman was so close to her. I can't contain my excitement. A branch snaps beneath my foot. My breath stops as she freezes and scans the trees. For a moment, I'm sure that I'm still invisible, but then I see the realization in her expression as her eyes zero in on me.

She sees me.

FORTY-NINE

Morris Lauber worked at an auto parts store in South Denton. Josie and Gretchen drove there in Josie's vehicle. Noah had been sent home for more rest after questioning Asher Jackson Jenks about the sweatshirt in his car. As expected, he denied owning it and said he had no idea how it had found its way under the seat.

Lies, Josie thought. Everyone lied.

But the sweatshirt bothered her. She still wasn't sure why. It had something do with that rogue thought in the back of her mind that she couldn't quite pin down. The one that had been born after spending hours on StoryJot. Round and round went the carousel of her mind.

Kayleigh. Felicia. The story. The Woodsman. Henry Thomas. Asher Jackson Jenks. The kids in Montour and Lenore Counties. The traps. Games in Danville and Fairfield. Savannah's favorite scrunchie. The handprint. The sweatshirt. The wildflowers.

Gretchen's voice interrupted it. "I don't understand why we're asking Morris Lauber about this, and not the kid you saw at Henry Thomas's cabin."

"As soon as I left the cabin, I ran the plate," Josie said. "That kid is twenty-five and we've already arrested him a dozen times on drug charges. He's a regular under the East Bridge."

Denton's East Bridge was the hub of most of the drug activity in the city.

"Maybe we should be talking to Zeke," Gretchen suggested.

Larry Ezekiel "Zeke" Fox—or "Needle" as Josie had nicknamed him as a child—was a lifelong drug user and dealer who lived in a shack near the bottom of the East Bridge. When Josie was a child and the woman she thought was her mother needed a fix, she called Zeke. Whether he meant to or not, he'd saved Josie from some of that woman's worst abuse. In adulthood, on the job, she'd come to a grudging truce with him. Then, he took a bullet for her. Josie wouldn't call them friends, but nowadays, she made sure Zeke had what he needed in terms of food, clothing, and shelter and in return, he answered all her questions honestly.

"Zeke isn't going to tell me what I need to know," Josie said. "I already thought of that."

"And Morris Lauber will?" Gretchen said.

Josie could hear the skepticism in her voice.

"Nobody knows Henry Thomas better than Morris Lauber," Josie said. "And Morris Lauber is more afraid of the law than he is of Thomas. We can get this out of him."

Josie and Gretchen found Morris behind the counter of the parts department at the back of the store. The moment he saw them, his mouth dropped open. Then, regaining his composure, he turned to his coworker and mumbled something. Before Josie and Gretchen could reach the counter, he was already around it, heading directly toward them. The flaps of his bright red work vest slapped against his sides as he walked.

"What are you doing here?" he whisper-shouted once they were in earshot of one another.

Gretchen said, "Mr. Lauber, we need to ask you some more questions about Henry Thomas."

"No. Not here. Come on, can't you wait till I'm off work?"

Up close to him, Josie smelled beer on his breath. "Do you think Kayleigh Patchett's parents can wait for her to be found?"

He rolled his eyes and pointed to his left. A door was nestled among the shelves that displayed various types of tires. Over the top of it a sign read "Exit" in glowing red letters. "Can we at least go outside?"

Josie stepped aside and gestured for him to lead the way. The door opened on to a narrow parking lot alongside the store. Just outside it was a standing ashtray. Morris fished a pack of cigarettes out of his vest pocket and lit one up. "I don't know what you could possibly need from me now," he complained. "You two damn near took my whole life apart the other day. Darcy still isn't convinced that I did nothing wrong. She thinks I'm hiding something."

"Are you?" asked Gretchen.

"You wanna know the truth? I got a couple of gambling debts I don't really want her to know about, but that's it. I told you, I ain't done nothing wrong."

Josie said, "We're not here about you, Mr. Lauber."

He flicked the ash from the end of his cigarette. "I know. Henry again. Well, I ain't talked to him since I last saw you, so I don't know what you want from me."

"You've known Henry pretty much his whole life," Gretchen said. "You know a lot about him."

"So?"

"What can you tell us about his conviction?" asked Gretchen.

Lauber shook his head. "You're kidding me, right? You're the cops. You don't know?"

Josie said, "We know that he held a young woman at gunpoint. Henry forced her into the basement and held her there against her will. Henry told us that her boyfriend owed him some money and that's why he was there. What we don't know is why he would hold his friend's girlfriend up for money."

Lauber said nothing.

Gretchen said, "You're friends. You think Henry would ever hold Darcy at gunpoint if you owed him money?"

"No. He'd never do that to me."

"Why not?" Josie asked.

He looked at her as if she was trying to trick him. "Because it ain't like that between us."

"Like what?" asked Gretchen.

When he didn't answer, she tried again. "Did you know the friend who owed Henry money?"

"Nah, I didn't know him or his girl."

"Did Henry ever talk about him?" asked Josie.

"Only to say he owed him money," Morris answered.

"Why did he owe Henry money?" Josie said.

"What?"

She repeated the question.

He hesitated, sucking on the end of his cigarette, staring at Josie over the end of it. "I don't know."

"You sure about that?" asked Gretchen.

He tossed his cigarette onto the ground and stubbed it out with his foot. "I'm sure."

"Okay," said Gretchen. "I'll tell you what. We're going to come back here tomorrow to check again. To make sure that you're sure."

Lauber's eyes bulged. "What? You can't do that."

Josie said, "Mr. Lauber, a girl is missing and on top of that, we've got another girl who was just murdered in the woods. I don't know if you've watched the news in the last twenty-four hours, but our investigation is heating up. The press is all over us to figure out what's going on in this city. Among our many leads and suspects, we are looking at Henry. We believe you have knowledge about him—specifically about his past—that is relevant to our investigation. We can come back as many times as we want."

Gretchen turned to Josie. "But maybe we're being unfair to Morris. How about this? We'll meet you at home instead. I think Darcy really liked me. I wouldn't mind seeing her again."

"Good God," Morris muttered. "You can't just—I don't know anything about this missing girl, or the dead one! I'm telling you I don't think Henry had anything to do with either of those."

Josie said, "But right now we're asking you about something that happened in Henry's past. Something he already went to prison for."

"Right," Gretchen agreed. "We're looking for a little more background on what Henry did back then. He's already served his time for it, Morris. We just want to fill in some gaps."

He regarded her with suspicion. "You're saying he won't get in trouble if I... fill in the background?"

Josie said, "How could he get in trouble, Morris? It's time served."

"I don't know. He might get mad at me."

"Mad enough to put a gun to Darcy's head?" asked Gretchen.

"I told you, he would never do that. Not to me."

"Why not?" Gretchen said. "The truth this time, Morris. That case was open and closed. We're not looking to add charges to something that's said and done."

With a heavy sigh, he took out another cigarette and lit it. "'Cause I'm a real friend to him. That guy whose house Henry went into? He owed him money for drugs."

"Henry sold him drugs?" asked Josie.

"No," said Morris. "Back then—and I'm telling you that this was years ago, before Henry went away. He's clean now. Back then, Henry ran in some circles. His dad always told him to get out of it, but it was too lucrative."

"Henry was a dealer?" asked Gretchen.

"No. Henry was a supplier. The guy whose house he went to was a dealer. Small-time. Back then, Henry had connections. He'd get a decent supply and then he'd get a bunch of kids to sell it. He collected the money."

"He was a middleman," said Josie.

"Yep."

"Where did he get his supply?" asked Gretchen.

"I don't know," Morris said. The cigarette dangled from his mouth as he held both palms face out in the air. "I really don't. I only know what I know 'cause I heard his dad talking to him about it and some things his dad told me after the fact."

"Where did he keep his supply?" asked Josie.

"I'm pretty sure he was keeping it in his dad's garage. He was living with his dad back then. After he got sent up, his dad told me that was the end of that. No more drugs in the house. I think he was always nervous that Henry would get him in trouble. 'Course, then he went and died while Henry was in prison."

Gretchen said, "How about after he got out? Did he get back into it?"

"Hell if I know. I don't think so, though."

"You sure about that?" asked Josie. "You're up at his place a fair amount. You ever see anything?"

"No. I never did. I don't think he would do that. It's what got him sent up. He missed his dad's death and his funeral and everything. Put a hurtin' on him. I think he means to stay on the straight and narrow now. He's got a good job, his own place. Why would he get back into that?"

Josie said, "You told us that teenagers come up his driveway all the time. You sure they're making wrong turns, and not there to get what they need to sell or to pay Henry what they owe him?"

Morris flicked his cigarette butt to the ground, beside the first one, and smashed it with his boot. "I never saw anything like that. But didn't you guys search there when you were looking for that girl? You didn't find anything?"

They hadn't. Just like they hadn't found any clear indication that Henry Thomas was behind Kayleigh's abduction or Felicia's death and yet, Josie was sure that Henry Thomas was hiding something. Maybe drugs. Maybe Kayleigh. Or both.

"Morris," Josie said. "If Henry did have a supply and it wasn't on his property, where would it be?"

"Hell if I know, and that's the truth."

FIFTY

"You think that Henry Thomas is still a drug supplier," said Gretchen.

They were back at the stationhouse after grabbing a quick lunch. Josie stood in front of Mettner's desk, staring down at his blotter. In the lower left-hand corner, in red ink, in what looked like Amber's handwriting, were the initials A.W. with a heart under it and then the initials F.M. *Amber Watts hearts Finn Mettner.*

Josie felt like the breath had been knocked out of her. "Oh God," she gasped.

Gretchen's chair creaked. "You okay?"

Josie tore her eyes from the blotter, instead looking at Mettner's computer screen, dormant for months now. "Yeah," she breathed.

Gretchen's chair creaked again, and Josie recognized the sound as her settling back into it. Josie swallowed over the lump in her throat and answered Gretchen's question. "Yes. Henry Thomas is still in the drug trade. I think that's how Asher knows him. Asher is one of his dealers. That's where Kayleigh was getting her stash, from Asher, who got it from Henry."

She put both hands on the back of Mettner's chair and held on, trying to get her breathing back under control. Her eyes drifted to a framed photo of his parents, brothers, nieces, and nephews. She quickly turned back to the computer screen. Soothing blankness.

Gretchen said, "That would certainly explain the teenagers in his driveway all the time. He meets them at the park—his legitimate job—brings them on as dealers and collects the money. But you know what else we didn't find on his property?"

"Large amounts of cash," Josie said. "I know. Or drugs, for that matter."

"You think if we find his hiding place, we find Kayleigh."

"Yes," Josie said.

"Maybe the snare trap he's been using, too," Gretchen added. "Maybe if the DNA comes back from the hair in his cabin, we can arrest him and we'll have some leverage on him. Maybe then he'll tell us what he did with her body."

Josie pulled Mettner's chair out and slowly sat down in it.

Gretchen said, "What are you doing?"

"Mettner handled Henry Thomas's case. The one that got him time in prison."

"Yeah," Gretchen said. "What are you looking for?"

Josie leaned down and opened his bottom-left desk drawer, which held rows of neatly labeled files. "Mett kept his own notes about cases he handled. He typed everything into the notes app in his phone and then he'd email those to himself."

"I know," Gretchen said. "Then he'd use them to write up his reports."

Josie began riffling through the file folders. Luckily, they were arranged alphabetically. "But he always kept his original notes, which included his impressions and theories, things that didn't make it to his final reports or to court testimony. He printed them out and filed them away here."

Gretchen's chair creaked once more, and seconds later, she

was beside Josie, looking over her shoulder as she pulled Mettner's Henry Thomas file from the drawer. "What are you looking for?" she asked.

"I'm not sure," Josie said. "I'll know it when I see it."

As she paged through the file, the carousel in her mind started again. The thought she'd been trying to pin down had become a little clearer, now a ghostly outline in her head, but it still eluded her.

Finally, she came to a page describing Mettner's interview with Henry Thomas's nineteen-year-old victim. Gretchen read along over Josie's shoulder. The victim had described Thomas as creepy. She'd said that he'd been at the house before on multiple occasions and approached her, wanting to talk to her because the year before, a man had broken into her home with intentions of raping her and she'd not only fought him off but killed him. The case was ruled self-defense. Mettner's notes indicated that the incident had taken place outside of their jurisdiction. The victim had moved to Denton for a fresh start. Except that Thomas found out about her history and became "obsessed" with her, wanting to know the details and whether or not it had felt good to kill a man. She related that hearing the details of her ordeal seemed to turn him on. He'd eventually made a sexual advance, which she had rejected. The day he forced her into the basement, he'd offered to forgive her boyfriend's debt to him if she dumped said boyfriend and went out with Thomas. Mettner's notes read: "*Become his.*"

"What the hell?" said Gretchen. "This is disgusting. Is this what you were looking for?"

"Sort of," Josie said.

"Well, if this guy is wandering around the woods, trapping and killing teenage girls, this isn't really surprising information."

"No, it's not."

Josie left the file open on Mettner's desk and stood, moving back to her own desk and firing up her computer. Gretchen watched her with narrowed eyes. "You're on to something, aren't you?"

"Chan took photos of the remnants of the trap we found where Kayleigh was abducted," Josie muttered. "She never could reconfigure it."

Gretchen joined her at her desk, pulling her chair along with her. She plopped into it and watched as Josie pulled up the photos that Chan had uploaded to the file. Josie clicked through them.

Gretchen said, "What are we looking for?"

Josie stopped at the photo of the pointed sticks that had been bound together with vine. "I'm not sure. I just know that we've been missing something big all along."

She clicked out of those photos and brought up a new set.

"What are these?" asked Gretchen.

"The crime scene photos from the cases in Montour and Lenore Counties. Heather Loughlin sent them to me, but I haven't had a chance to look at them."

She started clicking through them, stunned at how similar each one looked to the Felicia Evans scene. The bodies of Amanda Chavez and Sarah McArthur were laid out, legs straight, as if they had simply laid down to take a nap. Except that their heads had been smashed in. Josie studied their clothes and shoes and then she scanned the area around the bodies in both sets of photos, looking for some evidence of the traps. All she saw was mud, leaves, brush, twigs, and crushed purple wildflowers.

The thought she'd been chasing since reading Kayleigh's stories stopped squirming away from her, coming into focus finally.

"Holy shit," she said. She lunged across her desk and picked up her phone, pulling up the StoryJot app and locating Kayleigh's profile. Once she found what she was looking for, she returned to her computer screen, minimizing the crime scene photos and pulling up Google. In seconds, she had her answer. Her heart thrummed in her chest. Every cell in her body felt abuzz.

Gretchen said, "I'd really love to know what's going on right now."

"The missing piece," Josie said. "It's Kayleigh."

"I don't understand."

Josie pulled up the photos from Heather again. She sent one from the Chavez scene and one from the McArthur scene to the printer. As it lurched to life in the corner of the room, she went into the Denton PD files and found photos from the scene of Kayleigh's abduction and Felicia Evans's crime scene. She printed those as well. Grabbing them from the printer, she spread them across her desk. "What do you see?" Josie asked. "What's the same in every photo?"

Gretchen put her reading glasses on and peered at them. "Dead girls."

"No," Josie said. "Every photo. All four."

It took a moment, but then Gretchen saw them. "The flowers. The purple flowers. What are you saying? This is the killer's signature? He leaves these flowers at each scene? It's not a very good signature. They're trampled at every scene. They don't look like they were left there, they just look like people walked all over them. Typically, serial killers' signatures are pretty obvious."

"It's not his signature," Josie said.

"It's not a signature?"

"It's not Henry Thomas's signature. It's Kayleigh Patchett's. She's not a victim. She's a killer."

FIFTY-ONE

Gretchen slid her reading glasses off her nose. Lips pursed, one eyebrow arched, she stared at Josie, her eyes darkening as she considered what Josie had just said. Then she leaned back in her chair as far as it would go. In protest, the chair shrieked. Gretchen folded her arms across her chest. "Kayleigh met Asher Jackson Jenks on StoryJot."

"Yes," Josie said, relieved that Gretchen didn't think she was crazy.

"Asher is a small-time drug dealer. We know that because we found all that stuff in his apartment. Almost enough for a charge of possession with intent to distribute. He gets the drugs he sells from Henry Thomas, who we know now has a long history of being in the drug trade. Kayleigh met Thomas through Asher."

"Yes," Josie said.

"You can't prove that."

"Just run with this for now," Josie said. "Hear me out."

"For some reason, Thomas becomes... what? Obsessed with Kayleigh? Why?"

"I don't know," Josie said. "That's the part I haven't quite worked out but yes, he fixates on her, and they develop some kind of relationship. A secret relationship. No one knows about it. Not Asher, not Olivia. On some of the nights that Kayleigh snuck out, she could have gone through the woods to see him at his cabin."

Gretchen frowned. "I don't know. That's a hike."

"But not impossible. They could have met somewhere. Maybe he came to her. It would explain the handprint on the Patchetts' sedan. My point is that they became involved somehow."

"Sexually?"

"Kayleigh told Felicia that her boyfriend was going to kill her," Josie pointed out. "Who does that sound like? Asher Jenks or Henry Thomas?"

"Okay," said Gretchen. "Then what? They decide to become this killing couple?"

"Yes," said Josie. "He grooms her. He's got violent tendencies. He was turned on by the thought of a woman killing. We know that from Mett's notes. Kayleigh was even younger than that girl. Impressionable. Neglected and dismissed at home. Always outshone by her little sister in everything. Gretchen, no one saw this kid. Not even her parents. When Felicia Evans plagiarized her story, her parents never even considered that Kayleigh was in the right. Not even for a moment. No one believed her. The only person who did, who knew that she was telling the truth, was Asher and he refused to go to bat for her."

"Someone that beaten down and invisible makes for an excellent victim," Gretchen said with a sigh. "People like Thomas, child molesters, that sort, they never target the self-assured kids who are well-loved at home with attentive parents. Those kids would be too hard to turn."

"But with someone like Kayleigh, all he would have to do is make her feel special, important, make her feel seen for the first time in her life," Josie agreed. "Make her feel like she was number one. Since her sister was born, she's been like an afterthought in her house."

"Jesus," Gretchen said. "The Patchetts raised the perfect victim for someone like Thomas."

"Yes," Josie said. "They did. Gretchen, I read her stories on that app. While most of them revolve around sex, the ones that don't are more or less about her family life. In 'Bumper Cars,' the parents leave an amusement park without one of their daughters. She's left at the bumper cars, and they never even notice that she's not with them. It's the sister who reminds them that she's not there. The story that Felicia stole is also about sisters."

"And how the parents favor one over the other?"

"No," Josie said. "The parents send the sisters on quests. One of those quests is to find a flower called *Saintpaulia ionantha*. If they could find it, the kingdom would have protection from marauders for a hundred years, or something like that. I thought it was something that Kayleigh made up since it's a fantasy story, but Gretchen, it's a real flower. A type of African violet. Purple, and get this, it's also called 'Favorite Child.'"

"That's her mark," Gretchen said. "Her signature. The purple flowers. African violets don't grow around here so she uses purple wildflowers in their place. She's flaunting her involvement. Using something from her own writing. From the story that was stolen from her, from which no one believed her."

"It's fitting that it has to do with a favorite child, given her circumstances. When I was at the soccer field, Savannah gave me her scrunchie. She wanted me to give it to Kayleigh when we found her. She told me it was her favorite."

"That's been rattling around in your brain ever since," Gretchen said.

"One of the things, yeah. Not because of the scrunchie but because Savannah used the word favorite—"

"And Savannah is clearly the Patchetts' favorite child,"

Gretchen said. "Do you think Kayleigh killed these other kids? Where is she getting the flowers?"

"A bunch of them grow in Henry Thomas's driveway," Josie said. "I'm not sure which of them did the actual killing. I haven't figured that out either, but I think they've been doing this together."

"The trap that Chan can't put together," Gretchen said. "Did Thomas set that for her? Did things get out of control? Maybe he felt he needed to stop it."

Josie shook her head. "No. It wasn't a trap. It was a scarecrow. Think about it. The yellow sweatshirt with the holes in the outer arms? That's where it fit over the frame that Kayleigh built with sticks and vines so it would look like a man. Then she set it up, very much like a trap, so that if she tripped it at just the right moment, it would come flying down at her. From far enough away, it would look like a man rushing toward her."

"To an eight-year-old," Gretchen said.

"Yes. She took the sweatshirt and jeans with her. At some point, somehow, after her staged abduction, she ended up in Asher's car and stashed the sweatshirt there. Whether it was to get rid of it or to frame him, I'm not sure."

"You think he's seen her since her abduction, or that she put that into his car without him knowing?" Gretchen asked.

"He had to have seen her. I'd bet that's where she's been staying—or at least until we found him and started searching through his apartment."

"You think he knows about her and Thomas?"

"I doubt it," said Josie. "I think once we showed up on his doorstep, he probably told her to leave and never come back."

"So she was out on her own, with nowhere to go," Gretchen said.

"Except the woods. She was probably wandering around, keeping out of sight even before she started staying with Asher.

She couldn't exactly stay with Thomas, not with the searches and police scrutiny."

"You think she was hanging around the Stacks and saw an opportunity when Brody Hicks and Felicia Evans went into the woods?"

"Yes," said Josie.

"She just happened to have a snare trap on her?"

Josie shook her head. "I don't know. Or maybe she snuck back up to Thomas's cabin and they did it together. Maybe they went hunting together that night, and she just got lucky that it was Felicia who went in. She knew about the Stacks."

"But the other cases," Gretchen said. "The other counties."

Josie pointed to Sarah McArthur's body. "Look at her T-shirt."

Gretchen put her reading glasses back on and leaned in, studying it. "Lady Ironmen Softball."

"That's Danville's school team," Josie said. "They're in Montour County."

"The Lady Ironmen? Really?"

"I know, I know, but that's not the point," Josie said with a laugh. "When I went to the park to talk to the Patchetts, they were at Savannah's soccer practice and I overhead the coach telling the kids that they'd play Danville and then Fairfield. I couldn't figure out why it was sticking in my head."

"Fairfield is in Lenore County," Gretchen said. "Kayleigh would have played softball against the same schools in both counties. She would have come in contact with the other victims. Talked with them. Maybe even encouraged them to do the Woodsman challenge. She might have even discussed with them where they would do it."

"She was setting it up," Josie said. "Then she and Thomas would have some idea of where to hunt. She could have done this a number of times. We don't know how many times they were unsuccessful. We just know that those two times were the ones where they actually ran into the kids in the woods at night."

"And they took away anything they thought could be used to trace back to them, even rocks," said Gretchen.

"Yes. I doubt they kept the rocks, though. All they'd have to do is toss them somewhere not near the crime scenes. No one would find them, and even if they did, they'd never connect them to the scenes. Gretchen, if you look at the case through this lens, the pieces fit."

"True," Gretchen agreed. "Mostly. But if you're right, where's Kayleigh now?"

Before she could answer, Josie's cell phone rang. She picked it up from her desk and answered. It was the Chief. "Quinn. You and Palmer need to get your asses over to the Patchett household right now. I'll be right behind you. We've got a situation on our hands. Little Savannah Patchett is missing. Again."

FIFTY-TWO

They could hear Shelly Patchett's wails as they approached the front door. A uniformed officer stood on the front stoop, face impassive. Josie and Gretchen nodded a greeting and went inside. As she crossed the threshold and Shelly's cries became louder, Josie's heart thudded in her chest. Shelly was on the floor in a heap of limbs, her entire body convulsing. Dave knelt next to her, trying to pick her up under her shoulders, but her body went limp except for the trembling and the juddering rise of her chest and shoulders when she called out. "Savannah! Not Savannah! God, not Savannah!"

Her face was streaked with tears. Snot and spit dripped from her chin. Her eyes looked right at Josie and Gretchen but didn't register their presence.

Dave looked up at them, face pale and imploring. "Can someone help me get her on the couch?"

Josie raced forward and slid an arm around Shelly's waist. Together, she and Dave lifted her and moved her back to the couch. She slumped as soon as they got her onto it, nearly sliding off. Dave sat next to her and pulled her to him, holding her in place.

Gretchen looked around and spotted a box of tissues on a nearby end table. She grabbed them and offered them to Shelly. She ignored the box, but Dave took several from it and used them to dab at Shelly's cheeks. This only made her sob harder.

"Babe," Dave said. "You need to calm down. You have to tell the police what happened."

Josie knelt in front of her. "Mrs. Patchett, please, can you tell us what happened?"

"He took her!" Shelly shrieked. "The Woodsman took her! You said he wasn't real, but he is! He took both of my children. You lied to us and now Savannah is gone!"

Dave looked from Josie to Gretchen helplessly. All their gazes were momentarily drawn to the front door as it banged open. The Chief stepped inside and joined them in the living room.

Josie turned back to the couple. "Mr. Patchett, can you tell us what happened?"

"I don't know," he said. "I went to the store. My wife was here with Savannah. I came home and Shelly was hysterical. Savannah was gone."

Gretchen said, "Shelly, I know it's hard but the best thing you can do for Savannah right now is take a few deep breaths, try to calm down and tell us exactly what happened."

Shelly blinked, awareness coming back into her eyes. Her breathing slowed marginally.

"That's it," Josie told her. "That's great."

After ten deep breaths, Shelly had calmed enough to speak, although her voice shook as she told them what happened. "Savannah has been cooped up inside this house for days now, except for soccer practice. It's all been so scary and traumatic. She misses her sister. The practice today made her feel so much better, more normal. When we got home, she still wanted to practice her kicks so I told her she could. The net is out back. I was out there with her but I—I left my phone in the house. I wouldn't even have gone back for it except that I was worried that we might get some news about Kayleigh. You have no idea how much Savannah misses her. It's been hell."

"We understand," said Gretchen.

Fresh tears spilled down Shelly's cheeks. "I was only gone a minute. I came in and it wasn't where I left it. Or maybe it was and I just didn't remember. But I found it and went back outside and she was gone. Just gone."

Dave squeezed her. "When I got home, the police were already here, and she was hysterical."

"I called 911."

The Chief said, "I instructed dispatch to call me directly with any types of calls like this one instead of putting it out over the radio. I was trying to keep the press away. I was at the mayor's office, giving her an update when I got the call about Savannah."

Gretchen said, "Mr. and Mrs. Patchett, did you look for her?"

Dave handed Shelly more tissues and she blew her nose. "I went to the edge of the woods. I called for her. I went into the trees a little bit but I was afraid of getting lost like last time, so I just called 911."

The report that had come from dispatch was simply that Savannah had gone missing from her backyard. "Mr. and Mrs. Patchett," Josie said, standing up. "We'll need to do things that are simply protocol in situations like this, which means the first thing we need to do is search the house and make sure Savannah's not hiding somewhere inside. Is that okay with you?"

Dave sighed. "I don't care what the hell you do anymore. Just find my kid."

Josie, Gretchen, and the Chief set about clearing the house. In the kitchen, out of earshot of the Patchetts, Gretchen said, "Is this Kayleigh or Henry Thomas?"

"I don't know," Josie said.

"What the hell are you two talking about?" asked the Chief.

"Chief," Gretchen said. "Quinn has something to tell you."

FIFTY-THREE

Less than an hour later, the three of them stood at the foot of Henry Thomas's driveway, pulling on Kevlar vests and checking their radios. The Chief had asked for two additional marked units as backup. He spread out a piece of paper on the hood of his car and drew a crude map of Henry Thomas's property. The cabin, the vehicles, the driveway, and the woods all around. "We're looking for a little girl," he said. "Remember that. We don't have a search warrant. We're going to go knock on this guy's door and ask him about this girl, ask him if we can have a look around. We don't believe that he is armed but we know from his history that he is dangerous. There may be another person on the premises, Kayleigh Patchett. I'd like three of you to cover the sides and the rear of the cabin while we talk with Mr. Thomas. Be vigilant."

The walk up the driveway seemed endless. Sweat pooled at the base of Josie's spine and slid down the sides of her face. Whether it was from the warm weather or her nerves or both, she didn't know. Once they reached the top of the driveway and didn't see anyone in the vehicles, the uniformed officers spread out, walking around the cabin. The Chief waited at the bottom of the steps as Josie and Gretchen walked up and knocked on Henry Thomas's door.

"Mr. Thomas," Josie called. "It's Detective Quinn. I need to speak to you immediately."

Josie's heart felt like it was going to pound out of her chest. If he didn't answer, there wasn't much they could do. They had no concrete evidence that Savannah Patchett was inside or that Thomas had anything to do with her disappearance. They were there based on Josie's theories, which, while solid, weren't enough for even a search warrant. The Chief had proposed having Luke and Blue search for Savannah again. If they led Denton PD back to Thomas's cabin, then they would have enough for another search warrant.

Josie had worried that would take too long and advocated for approaching him and questioning him directly.

She knocked on the door again. "Mr. Thomas! Open up."

Footsteps sounded from inside. To Josie's relief, the door swung open. Clothed in a plain white T-shirt and black sweatpants, Henry Thomas stared at her. "You again," he said. Looking beyond her, he saw Gretchen and the Chief. Josie didn't miss the momentary flash of panic on his face. "What now?"

"Where is Savannah Patchett?"

He rolled his eyes. "We're back on that again. I told you. I had nothing to do with that girl going missing."

"Savannah Patchett," Josie said. "She's eight years old. Curly brown hair. Blue eyes. Kayleigh Patchett's sister."

"There are two of them missing now?" he said. "That seems like a you problem to me."

Josie pulled out her phone and brought up a photo of Savannah. She turned it toward Thomas. "You're saying you haven't seen this girl today?"

"Not today or any other day."

"Then you won't mind if we come in and have a look around?"

He stiffened. It was barely perceptible, but Josie saw it. A few beats went by. Josie spoke again. "Can we come in and look around, Mr. Thomas?"

Looking at his bare feet, he said, "Sure. Come on in."

Josie waved for Gretchen to follow her. Inside, the cabin didn't look much different than the last time Josie had been inside except for a blanket crumpled on the couch and two unwashed coffee mugs sitting in the sink. "You have company, Mr. Thomas?" Josie asked him.

He stood in the center of his kitchen, watching them. He didn't answer.

They moved down the hall, checking both bedrooms, looking anywhere small enough for Savannah Patchett to be hidden. She wasn't there.

In the bathroom, Josie checked the cabinet under the sink. Nothing. She pulled the shower curtain back to look in the tub and something flew at her, life-sized and thrashing, tearing the shower curtain down with it. Josie felt the impact of a body slamming into hers. They went crashing down, into the hallway. She heard Gretchen say, "Oh shit."

Then came the screaming. Like an animal. Josie looked up to see that Kayleigh Patchett was straddling her. Her brown hair hung down, brushing Josie's chest. Her lips peeled back from her teeth. Fingernails dug into Josie's scalp and down the side of her face. She reached both arms up, folding them over top of Kayleigh's forearms and levering them downward. At the same time, she planted one of her feet and bucked her hips, rolling the girl off her and onto the floor. The girl kicked and flailed, still trying to attack Josie. From the rear of the house, Gretchen approached just as Kayleigh got to her feet. One swift kick to the abdomen sent Gretchen onto her ass. Josie scrambled upright only to receive a swift kick in the ribs from Kayleigh.

Her body knocked into one of the walls. Kayleigh ran toward the living room.

Josie regained her balance and sprinted after the girl. She was in the kitchen, yanking drawers out of their housing, sending silverware crashing to the floor. From the corner of the room, Henry Thomas stared, impassive and stock-still. Gretchen drew up beside Josie just as Kayleigh found the biggest knife in Thomas's kitchen.

"Get out of my way," she snarled. "Or I'll stab you both."

Josie and Gretchen drew their weapons. Thomas threw his hands in the air and edged as far away from Kayleigh as he could get. The mess of flatware at his feet didn't give him much room. Josie took in Kayleigh's appearance. She was thin— thinner than in her photos—and her brown hair looked clean and freshly washed, tumbling over her shoulders. Only her eyes looked hollowed out and tired. She wore a T-shirt and sweat- pants that were several sizes too large. Thomas's clothes. Like him, she had bare feet. Josie wondered how long she'd been at the cabin. Had she been inside when Josie came to question Thomas about the handprint?

"Kayleigh," said Josie. "Put the knife down."

She waved it at them. "You're going shoot me if I don't put it down? Is that it?"

"I'd rather not," Josie said. "Kayleigh, the truth is that we just came here to talk."

"Bullshit."

"It's true," Gretchen said. "We know everything, Kayleigh. There's no point in ending this in violence. We just want to talk to you. To hear your side of the story."

"Isn't it time that you told your side, Kayleigh?" Josie added.

"You bitches don't know anything," she said, but there was a tremor in her voice that hadn't been there before.

"We know that Felicia Evans stole your StoryJot story," Josie said. "The one about the twin princesses, 'Reign.' She passed it off as her own in a contest at school, which she won, and because of it, she got a spot at Denton University's Youth Summer Writing program."

"We know that your parents never even considered that you had written it. They took Felicia's side from the beginning," Gretchen said. "Did they even ask you if you'd written it?"

The knife had lowered almost to Kayleigh's waist. Her eyes were wide with shock. "No," she said quietly. "They didn't ask."

"No one believed you. Only Asher, and he wasn't willing to come clean about your relationship in order to prove to everyone that you'd written the story," Josie said.

"Everyone failed you, didn't they?" Gretchen said, leaning into the psychological profile of Kayleigh that she and Josie had come up with earlier. "Your teachers, your peers, your boyfriend, and your parents. Don't even get me started on your parents."

Kayleigh's brows lifted slightly at this. She was interested in this particular bit.

Josie said, "They wouldn't let you quit softball no matter how many times you told them you didn't want to play. They were obsessive about you being involved in sports and yet, they barely even noticed you because all of their attention was and always is on Savannah."

Kayleigh nodded along with Josie's words.

"What we're saying," Gretchen said, "is that we know that no one saw you. It must have seemed like no one even cared about you."

The knife hung at her side now.

Josie said, "Until you met Henry. He saw you, didn't he?"

Even at the mention of his name, Henry remained silent. His hands were still in the air in a gesture of surrender. In the back of her mind, Josie was trying to figure out his angle. He wasn't fighting. He wasn't speaking. He wasn't engaging at all. From a legal standpoint, this was probably his smartest move.

He'd been caught red-handed with Kayleigh in his cabin. Why make it worse on himself by doing or saying something that might lead to more time in prison than he'd already be serving?

Gretchen said, "Henry finally made you feel like someone cared about the real you, didn't he?"

Kayleigh glanced at him.

Josie said, "He made you feel special, didn't he? Showered you with attention. The kind you'd never gotten before."

Kayleigh's lips twisted in a look of consternation.

Gretchen said, "It must have felt great to have that finally. Then he wanted you to do things."

Kayleigh raised the knife again. "That's enough."

Josie said, "We know that you and Henry trapped and killed kids here and in Montour and Lenore Counties."

"But Kayleigh," said Gretchen. "If that's the cost of his attention, is it really worth it?"

"What?"

"He groomed you, Kayleigh," Gretchen replied. "Manipulated you."

"No," she said. She looked at Thomas again, but he kept his eyes on Josie, unreadable. "That's not how it went. He didn't groom me." With her free hand, she pounded a fist against her chest. Eyes still on Thomas, as if she was talking only to him, she said, "I earned this. I did this. This is my masterpiece."

For one brief second, Thomas's eyes darted toward Kayleigh, and in them, Josie saw a sick sort of satisfaction. In her head, she recalibrated, pulling the pieces of her theory apart and trying to fit them together into a new order, one that fit the narrative that Henry Thomas had not actively groomed Kayleigh Patchett but that she had worked to impress him until she had his attention. What could she have done to impress a man like Thomas? It wasn't sex, Josie thought. Or it wasn't *just* sex. Henry Thomas had fantasies. Dark, violent fantasies. But

Josie was sure that Kayleigh had not killed anyone before she took up with him.

What had she done that would impress him? What was the one thing that Kayleigh had at her disposal? The one thing she was good at? The one thing that everyone overlooked? What had she told Asher after Felicia took her story, when she was bent on revenge?

What if I wrote a story so good and so big that it went viral? Then she couldn't steal it from me.

The final piece of the puzzle tumbled into place. "It was you," Josie breathed, her mind still grappling with the depth and breadth of what Kayleigh had done, what she'd created. "Kayleigh, it's you."

She thrust her chin forward, the image of pride.

"You're the Woodsman," Josie said. "No, no. You're the author of the story of the Woodsman. The legend. You created the myth. You spread it and made sure that it kept going until it became viral around here. Viral enough for kids to do Woodsman challenges, for schoolchildren to be scared of him, for there to be a hashtag on social media."

Gretchen gave a low whistle. "Then you made him real."

A smile spread across Kayleigh's face. The knife clattered to the floor. With a strange kind of grace, she stepped over the mess of silverware at her feet and offered them her wrists. "Now you've seen me."

FIFTY-FOUR

"Kayleigh," Josie said. "I'm not going to lie. You're in a lot of trouble. It would really help us out if you told us where to find Savannah."

Sitting in the back of a police cruiser, hands cuffed behind her, Kayleigh didn't even look at Josie, who sat in the front seat, talking through the divider that separated them. They had taken both Thomas and Kayleigh into custody without incident, which had seemed like a huge win, until Josie and Gretchen started questioning the two of them about Savannah's where-abouts. Across the driveway, in a different cruiser, Henry Thomas had only said four words: "I want a lawyer."

Kayleigh hadn't said any words at all.

Josie tried again. "However you feel about your parents—and for what it's worth, I don't blame you—I know that you love your little sister. She is innocent in all this, Kayleigh. She's just a little girl who loves and looks up to you. You're her protector. I'm asking you to be that to her now. Tell us where she is so we can make sure she's okay."

No response. Kayleigh leaned forward, resting her forehead against the back of the driver's seat. She started to hum softly.

Josie reached into her pocket and took out the scrunchie Savannah had given her at the soccer field. "Look at this. Savannah asked me to give this to you when I found you. She said it's her favorite scrunchie. She wanted you to have it. She loves you, Kayleigh. That must mean something to you."

Kayleigh didn't look at the scrunchie. Her humming intensified. A sick feeling swirled in Josie's stomach. Was Kayleigh so unaffected because Savannah was already dead?

Josie put the scrunchie back in her pocket. "You can ignore me all day, but you'll never get me to believe you don't love your sister. In fact, you went back to check on her today, didn't you? You were in the woods, watching the house. She came out to kick balls, and you got too close. She saw you. Then she followed you back here. What did you do with her?"

The humming grew louder, faster.

"Did Henry kill her?"

The humming paused but Kayleigh gave no answer. A commotion from outside drew Josie's attention. She got out of the cruiser but left the front passenger's side door open, giving Kayleigh some air. She looked across the driveway to Gretchen, who shrugged. Soon after, Shelly Patchett came running up the driveway, slipping and stumbling on the gravel. Behind her was Officer Brennan. "There was no stopping her," he called.

"It's fine," Josie said.

Shelly stopped between the cruisers. "Where are my girls?"

Gretchen walked over to her and said something into her ear. Her next words were a scream. "Well, where is she? Find her, find her!"

Josie turned back toward Kayleigh, whose eyes were now on the window, watching her mother. She said, "Let me out."

Josie opened the back door and helped Kayleigh out. When Shelly saw her, she ran over, gathering Kayleigh in her arms. After a long hug that seemed to make Kayleigh uncomfortable, Shelly released her. Touching Kayleigh's cheek, she said, "They told me. They told me that you... that you were involved. That that man made you do all these horrible things."

Kayleigh didn't speak but she jerked away from Shelly's touch.

"It's okay," Shelly said. "We'll get you a lawyer. Any judge will be lenient when they know how he manipulated and coerced you into those awful things. You're so impressionable." Tears fell from her eyes. She tried to touch Kayleigh's face again, but she stepped away, bumping arms with Josie. "So gullible," Shelly added. "But it's okay. It's okay." She stopped and scanned the premises. "Where's your sister?"

Kayleigh said nothing.

"Kayleigh, where is she? Where is Savannah?"

Quietly, Kayleigh said, "How would you feel if you never saw her again?"

Shelly pressed a hand to her chest. "What?"

She spoke louder this time, through gritted teeth. "How would you feel if you never saw Savannah again? If you never knew what happened to her?"

"I don't—I don't—why are you asking me this? Where is your sister?"

"Mother," Kayleigh said. "Do you remember when Savannah was just a baby, and I was eight years old? You took us trick-or-treating. Savannah was dressed up in her stroller. You were pushing it. We went somewhere—into the city or the park or something—somewhere we could walk around and get candy."

"I don't understand," Shelly said.

"Do you remember?" Kayleigh went on as if she hadn't spoken. "I was walking beside the stroller and somehow, one of its wheels rode right over the back of my ankle. It hurt a lot but I didn't want you to be upset with me because you'd already snapped at me several times that day. Nothing I did was right.

So I tried not to show it. I said, 'I'm okay, Mommy. I'm okay,' and do you remember what you said?"

Shelly was stunned into silence.

Kayleigh said, "You said, 'I don't care whether or not you're okay, Kayleigh. I don't care how you feel.' Then you pushed the stroller around me and left me trailing behind you. You never snapped at Savannah, not even when she got older, and she was annoying. Because you love her more than me."

Shelly held her hands out toward Kayleigh, in a begging posture. "No, no, Kayleigh, I—"

"I don't care, Mother. I don't care about your feelings." Turning back to Josie, she said, "I'd like to get back in the car now, please."

FIFTY-FIVE

Blue sat beside the El Camino and issued a single bark. It was dark. The ERT had arrived and set up the halogen lights they usually reserved for poorly lit crime scenes. Both Kayleigh and Henry Thomas had been transported to Denton PD headquarters to be processed hours ago, after it became clear that they were not going to divulge what had happened to Savannah Patchett. Noah had come on shift shortly after that and suggested they bring in Luke and Blue. If Savannah was nearby, he reasoned, they would find her. If, in fact, she'd gone into the woods on her own or because she was following Kayleigh and gotten lost rather than taken by Kayleigh and Thomas, and she was still out there, wandering on her own, Luke and Blue would find her.

They'd gotten a shirt from Shelly Patchett, who hadn't said more than two words since her conversation with Kayleigh. One of the uniformed officers had driven her home and returned with the shirt, but then Dave Patchett had simply driven her back. They were waiting at the end of Henry Thomas's driveway.

Josie was waiting for a miracle.

She walked over to Blue, who was now laying in the gravel, gnawing happily on the chew toy that Luke had rewarded him with after he'd alerted. His search hadn't taken more than ten minutes. He'd circled the cabin, gone inside, and come back out to the driveway, where he'd dutifully given his indication that he'd located Savannah Patchett.

It was the same place he had alerted the night they followed Kayleigh's scent to the cabin.

Josie said, "That's an active alert."

Luke frowned. "Yeah, but Josie, I told you. Dogs can have false alerts."

Blue's tail thumped against the gravel when he noticed Josie staring at him. "Twice?" she asked. "In the same place?"

"Sure. I mean, maybe both girls were taken from this spot. Well, I don't know about Kayleigh. Maybe she got into a car here and left."

"But Blue doesn't usually alert when he loses a scent, Luke."

Luke gave her a pained smile. "Blue is good, Josie, but he's not perfect."

Behind the two vehicles, Noah stood in a line with Gretchen, the Chief, and a couple of uniformed officers. He met her eyes. They didn't have to speak. She knew he was thinking the same thing as her.

Josie looked into the dog's eyes again. "Blue is perfect, even if his record isn't." She spun around in a slow circle. Savannah wasn't there. They'd checked the cabin again. They'd been all over the property. They'd searched inside both vehicles and under them. Still, Josie glanced inside the windows of the El Camino and its rear bed again, even though she knew both the cab and the bed were empty.

Why did she feel like she was missing something huge?

For the second time in a week.

She said, "Luke, if Henry Thomas killed Savannah and buried her here, would Blue alert?"

Luke stamped a foot against the gravel. "Here? In his driveway?"

"Would he alert?"

"I taught him a passive alert for cadavers but Josie, there's no way Henry Thomas would have had time to bury an entire body right here in the middle of his driveway and cover it with gravel before you all showed up, even with Kayleigh Patchett's help. Gretchen said you were here within an hour of the 911 call, and Noah said this car doesn't have a torque converter, which means it doesn't move." He kicked some of the gravel and watched as it flew toward the El Camino, careening off the undercarriage.

Josie squatted down in front of Blue and started clearing gravel away with her hands. Her chest constricted. Had Thomas and Kayleigh really done this here? So close to the burial grounds? Buried the body of another young girl in a place that had held the secret bones of so many other girls for almost a hundred years? Had Kayleigh really done that to her own sister? She had already killed, and she was willing to go to jail without ever revealing Savannah's whereabouts, Josie thought. It wasn't a stretch to think that she could murder her own sister.

"Josie," Luke said.

Noah appeared next to him. "Hey," he said softly, squatting down beside her.

As if sensing her distress, Blue whimpered. He stepped forward and licked Josie's face, his long tongue drawing a slobbery trail from her chin to her forehead. "Blue!" she said. Under any other circumstances, she would have laughed. In the moment, she wanted to throw her arms around the dog's neck, bury her face in his fur, and weep for all the horrible things that had happened on this mountain—for all of the things this mountain had stolen from her personally and for what it was now stealing from the Patchetts. She might not respect their parenting, but she couldn't bear the thought of Savannah, a classmate of Harris's, being coldly and savagely murdered, in part by her own sister. Josie settled for scratching behind one of Blue's ears. She used the back of her other wrist to wipe the slobber from her face, turning her head into it.

She almost missed it.

Noah put a hand on her back. Blue stood up and nudged her, his wet nose pressing into her neck. Her eyes were locked on the rear driver's side tire of the El Camino. "Just a second, boy," she murmured. "Noah." She stood up and walked closer to the car, bending to get a better look at the tire. Noah followed and watched as her fingers touched mud caked in the treads. It was soft, moist. Straightening, she looked around.

"What is it?" Noah asked.

"Just a second." She walked around the El Camino to where the gravel driveway ended, and the grassy part of the property began.

"When I was here last, Henry Thomas was outside, working on the car. He was going to paint it."

"Doesn't look like he did," Noah said.

"No. We got interrupted."

She crossed the boundary between the gravel and the grass. It spread out about ten or fifteen feet before it met an uneven line of trees. In the direction of the cabin, it narrowed and meandered around to the back of the structure. In the direction of the road, it curved into a barrier of knee-high weeds and brush. Josie followed the weeds until she found what she was looking for—an area of the brush that had been tamped down. Not enough that anyone would notice unless they were looking for it. From the driveway it didn't look like much but now that Josie stood over the top of it, she saw the mud and the light tire tracks.

Returning to the El Camino, she looked at the rear passenger's tire. It was clean. Looking back to where she had seen the tire track, she tried to envision it. "Can we get the hood open?"

Luke raised a brow but said nothing.

Noah said, "What for?"

"To see if the torque converter is there."

Luke said, "You won't see it by looking under the hood."

"Yeah," said Noah. "You'd have to be under the car. We'd need lights. Maybe a lift of some kind. Even then, I'm not sure it would be visible without removing some stuff. Wait—you think it's there?"

"Yes," Josie said.

"But how?" Noah said. "The torque converter was not in here when Hummel impounded the car. I'm telling you. I saw it with my own eyes. The mechanic had it up on the lift. He showed us where it should have been."

"Well, Henry Thomas got one after the car was returned and installed it. He's probably had it all along. He installs it when he needs it, like to travel to Montour or Lenore Counties and not leave a GPS imprint."

Luke said, "And what? He just takes it out when it's here? Josie, that's no easy feat. He'd need a lift. He'd have to lift up this whole car and remove the transmission."

"How long would it take?" Josie asked.

"I don't know. A couple of hours, maybe more, but I don't know about doing that in this driveway. This is gravel."

"But could you do it?" she asked.

Luke studied the car. "I mean, I guess, but you'd need at least four jacks with jackstands and a piece of cardboard or plywood to put over the gravel to steady them. It would be difficult but not impossible. I don't know about doing it over and over again."

"Then maybe he only did it recently," Josie said. "After Kayleigh staged her own disappearance and he realized that the police were going to come looking for him. He would have had time. He had cardboard. The last time I was here. He was getting ready to paint the car and he was standing on it. A big piece."

Luke gestured toward the car. "This hasn't been painted."

"I know," Josie said.

"He's got the jacks and jackstands, too," Noah said. "We found those the night we searched his cabin."

"But why would he go to all that trouble?" asked Luke.

"So that we would have nothing on him," Noah said. "Or to buy himself some time until the DNA from the cabin came back as Kayleigh's."

"Or so that he could hide all his secrets," Josie said. She walked back to the El Camino, getting down on her stomach and shimmying underneath.

Luke said, "You might not be able to see the torque converter from there."

"That's not what I'm looking for," she called back.

Then came Noah's voice, "What makes you think the torque converter is there now?"

"Henry Thomas moved this car. Recently. There's mud on the back tire. There was no mud when I was here the last time. These tires were pristine."

Noah's face appeared, upside down, near the car's under-carriage. "I'm having someone search the cabin for the keys now."

Under the car, she started clearing gravel away.

Luke's face appeared on the other side, also upside down. "If there was something under there, wouldn't the ERT have seen it when they impounded the car? Or brought it back?"

Josie kept pushing gravel away. "Not if it was hidden well enough."

Her hands were raw from digging through the gravel. She was about to give up when she felt something smooth under her fingertips. She tapped a nail against it. Plastic. She tapped again, harder.

From deep within the earth came a shriek.

Josie's heart did a double tap.

She squirmed out from under the car, heart pounding so hard now that she was sure both Luke and Noah could hear it. Standing, she wiped dirt from her clothes. "She's under there," she said, voice high-pitched.

Blue barked.

"She's under there. I heard her. It's plastic. There's some kind of structure under the car. Noah, I need those keys."

He spun away from her and jogged up the steps of the cabin, disappearing inside. Moments later, he emerged, holding them high over his head. His feet pounded back down the steps. Throwing open the driver's side door, he slid inside. His fingers trembled as he fit the key into the ignition. For a split second, Josie wondered if the car would really start. It took a couple of tries but finally, it roared to life. Noah pulled the door closed and threw the gear shift into reverse. "Watch out," he yelled.

The officers in the driveway scattered as he backed up the car. Josie and Luke were already on their knees, clearing more gravel until a plastic hatch came into view. Noah joined them.

Luke said, "This is a septic tank. She can't be in here."

"Shhh," Josie said. "Listen."

She banged on the lid. The screams were clearer now.

"Jesus," Noah said. "Get the rest of this cleared. We have to get in there."

Moments later, they cleared the rest of it and Josie yanked the lid open. Light cut through the darkness below. Eyes shut tight against the light, pale, dirty, with her curls pasted to her cheeks, was Savannah Patchett.

FIFTY-SIX

Josie stood at the edge of the crime scene tape that the ERT had erected around Henry Thomas's cabin and watched as Hummel's team moved around, taking photos, laying evidence markers, and making sketches. She heard the crunch of gravel behind her from the direction of the road. She didn't turn. It was one of her team. The area was safe now. Noah drew up beside her. "Ambulances just left. Savannah seems uninjured but pretty traumatized."

Josie shivered at the thought of the girl in the small, dark space. It was literally Josie's worst nightmare. Because she had lived it. In a closet, not a chamber in the ground, but still, it had left psychic scars that would never heal. "Of course," she said.

"But she's alive."

It was a miracle.

In their line of work, children weren't found alive and if they were, the damage done was so severe, they had no chance at having a normal life ever again.

"Did she say anything?" asked Josie.

"You were right. She saw Kayleigh in the woods and followed her. Kayleigh tried to get her to go back home but

Savannah wouldn't leave her. When they got here, Kayleigh convinced her that she had to get into the tank so the Woodsman wouldn't get her. She never saw Thomas."

More gravel crunched behind them, the steps faster. Gretchen this time. "I checked the property records," she said. "When this place was built, they installed the tank that Savannah was found in, but it was never operational. There's another tank out back, from one of the old properties. That one is in use."

They watched as Hummel emerged from inside the house, a clipboard in his hands. He walked over to the septic tank hatch. One of his officers had lowered himself inside. For a long time, the flash of light from a camera was the only thing they could see from the hatch. Then another officer stationed himself on the ground at the opening. Soon, the officer inside was handing up evidence bags to the officer outside. Hummel had a brief conversation with them, peeked inside the bags and scribbled on his clipboard.

"How did she breathe in there?" Gretchen asked. "She was in there for hours."

Hummel walked over to them. "We found a lot of drugs in the tank. Weed, ecstasy, Oxycontin, and we think some Adderall, too. It was clearly where he kept his stuff. We also found a large amount of cash as well as some clothes and a few snare traps—some of which have dried blood on them. We also found two pairs of digital night vision goggles used for hunting. In addition to that, it looks like Thomas rerouted the pipe that connected the tank to the house and built out some kind of makeshift ventilation system. There was also a small storage space in the wall where it came into the house. It looks like a heating vent, but inside is a space to keep things and the pipe that leads to the tank. More cash and drugs and a few oily rags."

"Like the kind you use to work on a car?" Noah said. "Maybe that's where he kept his torque converter."

"It was right in front of our faces this entire time," Josie said. "All of it. Blue knew it. Those weren't false alerts. The girls were right under his nose. Kayleigh probably hid in there the night she staged her abduction. We were so far behind that Thomas would have had time to get the car moved, get her inside, and cover it up. Then all he had to do was wait until things settled down and then take her out."

Gretchen said, "That was probably when she went to Asher's. Too much heat on Thomas up here for her to stay in the cabin with him, and the septic tank wasn't a long-term solution. I bet we can get Asher to fill in some of the blanks."

"We'll bring him in," Noah said.

"I think the torque converter was already in when I spoke to him earlier," Josie said. "We had returned the car to him after it was processed. He would not have expected us to impound it again. He probably put it back then while the car was sitting right here. That's why the tires were still clean."

"He probably wanted it ready," Noah agreed. "In case he needed to access the tank."

"Which he did," Josie said. "Clearly. When Kayleigh showed up with Savannah, he simply turned the car on and reversed it so that they could get her inside."

"Imagine if you hadn't seen the mud, bos—Josie," said Gretchen.

A shudder worked its way up Josie's spine. "I don't want to imagine that."

FIFTY-SEVEN

Josie watched from across the table as Harris picked up a slice of pizza that was twice the size of his head. His small hands struggled to hold it as he brought it to his mouth. Half the cheese slid off and onto his paper plate. Beside him, Noah laughed and picked up the cheese with two fingers, slopping it back onto the slice. "You have to fold it up, like a book," he told Harris. He used his own slice to demonstrate. Harris studied the technique and tried it on his own. Some of the cheese still spilled over and fell back to the plate, but he managed a bite.

"Or," said Misty, who sat beside Josie. "We could ask them to give us smaller slices. Who could possibly eat slices this big?"

Noah popped the last bit of crust into his mouth and grinned. Harris stared up at him in amazement. "Uncle Noah can!"

Josie smiled and shook her head.

Misty said, "Harris, you don't have to finish that. Just eat what you can."

But his attention was already on the front door of the establishment, a new pizza parlor that featured an extensive arcade called Play Pizza Play. A boy that Josie recognized from Harris's

Little League team walked in, hanging from his father's arm. He pointed toward the arcade and the father nodded. The boy ran toward the games while his father headed toward the pizza counter. "Is that your friend from baseball?" asked Misty.

"Yeah," said Harris. "Can I go play with him, Mom?"

Misty scanned the large room. "Sure," she said. "But what do we always say?"

Harris stood and brushed crumbs from his shirt. "I have to stay in your eyesight."

"Eye line," Josie corrected. "You have to stay where we can see you and you can see us."

Harris glanced at the arcade again, searching for his friend. His shoulders slumped when he couldn't find him. Noah tousled his hair. "Why don't I go with you? You need a game card anyway, right?"

Harris's eyes lit up when Noah produced one from his pocket. Then they were off. Misty sighed and picked at her pizza. "Noah is so good to him."

Josie felt a pleasant warmth in the pit of her stomach. She moved her hand over it.

Misty said, "Any luck?"

Without looking at her, Josie shook her head.

Aware of a strange silence filling the place, they both looked toward the door where two adults and a young girl had just walked in. Whispering, Misty asked, "Oh my. Is that that family? The Patchetts?"

Shelly and Dave kept their heads down while Savannah skipped toward the counter, blissfully unaware of the stares directed toward them.

"Yes," Josie said, tearing her gaze from them.

It had been two months since Kayleigh Patchett and Henry Thomas were taken into custody and charged with a slew of felonies, including three counts of first-degree murder for the deaths of Amanda Chavez, Sara McArthur, and Felicia Evans.

Still, Kayleigh was the talk of the city. Josie had seen the endless questions and lambasting of the Patchett parents on social media with every update on the case, whether the post came from WYEP, Denton PD, the state police, or the prosecutors' offices.

How did they not know? There's no way they didn't know she was so sick in the head!

What did they do to her that made her that way?

Those freaks shouldn't be allowed to raise any more kids. Look how their first one turned out—a cold-blooded killer.

They ordered food and found a table far from where Josie and Misty sat—in the corner of the dining area, away from others. Dave and Shelly ate quietly while Savannah ran toward the arcade, quickly leaving their sight.

Misty said, "What a horrible tragedy."

It would be a long road for the Patchetts. The wheels of justice were slow to move once a case reached the court system. It could be years before Kayleigh went to trial. There was still some debate as to whether or not she would be tried as an adult. At first, her defense attorney had appeared on every news program that would have him, talking solemnly about how Henry Thomas had taken a young, impressionable girl and twisted her mind around until she was so frightened of him, she felt she had to kill. Clearly, this was the defense he intended to use when the cases went to trial—if they did—or while he was trying to negotiate plea deals. Kayleigh, however, told a very different story to investigators when she was interviewed. Josie had been present for one such session where she thought the defense attorney might have a serious medical event listening to Kayleigh give a completely different account to what he'd been spinning in public. She sounded proud of the story she had created and seemed to think she deserved recognition for it. Her attorney had ended all police interviews shortly thereafter.

Henry Thomas still had not said a word. He'd retained an attorney and that attorney had declined all requests by police or prosecutors to ask him any questions. Luckily, between Kayleigh's accounts and the DNA evidence, when it finally came in, the evidence against both of them was pretty damning. Kayleigh's DNA had been found in Thomas's cabin in multiple places. The DNA found on Felicia Evans's sneaker had matched to Kayleigh. The snare that had been found in Thomas's septic tank vault had yielded DNA from all the victims as well as him and Kayleigh.

Asher Jackson Jenks had filled in a lot of the rest. Kayleigh had met Thomas through him when he'd gone to Thomas's cabin to turn in his profits and get more drugs to sell. He'd felt uncomfortable about how much interest Thomas had shown in Kayleigh, but had simply stopped taking her with him. However, forty-eight hours after her supposed abduction, she had shown up at his apartment looking like she'd just spent the prior two days in a dungeon—which she basically had. She'd told him that she was the author of the legend of the Woodsman and that, to make it more real, she'd staged her own abduction. He'd let her stay at his apartment because she had promised to turn herself in after a few days. She'd say she'd simply been lost in the woods. He had no idea she was involved with Thomas until after the two of them had been arrested. After a day, he got nervous and told her he was going to take her to the police station with some story that he'd found her along the road. They'd driven a few miles when she tried to convince him to turn around and hide her for a bit longer. He refused and kicked her out of the car. He theorized that this was when she had left her sweatshirt under his seat, unbeknown to him.

However, she had returned a day or two later, begging him

to let her stay just one more night, to let her take a shower. He'd relented. She had been hiding in his apartment when Josie and Noah showed up at his house. By the time they returned with search warrants, she had fled. Asher had not seen her after that.

"Josie?"

Misty's voice brought her back from thoughts of the case.

"What's that?" Josie said, turning to her friend.

"I asked if you were sleeping or if you're still having the... dreams?"

"Still having the dreams," Josie answered.

Misty put an arm around Josie's shoulders and squeezed her. "Stress can make it hard to conceive. You know, Noah told me that Dr. Rosetti recommended a retreat..."

She trailed off and Josie realized that Noah hadn't casually told Misty about the retreat. He'd asked her to talk Josie into it. She'd be angry, but she was too grateful that the two of them cared about her enough to try to help her.

"I missed the summer retreat," Josie said.

"But?"

Josie sighed. "There's another one in the fall or winter, I think. Dr. Rosetti said she'll make some calls."

Before Misty could say anything else, Harris came barreling toward them. Misty withdrew her arm just as he leaped onto Josie's lap and wrapped his arms around her neck. His cheeks were damp with sweat. "Aunt JoJo! Aunt JoJo! Uncle Noah said no one could beat him at Mario Kart. I tried but I couldn't. Can you beat him? Can you?"

Josie stood up and swung Harris around her body until he was in piggyback position. When he giggled, she felt a wave of joy wash over her. "Are you kidding me?" she said. "Of course I can beat him."

A LETTER FROM LISA

Thank you so much for choosing to read *My Child is Missing*. If you enjoyed the book and want to keep up to date with all my latest releases, just sign up at the following link. Your email address will never be shared, and you can unsubscribe at any time.

www.bookouture.com/lisa-regan

As with all of my books, I have done my very best to keep things as authentic as possible. I put a great deal of research into each book, and I am lucky to have experts and consultants as well as friends and family who are so willing to give their time and knowledge. Still, there are times I have to modify the narrative for the sake of pacing and entertainment. This is fiction, after all. That said, any inaccuracies or mistakes are my own.

I am so grateful for all of my readers—old and new. I love hearing from you. You can get in touch with me through my website or any of the social media outlets below, as well as my Goodreads page. Also, I'd really appreciate it if you'd leave a review and perhaps recommend *My Child is Missing,* or perhaps other books in the series, to other readers. Reviews and word-of-mouth recommendations are still a huge factor in helping readers discover my books for the first time. Thank you so much for your loyalty to and passion for this series. Josie and I are in no way finished! I hope to see you on Josie's next several adventures!

KEEP IN TOUCH WITH LISA

www.lisaregan.com

 facebook.com/LisaReganCrimeAuthor
twitter.com/LisalRegan

ACKNOWLEDGMENTS

Lovely, amazing readers: I say this all the time, every chance I get, and it's always true. You are the very best readers in the world. I am so grateful for each and every one of you. You make every word worth writing. I am blown away by your continued passion for this series even after eighteen books. I don't ever want to stop writing for fans like you. You are truly wonderful. I am astounded on a daily basis by your enthusiasm and engagement when it comes to the Detective Josie Quinn books. I love how much you keep in touch via social media and email. I could use all the words in the world and they would never be enough to thank you for your loyalty and the excitement you bring to this journey. Thank you for staying by my side throughout so many books.

Thank you, as always, to my husband, Fred, for talking me down off so many first draft ledges and helping me work through plot issues as well as providing me with excellent ideas for various twists and other fun stuff in this book. You are my rock, and an amazing wealth of information and brilliant ideas. You are an incredible storyteller in your own right and I'm so grateful to have you on my team. Thank you to my daughter, Morgan, for giving up so much time with Mom so I can write this series. Thank you for always knowing exactly what to do when I am most stressed on a deadline. Thank you for making me laugh when I need it most. You are a gift that I cherish each and every day.

Thank you to my absolutely incredible assistant, friend and

first reader, Maureen Downey for making all things possible. You somehow manage to hold me up through every step of the process and remind me at the most critical junctures that I can actually do this. Thank you to my first readers and friends: Katie Mettner, Dana Mason, Nancy S. Thompson, and Torese Hummel. Thank you to Matty Dalrymple and Jane Kelly for being there for me on a daily basis for anything I need. I don't know what I would do without you!

Thank you to my grandmothers: Helen Conlen and Marilyn House; my parents: Donna House, Joyce Regan, the late Billy Regan, Rusty House, and Julie House; my brothers and sisters-in-law: Sean and Cassie House, Kevin and Christine Brock and Andy Brock; as well as my lovely sisters: Ava McKittrick and Melissia McKittrick. Thank you as well to all of the usual suspects for spreading the word—Debbie Tralies, Jean and Dennis Regan, Tracy Dauphin, Claire Pacell, Jeanne Cassidy, Susan Sole, the Regans, the Conlens, the Houses, the McDowells, the Kays, the Funks, the Bowmans, and the Bottingers! As always, thank you to all the lovely bloggers and reviewers who faithfully return to Denton with each book to solve crime with Josie and her team, as well as the ones who've only met Josie and her team in this book. I appreciate your time and your invaluable support!

Thank you, as always, to Lt. Jason Jay for answering my endless stream of questions so thoroughly and with such patience. I am so incredibly grateful to you. Thank you to Stephanie Kelley, my wonderful law enforcement consultant, who reads every word and goes into great detail to help me get things as accurate as fiction will allow. I learn something new from you with each book, and I am so blessed to have you in my corner. I am so grateful for you! Thank you to Andy Brock for answering so many of my youth sports questions! Thank you to Cindy and Michael Rex for the soccer info! Thank you so very much to Lonnie and Tammy L. Grace for figuring out how

Henry Thomas could fool police into thinking his El Camino didn't work! Brilliant stuff. I can't thank you two enough for taking the time to answer my endless questions on the subject.

Thank you to Jenny Geras for your steady hand, reassurance, and brilliant suggestions. Your insight made all the difference in turning the first draft into something I feel proud to share with readers! Finally, thank you to Noelle Holten, Kim Nash, my copy editor, Jennie, and proofreader, Jenny Page, as well as the entire team at Bookouture.